INFINITY 7:

GODS AMONG MEN

INFINITY 7:

GODS AMONG MEN

Braxton A. Cosby, Keshawn Dodds
&
Chayil Champion

INFINITY 7: GODS AMONG MEN

Published by Cosby Media Productions.

www.cosbymediaproductions.com

Cover art: Cosby Media Productions

Art Design: Braxton A. Cosby

Editor: CMP

ISBN: 9781793392619

TABLE OF CONTENTS

ACT I

CHAPTER 1

A NEW DOMINION

"He'll be the most unstoppable being ever created," Judge Amaruk Tahim said, arms folded behind his back. He donned a long black coat that covered his black pants.

"I thought the antichrist would have been a bigger man," General Swadin said, standing next to Judge Amaruk.

"Oh, but he will be, General. He chose to house himself in a lesser vessel because he knew he would inherit a greater body later – an improved resurrection, so to speak. That time is now."

The two stood facing three large silver containment units aboard Judge Amaruk's spacecraft as the enormous vessel continued its journey towards Earth. The containment unit had a timer on top that was counting down with only two minutes left.

"When those doors open, Natas Selur won't only be larger, but his power will be amplified," Judge Amaruk said. "I've had six dominion archetypes that I have built over the course of time, each one besting the previous. I was told by a great being of prophecy that my seventh would be my last and greatest one yet."

"Enlighten me, sir," said the General. "What exactly are the dominion archetypes?"

"They are indestructible bodies, colossal in size that I have constructed for each of the antichrist figures. The bodies are produced from an ancient element with many names, equivalent to that of Oramite with a tad more density and more reflexive, more reactive. The bodies are fused with the ancient element in order to make the antichrist body indestructible."

"What element do you speak of?" General Swadin asked. "I thought Oramite was the strongest element there was."

"Oramite is indeed exceedingly strong, and it is adaptive to its host, giving him or her very unique abilities. Several humans have been exposed to it, which is how they were able to defeat Natas in his Earthly body. His cosmic body will be a different story. You see, General, Oramite is more than just some element. It is an element made up of microscopic, intelligent, living organisms who are selective in whom they choose to bond with. In many cases, it is under the control and protection of angelic hosts. Very few times has it been found unattended in remote areas throughout the galaxies. Oramite, however, can be wielded and used by unselected recipients. Still, it is a tedious task and takes brilliant minds to figure out how to stabilize it and engineer it. Natas figured it out and used it for the giants. As for him, his demonic consciousness will be fused with a new body built with the element called Sinathyst."

General Swadin slowly turned to Judge Amaruk with a look of confusion.

"I can't say that I've heard of that, sir."

"Not too many have," Judge Amaruk said. "It is a very ancient element that I came across in my intergalactic journeys, found in the most furtive depths of the cosmos. No beings have ever traveled there. I studied the element, learned its secrets, its composition, and how it works. I knew I would be using it for such a time as this. Nonetheless, every habitable planet in all seven galaxies is at the reckoning of an antichrist figure in their respective realm. Judgment is at hand."

The two stood in anticipation as the timer finally hit zero. Steam hissed out of the top of all three containment units, and slowly, the doors opened. The giants exited the units suited in dark silver metallic outfits that looked like a leathery armor built with ultramodern technology. Gath studied his hands, which were also covered by the new material. He then studied the new armor for a few seconds and smiled malevolently. Siph opened and closed his fist, testing the elasticity of his new suit. A few seconds later, Natas Selur emerged from his container wearing a red suit made of the same material as the giants' suits. He was now as tall and as brawny as the giants as he occupied a new body – a body that had been cleverly constructed. His face was completely changed, and his large muscles filled out the definition of the suit. Defined jaws accentuated his face, and his short, black, wavy hair remained perfectly still due to its unbendable make-up in metallic texture.

Natas rolled his shoulders a few times, testing out his new body and its limbs. He admired his new physique as he took a few steps, checking out his legs, which now looked like tree trunks. The two giants looked upon their leader with amazement. Siph touched Natas on the shoulder.

"You look great, Father," Siph said, grimly smiling. "The Majesties of Canaan will no longer be a match for us. We will be invincible."

"Not so fast," Judge Amaruk cautioned. "Everything has to be tested. Yes, the three of you have size, and you're intimidating to the eye. However, your adversaries on Earth are powerful, and you must know your strengths and their weaknesses to defeat them."

"What would you have us do?" Natas asked.

Judge Amaruk waved the others along. "Follow me."

Natas and the two giants followed Judge Amaruk down to the simulation chamber on the space vessel where Judge Amaruk tested new weapons. The room was large, with four walls made of steel. It had glass windows at the top where on-lookers could watch the testing of weapons, or, in this case, the giants.

"Sinathyst is powerful, much like Oramite," Natas said. "It is what your new suits are made of. Also, much like Oramite, it has live and acting microscopic agents within its molecular structure. It's not quite selective as Oramite is, but the more you practice with the suit on, the Sinathyst develops memory, and it stores it to the point that it begins to enhance your fight patterns. It could even take over the fight for you if you let it. As for you, Natas, your new body is created by the element itself. The suit just gives you extra armor. Nonetheless, for it to truly know who you are, the Sinathyst must bond with you in battle. We will test that now."

"Who are we going to battle?" Gath asked, sounding somewhat concerned.

Judge Amaruk raised an eyebrow, and a slight smile split his jaw. After hesitating a bit, he finally spoke. "You're going to battle me."

"We're going to battle you?" said Gath mockingly. "You're tall to the average man, but to us, you're puny."

"To a twelve-foot specimen such as yourself, I can see where that sentiment might come from," Judge Amaruk said. "But, let's not forget that, before you were brought aboard my ship, you had your asses handed to you by men and women who were much smaller than you."

"They didn't defeat us!" Gath bellowed defiantly. "The portal dweller used his power to send us into space. Their weapons couldn't harm us."

"Gath, your father was missing two arms, had a hole in his chest, and the three of you were floating aimlessly in space," Judge Amaruk said. "That's defeat if you ask me. Now, I know humility doesn't reside in our culture, but at the same time, don't allow your pride to make you misjudge your enemy. Now, let's quit talking and put those suits to the test. Your gloves can absorb anything fired at you. They also allow your fingertips to fire deadly rays, beams, lasers, and invisible pulses of energy at your opponent. Your father already possesses the power of telekinesis, but your suits will allow you to have some leverage in that area as well."

"So you want us to fight you?" Natas questioned. "That sounds like fun."

Judge Amaruk nodded. "Oh, and Natas…"

"Yes," Natas replied.

"Don't hold back."

"I won't."

"Let's get it on, then," Gath said as he charged Judge Amaruk.

Gath ran up to Judge Amaruk at full speed, cocked his fist back, and threw a viciously hard punch that would have easily killed a human. However, Judge Amaruk stuck out his hand and stopped the giant's punch with the palm of his hand – which was considerably smaller than Gath's fist. Though standing at seven-plus feet, Amaruk was dwarfed by Gath, who stood puzzled at how one much smaller than he could block his punch. Before he had time to process it, Judge Amaruk grabbed the giant's arm and flipped him, slamming him on his back. Siph, angry at seeing his brother tossed on the ground, charged Judge Amaruk in the same manner as his brother had moments ago. Siph jumped in the air as if he had intentions to stomp on Judge Amaruk like a child would stomp on an ant. As he was coming down, Judge Amaruk caught him in midair with the power of telekinesis. With his arms extended and the giant suspended as if he was dangling on an invisible wire, Amaruk motioned down swiftly as if he were slamming an invisible vase on the floor. The giant crashed into the floor with a thunderous boom that vibrated through the space vessel. Others on board thought they were under attack.

Natas watched calmly as Judge Amaruk, the bald extraterrestrial, handled his giant spawns as if they were little kids on the playground.

"What's the matter, Natas?" Judge Amaruk asked, nonchalant. "Do you hesitate because you are apprehended by doubt or fear?"

"Not at all," Natas replied. "I gave my giants the chance to attack first so that I might have a few moments to study you and see your fighting style. You're well adapted in both the physical and telekinetic, I see. That's right up my alley."

Without saying another word, Natas stretched out his right hand toward Judge Amaruk. He then lifted his hand. As he did, Judge Amaruk elevated off of the ground involuntarily. Natas then closed his hands as if he were squeezing the juice out of an unpeeled orange. Judge Amaruk's body began to constrict with pain; the tighter Natas squeezed his fist. It was as if he was being crushed by an invisible boa constrictor.

"You're not the only one with the gift of psychokinesis, Judge Amaruk," Natas said. "I've been doing this for centuries."

At the same moment, Gath was picking himself up off the floor. Seeing Judge Amaruk suspended in midair, the giant felt inclined to exact a little payback. As Natas held Judge Amaruk suspended with his invisible grasp, Gath swung with another powerful blow that landed on the side of Judge Amaruk's head and sent him hurling right into the wall. Judge Amaruk hit the wall, and after leaving a slight dent, he bounced off like a deflated ball and landed flat on the ground with a smack. As he was picking himself up, he saw Siph's foot coming at him. He did not have enough time to react as he was kicked against the back wall by the second giant.

Again, he hit the wall, and this time he fell flat on his face. He saw double due to the wooziness from the crushing blows the giants had just dished out to him. He picked himself up off the ground as the giants stood over him, waiting to see if he was going to retaliate. He shook off the dizziness and wiped the sleeves of his black overcoat.

"Would you like to call it a day, Judge Amaruk?" asked Natas slyly. "Those hits look like they hurt."

Judge Amaruk wiped the blue blood that leaked from his mouth and nose and smiled. "You're going to have to do a lot better than that," he said. "I told you all not to hold back."

The two giants looked at each other with astonishment. Judge Amaruk now seemed to be fully recovered from the hits as he mocked the three behemoths. Using the giants' moment of disbelief to his advantage, Judge Amaruk charged at Gath with the speed of a bullet and punched him square in the abdomen. The giant sailed across the room and smashed against the wall. With the same speed, he ran over to Siph and launched himself into the air with a flying kick that landed in his chest. Siph slammed against the wall just like his brother. Speedily, Judge Amaruk flew through the air, defying gravity and hovering so that he was face to face with Natas. He immediately began throwing a series of haymaker punches that were landing on Natas' face with the force and velocity of a jackhammer.

Natas stumbled backward with each blow. His head snapped back and forth rapidly with each hit. Suddenly, Natas steadied himself underneath the strikes as each hit became less effective. Natas' body and face strengthened after each punch.

"Ha!" Judge Amaruk exclaimed, bringing his punches to a halt. "The Sinathyst is already protecting you. It has made you immune to my attacks."

"Yeah. But are you immune to mine?" Natas said as he angrily snatched Judge Amaruk out of the air by his feet and slammed him violently against the wall three times. He then hurled him across the room as if he were competing in the Olympic hammer throw.

Judge Amaruk soared through the air but suddenly stopped as he escaped the forces of momentum. He twirled out of his flight pattern into an upright position and hovered above the giants and Natas.

"Alright! Enough," Judge Amaruk shouted, unfazed by Natas' counterattack. "That was a great exhibition, to say the least, but all three of you will become more familiar with your new faculties as the Sinathyst adapts to your genomic composition. Gath and Siph, you don't have the enchanting capabilities that your father does, but your suits give you plenty of accessories to make up ground in that area. You have force fields, sonic blasters, magnetic negative and positive proficiencies, and saying that the suits are bulletproof is an understatement. One could fire a nuclear missile at you and the Sinathyst would absorb it. Given your size, the indestructibility of the suits, and the Sinathyst coalescing with your molecules, I would say you stand a better chance against the Majesties of Canaan and the other Super-Normal beings that partner with them. No more chopped limbs for you, Natas."

Siph eyed Judge Amaruk through narrowed slits, clenching his fists. "Are you making jokes about our father? I still owe you for that kick."

"Settle down, Siph. I am not your enemy," Judge Amaruk said. "We are on the same side. Besides, we have plenty of enemies on Earth and abroad."

"And you? What is your role in all of this, Judge Amaruk?" Natas asked, curious. "You seem to possess great abilities as well. Where will you be when we bring the reckoning to Earth?"

Judge Amaruk slowly floated down to the ground, landing softly as he approached Natas and the giants. “I will be right there with you, fighting by your side. I didn’t rescue you by coincidence or happenstance, Natas. This was calculated and thought out with much patience. When we are finished laying waste to Earth, we will move throughout the galaxies assisting the other antichrist figureheads.”

“There are other very talented individuals who do not play nice with the Majesties or their Super-Normal constituents,” Natas said. “Perhaps we can find these individuals and persuade them to partner with our cause. I reckon we will need all the help we can get.”

“Indeed we will,” Judge Amaruk said. “As the Master says, ‘the more, the merrier.’“

“I have unfinished business with the portal dweller,” Natas said. “He serves of great importance to my plan. We will need to figure out how to neutralize and eradicate the others, starting with the speedsters. Killing him will be personal.”

“Patience, Natas,” Judge Amaruk said. “We will be upon Earth in two days. That is enough time for you and the giants to become more acquainted with the Sinathyst and the abilities it lends to you. It also gives us enough time to come up with a plan. We must move with shrewdness and precision. If we do, we will prevail.”

Judge Amaruk extended his hand to Natas, who studied him with skepticism for a moment before extending his hand. Finally, the two shook hands in an agreement of solidarity. The large vessel continued its course towards Earth with demolition and destruction trailing in its wake.

CHAPTER 2

NOT SO FAST

"I'm not falling for that again," Paladin said, looking at Blurr as she stood over him.

"Come on, one more time. You'll knock it out easily, and then we can go home," Blurr said with a wink. She offered him a hand.

"You clearly cheated on the last run," Paladin said.

"Did not! Ran you down fair and square," Blurr said.

"Slamming through an abandoned building counts as fair these days, huh?" Paladin pointed out.

"Sore loser face imminent. I can see it through your mask."

"Cannot."

"Can too."

"Uh, alright," Paladin said, taking her hand as she gave him a tug and lifted him from the ground. The Chicago skyline glistened in the glow of the early morning sun, as sunlight reflected off the sides of the numerous window-tatted buildings. From their vantage point atop the John Hancock Center, they could see everything. "B.R.A.I.N., how is the S4 looking in terms of power?"

"It's running at approximately seventy-three percent. Levels are holding strong. You started out at eighty-nine," B.R.A.I.N. said. "That new power cell charger is performing admirably."

Blurr dusted off her hands and came alongside Paladin, flipping a coin in the air. "Okay, honey buns, call it in the air."

The coin tumbled upwards through the sky, and as it turned groundward, Paladin cried out, "Heads!"

Blurr snatched the coin and slapped his against the back of her opposite hand. She pulled her catching hand back to reveal the face of the coin. "Tails it is."

"Again?" Paladin asked.

"What? You got a problem with tail all of a sudden?"

"I've picked heads every time, and I still haven't won."

"Never heard you complain about too much *tail* before."

Paladin smiled behind his mask. "I can never get enough of that. Hope I'm not too much man for you."

"Please, as if," Blurr said with a raised eyebrow.

"But you're not a cat anymore. So be careful what you say. Gotta keep those promises, you know," Paladin said, wagging a finger.

"Never needed to be Cheetah-Girl to give good tail."

"Eww, gross. Could you guys spare me, please? Your Inner Ear Piece Comms are on, you know," Lydia interrupted.

"I concur. Just get on with the last speed test," B.R.A.I.N. said.

"B.R.A.I.N., what are you tripping for? You're an A.I., for crying out loud. This type of talk shouldn't bother you one bit," Paladin said.

"It doesn't bother me; just annoys me a little. Recall that I have to see and hear everything that goes on in that bedroom of yours at The Beacon every night," B.R.A.I.N. said.

"Every night?" Lydia asked.

"*Every* … night," BRAIN said.

"Geesh, what's the secret, you two?" Lydia asked.

"It's simple. Love makes it all possible," Blurr replied.

"Since we're asking questions, what's with all the hanging from cables about? Does that improve the experience?" B.R.A.I.N. asked. There was a deliberate pause in the conversation, and just before Paladin could respond, B.R.A.I.N. chimed back in. "Asking for a friend."

"Alright, that's enough Q and A for now. Let's get the test over with, can we?" Paladin said.

"Lydia, map it out," Blurr added.

"Okay, I've got three NAV points plotted out on Washington, Hewitt, and Langston. I'm uploading to both of your HUDs now," Lydia said.

"Got it," Paladin said.

"Still uploading," Blurr said, a hint of irritation in her voice.

"We're still trying to work the kinks out of the HUD system in your goggles, girly. Give it some time," Lydia said. "Recall that we're on the fourth version of Paladin's suit. Optimization is an afterthought for him."

"You're telling me something about time?" Blurr asked mockingly. "Sister, that's something I'm never short on. But even us *Conduits* have our limitations."

"You still gloating on that mythos babble Zenith shared with us?" Paladin asked, sounding somewhat annoyed.

"Hey, I don't think it's just babble. You saw it for yourself. The vortex, those voices. It was all real," Blurr said.

"I know what I experienced, but that was weeks ago," Paladin said, leaning over in a three-point running stance. "We haven't seen or heard a peep from him since then, and you haven't had any more time window visions since then. I just don't know if he was manipulating us for his own agenda or not."

"Well, I believe him," Blurr said, getting in a crouched running position too. "I don't recall everything that happened out there on the battlefield when we tried to retrieve Q-18, but every now and then, some flashes of memory bounce through my head."

Paladin stood. "What! Really? Why didn't you tell me?"

"They're not serious or painful. Not like before. They feel more natural, like, you know, *normal* memories. Like playing with kids on the playground type stuff."

Paladin's voice weakened. "What do you see?"

Blurr stood. "Images … people … places. I can't explain them in detail, but I feel some kinship with them. It's like I'm linked to the memories in a way that feels real."

"Newlyweds, that's it," Lydia piped.

"What!" Paladin and Blurr said simultaneously.

"That's it. That's the secret to all the marathon lovemaking. I get it now. Give a few months, it'll die down," Lydia said.

"There you go hating again. Save the shade for yourself, will ya, cousin?" Paladin said, shaking his head.

"Don't mind me, cousin. I wish you guys all the best. You deserve it.," Lydia said.

"You're only hating 'cause you're in love quarantine. That little romance with Thief fizzled out already?" Paladin asked.

"Don't tease her love, she's dealing with Thief here. That's one tough nut to crack when it comes to sharing and expressing feelings," Blurr said.

"We're just…I mean, things are complicated with Alice," Lydia said.

"I'm still not getting over the fact that's his real name," Paladin murmured.

Blurr elbowed him. "Always are with that one, Lydia. Been there, done that, got the T-shirt to prove it. Hang in there, Lydia. He's got a good heart, way deep down in that iron vault chest of his. Give it time."

"I know, I know. That's the only reason I keep trying," Lydia said. "It can be a headache, but I think he's worth it."

"Alright, HUD is active," Blurr said, tapping the side of her goggles. "Let's do this."

Blurr and Paladin both leaned into runner's stances. "Okay, you both have your NAV points laid out in front of you. On my mark, take off."

"Um, real quick, before we start. I'm up four to two, right?" Paladin asked.

"No, it's tied, lover boy," Blurr said.

"I distinctly recall winning the last two," Paladin teased.

"Keep lying to yourself," B.R.A.I.N. said.

"Really, B.R.A.I.N.? Whose side are you on?" Paladin asked.

"I thought I made that pretty obvious," B.R.A.I.N. said. "I'm on your side, but I have to keep you honest. We did away with spreading fake news years ago with that *delus*ional ex-president of ours."

"Aww, I knew you cared," Paladin said.

A pair of E.I.E.s dropped in to view. "We've got company," Blurr said.

"Give the people what they want," Paladin said.

"Go!" Lydia barked.

In a flash, Blurr and Paladin exploded from the side of the John Hancock Building, mere smudges to the naked eye. "NAV one approaching," Paladin said, eyeing a circular hologram before them as it grew in size the closer they got to it. He and Blurr were running neck and neck.

They rounded the first NAV point and banked a hard left. Paladin hugged the ground while Blurr took the scenic route, skimming along the surface of an adjacent building and angling up towards the top of it. She pushed off with her right leg and sprung forward, taking a slight lead over Paladin as they headed towards the next NAV point. "Closing," she said. Just as they were about to pass through, something in the corner of Blurr's eye caught her attention. "What?" she murmured.

"What, what?" Paladin asked.

"Saw something," Blurr said.

Blurr broke from the coordinates and headed after it. "Saw what?" Paladin asked.

Blurr didn't respond, but pushed the pace, picking up speed. Paladin broke off after her, hitting a turn so hard that he failed to overcompensate, and the inertia of the turn caused him to sail him off course. He righted himself and climbed the side of a building, tiptoeing along the concrete framing in between the windows, careful not to break them. Once he regained his composure, he quickly reset, bounded into the sky, and closed the gap between him and Blurr.

"Blurr, what are you doing?" Paladin asked.

"I'm … incoming!" Blurr screamed.

Before Paladin could move, Blurr whipped to his right, dodging a wave of toppling cars headed in his direction. Instinctively, the S4 switched variants from speed to strength, mere milliseconds before he was slammed by an SUV. He was sent reeling backwards into a row of parked cars on the busy side street.

"Cousin! Are you okay?" Lydia screamed.

Paladin lifted the SUV overhead as he stood and tossed it aside like it was a Tonka Truck. "S4, remember?" he asked, dusting his hands. The HUD in his helmet locked onto the source of the commotion. Standing some one hundred feet off in the distance was Slingblade. "What the hell? What do you think you're doing?" Paladin asked.

"Don't mind me, Paladin. I'm just fishing," Slingblade said.

"Well, you better start digging in your pockets for some coins. You just wrecked about six or seven cars. I hope you caught something big enough to pay the people of Chicago back," Paladin said.

"It's all worth it. Trust me. They'll thank me later," Slingblade said.

"Well, I've got time now. Let's chat it up," Paladin said, bolting towards Slingblade instantly. Before Slingblade could lift a finger to his forehead, Paladin was upon him, connecting a jab to his face and dropping him on his back. "Still playing with knives, huh?" Paladin said, noting the weapon in Slingblade's off-hand. "Come on in. I'm sure we can help you with whatever you're doing."

Slingblade shook his head, rubbing his forehead. "That really smarted."

"Sorry, man," Paladin said, offering him a hand.

A small sedan rammed into Paladin from the side and pinned him against another vehicle. Slingblade stood. "Gotta watch your nine, soldier."

Suddenly, Slingblade was whisked away about fifty feet into the air and sent crashing against a wall, courtesy of a speeding shoulder charge from Blurr. "And your six, *soldier*."

Paladin emerged from the rubble. "You good?" he asked Blurr.

"Peachy."

"Funny, I never liked peaches," Slingblade said, stepping from the broken wall, eyes glowing.

"What's wrong with you? Asking all Zenith and stuff," Blurr said.

"Supersonic Sound Blasts!" Slingblade yelled, casting a sea of translucent yellow discs in both of their directions. Both Blurr and Paladin, now sporting the speed variant of the S4, made haste and narrowly dodged all of them, swirling around the city streets like a set of windmills pushed along by hurricane-force gusts. Slingblade continued his barrage, careful to keep them at bay. He paused for a moment, shoulders bouncing up and down as he took a moment to regain his composure.

Paladin and Blurr dropped to the street. "Wearing down, Slingblade? You don't have to do this. Whatever is going on, trust us. We've been on the other side of the law. We can help."

Slingblade reached into a satchel around his waist and pulled out an old-style, golden flip pocket watch and pointed it to his right. A vortex materialized, reminiscent of the one Zenith conjured just a few weeks ago. "See you around."

Blurr darted in Slingblade's direction. But just as she was about to grab him, he safely jumped inside, and the vortex closed. She slid to a halt, staring at her hands. She turned to Paladin with anger in her eyes. "Damnit." She squeezed her eyes shut.

Paladin came to her side, rubbing her back. "It's not that serious, baby. I'm sure we'll find Slingblade again."

"It's not that."

"What is it, then?"

Blurr opened her eyes again. "I had another series of visions."

"And?"

She looked at Paladin. "And they're all bad."

CHAPTER 3

SOLAR WARRIORS MEET THE MAJESTIES

"Man, where is this guy?" Michael mumbled, looking into the sky. He was standing in a secluded area on top of Mount Tom, just outside of the city as the sun was dropping below the skyline. "He's always running late. I have to remember to tell him to meet an hour earlier; maybe his internal clock will make up for it."

"I heard that," Jeffery said, landing on the ground right behind Michael. "Now you know dang on well that I had to finalize our story to keep the girls from wondering where the heck we were. My parents did a great job covering for us."

"I'll let this one pass; we have bigger issues to deal with," Michael said, walking over to his friend. They shook hands as he continued. "So, Menzuo is off on his own *personal* journey to figure out things without Solar by his side?"

Jeffery nodded. "Yeah, he is. I'm not sure where he will go, but he said that he had to travel out of Earth to gather his thoughts. It's only been a month since our friends headed back home, and things have been relatively quiet since that battle against Queen Eaziah, but Menzuo has been really off."

"Hell, you'd be off too if the protector that you started this journey with was no longer fighting with you," Michael said. "That was a big loss for Menzuo. Solar has his body back and is now on Yardania, getting familiar with life again. And those visions that Lord Fetid put into Menzuo's mind about the future … that is a handful to deal with."

"Speaking of those thoughts," Jeffery said. "Menzuo had visions of us meeting these so-called Majesties of Canaan in Jerusalem. These four fighters are supposed to be key to helping us with the next phase of our journey."

Michael nodded. "Menzuo said that we need to find a girl named Rekluse, some Jamaican guy named Slaycick, another guy named Tenan and their leader, known only as Blessed. These four are somehow tied to whatever we're supposed to be searching for."

"Man, it's going to be like trying to find a needle in a haystack," Jeffery said, pacing. "So, tell me again where we need to start."

"We need to head to Tel Aviv first and check in to our room. By the time we get there, it will be morning. From there, we can search the city until nightfall. Hopefully, we can ask people to help us locate a man that has arms made of Oramite."

"Okay, okay, okay … What the heck is Oramite again?" Jeffery asked.

"Oramite is the strongest element ever found in the universe, and, somehow, these Majesties have obtained it to keep peace on their war-ravaged continent," Michael replied.

"Got it," Jeffery understood. "At least we know that they are on the good side of things."

"My question is," Michael said, "what are we supposed to say if and when we find them? Hey, we're superheroes from America, sent here to get answers from you about something that we have no freaking clue about?"

"Kind of like that," Jeffery said, chuckling. "Hopefully, we can figure out what we need to find."

"Hopefully, they don't try to kill us," Michael replied.

"I didn't think about that," Jeffery said. "Dammit! We're also supposed to keep our powers hidden. This is going to make it that much harder."

"At least we can use our powers to fly to Tel Aviv," Michael said. "It shouldn't take us more than a couple of hours. It will only take us that long because we have to fly undetected. We can't use super-speed at any point."

"Understood," Jeffery replied, and then powered up. "I guess we should get to it, then."

Michael did the same, muscles flexing. "Man, it feels good to have this power suit on again."

"I think we should use our real names moving forward," Desmurose said.

Allucio agreed. "I like that. Let's get to it. We have a serious mission ahead of us."

"I just hope the food is good when we get there; I'm starving," Desmurose said.

Allucio shook his head. "You're always thinking about your stomach. Let's go!"

Both warriors shot up into the sky, high above the clouds, and instantly made their bodies invisible so that no satellites or passing aircraft could detect them.

Breaking through the clouds, they quickly flew over the Atlantic Ocean and headed down closer to the water, just under the cast of any radar signals. As they continued on, they noticed a large pod of whales making their way to the surface and then slowly descending back towards the ocean floor. It was a calming sight to see the peacefulness of life in the open sea.

In the distance, the continents of Africa and Europe closed in from their right and left, respectively. Allucio and Desmurose decided to fly through the Strait of Gibraltar, as they knew that it would be the best route to Tel Aviv.

"We're almost there," Allucio said. "Let's make our way above the clouds to scan for a safe place to land."

"Got it," Desmurose said. "I'll follow you."

They both shot high into the sky again just as they arrived above their destination. As they slowly materialized into view, Allucio and Desmurose scanned the ground below.

"It's still very early in the morning. There isn't anyone on the streets," Desmurose said, peeking through the clouds.

"Let's find an alleyway to land in," Allucio said.

"Roger that. This is the beginning of a new journey," Desmurose said.

"I hope this search for our needle in a haystack won't take that long," Allucio replied.

"I hope it doesn't either," Desmurose said. "Okay, let's get down there before people begin to make their way into the city."

Both warriors dropped out of the sky and landed behind two buildings in a deserted alleyway. They made their power suits disappear and were now back in their regular clothes.

"Okay, do you have the pictures of Blessed that Menzuo gave you?" Desmurose asked.

Allucio reached into his pocket and pulled out the two pictures from their research on Blessed. "Here they are."

The picture showed a man charging in action. His bald head was glimmering, and his beard slightly covered his angered grimace as he looked to be on the attack. His fatigued military shirt had a symbol on it with the initials "M.O.C." and his arms looked to be chiseled out of some dark and shiny form of metal: possibly the Oramite element.

Desmurose took one of the pictures. "This man looks like he's no joke. Let's try not to piss him off, okay?"

"I can't promise you anything," Allucio replied. "You know when I'm nervous, I say stupid and slightly offensive things. It's how I cope with uncomfortable situations."

"Please help me," Desmurose said, looking towards the sky. "Okay, I'll try to stop you from embarrassing the both of us. After we check into our hotel, we can go out into the city to search for Blessed and his team."

"That sounds like a good plan," Allucio replied. "I'm seriously hungry after that flight, and honestly, I don't know about you … but I have to pee badly. Flying over that ocean didn't help."

"Who are you telling," Desmurose said. "That wasn't a well thought out plan, but we're here. Let's get to the hotel, then we can relax for a bit."

Allucio and Desmurose walked out of the alleyway, down the street and out towards their hotel. They were just a few hundred yards from where they were staying.

After they checked in, both young men headed down to the hotel restaurant. The food gave them enough energy to begin their search. When they exited the hotel, Allucio and Desmurose headed out to a much more populated city. Within just a few hours, Tel Aviv almost looked like New York City; a beautiful city with a modern skyline took the two young warriors by surprise. They felt right at home as they walked the streets.

Desmurose turned to Allucio. "Let's split up and start asking around to see if anyone has noticed this *Blessed*."

Allucio nodded. "Okay, I'll take the beachside, and you can take the area around all of the restaurants. We both know you like to eat anyway."

Desmurose smiled. "Sounds good to me, but don't get stuck looking at all of the pretty women on the beach; your concentration is weak when you get around women. You're not a ladies' man. We have a mission to focus on."

"Oh, yes I am," Allucio said. "You know the ladies think I'm cute!"

"Please don't make me sick," Desmurose said.

"You just don't go and get yourself sick, eating everything in sight. As long as you promise to minimize your eating while you search for Blessed, I'll do my best to focus on the mission and not the hot ladies."

Desmurose shook his head but agreed. "Then let's get to it. We can meet back here in a couple of hours. If you find anything before then, just give me a call. Remember, don't use your powers. We can't risk the exposure."

"Right," Allucio replied. "We have no idea what threats are out here. See you in a bit." Allucio walked off. As he headed for the beach, he slowly removed his shirt.

"This is not going to end well," Desmurose said, walking down the street and entering the restaurant district. He pulled the picture out of his pocket and studied the target's face and features. He looked into the crowd; there were hundreds of people walking past. Desmurose sighed heavily. "At least I know Tel Aviv has some of the best sushi restaurants in the world. I might as well enjoy this as much as I can." He continued on.

As the young warriors took in the sights from the beach and in every restaurant, they half-heartedly searched for Blessed.

Allucio tried his best not to get too caught up watching the beautiful ladies in their bikinis. Although his mission was to show every woman the picture, it was also the perfect excuse to talk to them. His slick mouth had gotten him slapped and cussed out a few times, but it didn't matter; he was enjoying every minute of it.

Desmurose didn't have any better luck. He found himself eating more sushi than he bargained for. From time to time, he would ask the person next to him if they knew of the man in the picture. Unfortunately, the people that he asked were more interested in the food than helping him out.

After their time for searching was up, the two young men met up back in front of the hotel. "Any luck?" Desmurose asked.

"None at all," Allucio replied.

"How hard did you try?" Desmurosed asked.

Allucio looked at his friend's shirt, noting a few splats of soy sauce on it. He looked up into his eyes with a half-smile. "I guess as hard as you did."

Desmurose looked down at his shirt and chuckled. "Good one. Look, I'm still tired. Let's get some rest and come back at night."

"Yeah, it's been a long day, and this jetlag isn't helping. Hopefully, we'll have better luck when it's dark."

They both went up to their rooms and quickly fell asleep.

***

That evening when they finally woke, they decided to head down to one of the most famous night clubs in Tel Aviv. Inside, there were ladies wearing bikinis dancing in glass cases throughout the club. A large club room-sized fish tank was perched up on the stage and an amazing laser light show with loud music kept the crowd dancing. The energy was electric.

"I'm going to get something to drink at the bar," Desmurose said.

"A drink?" Allucio asked. "Not a *drink*-drink?"

Desmurose shook his head. "No, I'm just thirsty, and this place is packed with people. I just need to get out of this crowd."

"Okay, I'm right behind you."

They both walked to the bar. Desmurose worked at getting the bartender's attention for almost five minutes. "This guy must be blind. I've been calling him for a while now."

Allucio looked at everyone that the bartender was serving and smiled. "If you want a drink, then you will need to transform into a girl because that's all he's serving. Last time I checked, you can't shape-shift, so you're basically out of luck, buddy."

Desmurose sighed as he watched the bartender pass by him again. "Thanks for noticing me!" he shouted. As he continued to try to get the bartender's attention, a beautiful lady squeezed her way between him and Allucio.

"Pardon me, gentlemen," she said.

Allucio turned as he felt someone bump him. His eyes widened and his mouth dropped at the sight of this amazingly beautiful woman. "Whoa!"

She whistled to grab the bartender's attention. He made his way over. "What will the fine lady have this evening?"

"I'll have a lemon drop martini," she said, then looked to Desmurose and Allucio. The lady focused her attention back to the bartender. "And give these two whatever they want and put it on my tab."

The bartender's face quickly turned sour. "What you want," he said.

"I'll have a glass of milk," Desmurose replied bitterly.

"Are you serious?" the bartender asked.

Desmurose's anger was rising. "Yes! A glass of milk, dammit, and don't jimmy it with any liquor."

The bartender shook his head then focused his attention on Allucio. "Milk for you too, lil baby boy?"

Allucio's eyes never left the lady that finally got the bartender to notice them. It was as if he was stuck in a trance by her beauty. "I'll have her hand in marriage. I'm in love."

The woman smiled. "That's cute, but I think you're a little too young for me, and I'm spoken for. Maybe in the next life."

Allucio puffed out his chest. "Age ain't nothing but a number baby, and what does your man have to do with me?"

She walked off with a smile. "What a little charmer you are. Have a good night."

Desmurose smacked himself in the forehead. "You just spit two cheap song lyrics to try to get that woman's attention?"

"I think it worked," Allucio said. "She's the first woman in Tel Aviv that didn't either smack or cuss me out. I think I'm in love."

"Dude, she said that she's taken. Are your ears cleaned out?" Desmurose replied. He was still angry about the treatment that he got from the bartender. "Forget about her. After I get my drink, we need to seriously try and search for Blessed. We already wasted an entire day. Snap out of your fantasy and focus."

Allucio nodded as he kept his eyes on the woman walking back to the dance floor. As soon as Desmurose turned back to the bar to grab his milk, Allucio walked off as if a magnet was pulling him towards the lady.

She was swaying her hips, keeping on beat with the music with her drink in her hand, not dropping one bit of it. Allucio was stuck on trying to get her attention.

Desmurose turned around and started to speak again. "Okay, I'll take the right side of the club and..." Desmurose paused, noticing Allucio wasn't next to him. "Now, where did that fool go?" He scanned the crowd. Allucio was approaching the lady on the dance floor. "This isn't going to end well." He leaned back against the bar and watched the action take place.

As he got closer, Allucio started to dance to the music. He was directly behind the lady and decided to do his best to get her attention. He danced in a circle until he was directly in front of her.

When he finally caught her eye, a smile splashed across her face. "You again?"

Allucio was bopping to the music. "Yep, just your future husband looking for a dance."

She chuckled. "You might want to leave before my man gets upset."

A smile fell upon Allucio's face. "If he gets upset, then it's his fault. He shouldn't leave such a beautiful lady to dance by herself."

"You're a brave soul, but I think you should go," she said. The woman looked to her left, where the booths were.

Allucio looked in the same direction, noting three men in the area. One man with a bald head and beard was smoking a cigar, while the other two were standing, looking right in his direction. The one to his left was dark in complexion, stood about six feet tall, and his braided hair was pulled back just above his shoulders. He was leaned against the bar post, shaking his head. The man to his right was fair-skinned and just about the same height as his friend. He stood with an angry scowl, and his piercing eyes looked right through Allucio.

"That must be your man. He looks pissed," Allucio said.

"Oh, he is," the lady replied. "I think it's best you walk away."

Allucio kept dancing then shook his head. "I think I like the company."

The lady chuckled. "Then, it's your funeral."

Desmurose saw the three men in the sitting area. One of the men was posturing, as his attention was locked in on Allucio. "Oh c'mon! This is about to get ugly," he shouted. Placing his milk back onto the counter, Desmurose tried to fight through the crowd to get to his friend.

As he pushed through the crowd to get to Allucio, he directed his focus back to the three men. He watched the guy next to the woman – who was most likely her boyfriend – tap the side of his head. As he did, an energy surge climbed and shot towards the dance floor, directly in Allucio's direction.

Just as Desmurose made his way to the center of the dance floor where the woman was dancing, he noticed that Allucio had disappeared. He quickly looked around for his friend, then directed his attention to the lady. "Excuse me, where did my ignorant and brain dead friend run off to?"

The lady kept dancing. "He didn't run off, he just needed to find a way to get cooled off," she said, pointing above the stage to the fifty-foot fish tank that faced the crowd.

"How in the …" Desmurose said. Allucio was swimming near the bottom of the fish tank with all of the exotic fish. "You have got to be kidding me!"

He quickly jumped onto the stage and climbed up the ladder. Allucio swam to the top. Desmurose quickly helped him out. "How the hell did I end up in this tank?"

The lady walked over to the sitting area, and the man was still visibly upset. She tried her best to calm him down as she motioned to the group that it was time to leave. The bald man who was still calmly sitting at the booth put out his cigar and finally stood. As he did, Desmurose noted that both of his arms were black and his features resembled the man they were supposed to be looking for.

"Well I'll be damned, I think I have an idea of how you got in there," Desmurose said.

"Man, this sucks. I was breaking her down until this freak accident happened," Allucio said.

"I doubt that it was a freak accident. Someone placed you in that tank," Desmurose said.

"Who?" Allucio asked.

"A Majesty," Desmurose replied.

Allucio was dripping wet as he stood on the stage. His anger subsided as he quickly tried to focus on the crowd. "Where did you see a Majesty?"

"I think your taste in women found them. If I am correct, that lady and her friends are the ones that we are looking for. I believe that her boyfriend teleported you into this fish tank. I felt a surge of energy go straight towards you when he placed his hand onto his head," Desmurose said. He climbed down the ladder, keeping his eyes on the group as they exited the club. "C'mon, Wet Willie, they're leaving. We can't lose them."

"I'm coming, sheesh!" Allucio said. He climbed down the ladder in his wet clothes and followed behind Desmurose out of the club.

As they hit the city streets, they noticed the four people getting into a truck. "We need to get a ride," Desmurose said.

"Why don't we just fly behind them?" Allucio asked.

"Remember, we can't use our powers. We don't want to let people know who we really are, especially them," Desmurose said. He noticed a man standing by his car with a taxi sign on the top. "Hey, can we get a ride?"

"Do you have American money?" the driver questioned.

"Of course," Desmurose replied.

The man looked at Allucio. "It will be extra with your wet friend in tow. I hope that's not piss on you. Too many drunk Americans leave the club forgetting to use the damn bathroom."

"It's not piss!" Allucio shouted. "We can argue about my wetness, or you can take your money and shut it!"

Desmurose noticed the truck pulling off. He pulled out a bunch of money from his pocket. "Enough! We have to go. Extra it is. I'll pay."

"Get in, gentlemen. I'll take you to the moon and back for all of that money."

"Now he wants to be nice," Allucio said.

"Money talks, my friend," the driver said. "Where would you like to go?"

Desmurose pointed forward. "Follow that car," he looked to Allucio. "I've always wanted to say that."

Allucio shook his head. "And you call me corny?"

They drove off, following at a safe distance behind the truck, with the intent to not be detected.

After a short while, they ended up in the city of Abu Tor. The truck pulled over in front of a building. The three men and the woman exited the truck and went inside.

The driver pulled over just a block away from the parked truck. He pointed at it off in the distance. “I guess this is it, gentlemen. Your friends are up ahead.”

“Thank you,” Desmurose said, giving the man the money.

“This will be enough to cover the cleaning of my wet seats.”

Allucio started to wring out his shirt onto the seat just to leave a little more water on it. “I hope it stays wet,” he said, exiting the cab. The driver sped off before Allucio was completely out, almost spinning him completely around. “How rude are the people in this country?”

“You’re lucky we found a ride with your soaking wet clothes,” Desmurose said, chuckling.

Allucio quickly used his powers to dry off before anyone could notice. “I know, I know…no powers, but I wasn’t staying in those wet clothes any longer.”

“That was acceptable, but we have to keep our energy level down,” Desmurose said. He looked in the direction of the building. “Let’s try and sneak in there. That’s where they went.”

“I’m right with you,” Allucio said. “Do you think it’s them, the Majesties?”

Desmurose nodded. “I do. The bald-headed man’s arms were all black, and I know that the lady’s boyfriend has some powers. If it’s not them, I’d be seriously surprised.”

“Then let’s get to it,” Allucio replied.

Just as they took a step forward, a flash of light flew past them. “What the heck was that?” Desmurose shouted.

“Wah gwan my yute?” A man with a strong Jamaican accent spoke from behind them. “Mi don’t know way mek yuh following wi, but yu mussi looking fi action, eh?”

Allucio looked at Desmurose very confused, “What did he say? I didn’t get that at all.”

“Me either,” Desmurose followed. “I’m sorry, what was that?”

The man looked at Allucio. “My fault, I forgot you Yankees can’t speak Patois. You’re the kid that Tenan put in that fish tank.”

Allucio’s eyes lit up as the man spoke perfect English. “Yes, your boy put me in that tank. He got lucky, where is he?”

The man laughed. “You must be crazy trying to mess with his girl. He’s a very jealous man, you know?”

“Jealous isn’t the word,” Allucio said. “But you have to admit, she is fine.”

Desmurose broke up the conversation. “Enough of the small talk, who are you, and how did you know that we were here? As a matter of fact, how in the world did you get over to us so fast?”

“They call me Slaycick, and don’t worry about how I got here so fast. Just know that I could hear the both of you a mile away, plus your stalking abilities suck! What do you both want? I know it’s not about the girl.”

“Why wouldn’t I be here for the girl?” Allucio replied, feeling confident in his persuasive abilities to attract women.

“Because I felt an energy surge when your dumb ass tried to dry off without anyone noticing you,” Slaycick said, looking at Allucio.

Desmurose punched Allucio in the arm. “I told you not to use your powers.”

“So the both of you have powers? You must be a threat to the Majesties.”

“Threat … no … we are …”

“Did I hear a threat?” a voice came from the building. In an instant another man appeared in front of Allucio and Desmurose.

They both jumped as a portal formed right in front of them and caught them both off guard. Tenan walked through. “Whoa!” Allucio said, focusing on the man that now stood in front of them. His eyes widened. “Hey, you’re the one who put me in that tank. You must be Tenan, that lady’s boyfriend.”

"You're damn right, I am. No one hits on Rekluse and disregards me," Tenan said.

Allucio raised his hands. "You've got to admit, your girl Rekluse is fine!"

Tenan's anger started to rise even more. Desmurose jumped in. "Please excuse this fool's mouth. He speaks too much when he's nervous."

"Then, you might want to shut him up!" Tenan said.

"Why do I have to shut up?" Allucio said. "I'm not lying. If Rekluse was my girl, I wouldn't let her on the dance floor without me. I mean, what did you expect? Any man with a pulse would shoot his shot at her."

"Well, keep it up pal, and I'll stop your pulse right now!" Tenan shouted.

"I like this young fool. He has heart," Slaycick said chuckling.

Tenan slowly raised his hand to his head.

"We didn't come here for a fight," Desmurose shouted. "We're only following you all because we're looking for someone important."

"No, no, no! Bro, I think I wanna fight!" Allucio said, pushing in front of Desmurose and puffing out his chest, trying to show his bravado. He hopped around like a boxer in the ring. "You put me in a damn fish tank, people think that I pissed myself, women have been insulting all day in this damn country, and, honestly, I think I ate a little fish poop. So yes, I think we should fight for Rekluse. Hell, it's worth a beatdown just to say hi."

Slaycick started to laugh. "Tenan, you might want to watch yourself. This young man is truly testing your patience."

"My patience is gone!" Tenan said.

"Bring it, buddy!" Allucio replied.

Just as Tenan was about to form a portal to put Allucio in, another deep voice shouted out. "Tenan! Enough!"

Slaycick sucked his teeth. "Damn, just when it was about to get good."

Tenan relaxed his energy as the man walked out of the building. "Who are you two, and what do you want with me?"

Desmurose and Allucio watched as the man walked towards him. His black arms were shining as the reflection of the moonlight hit them. Rekluse walked right by his side. Allucio waved with a love-struck look on his face. Desmurose punched him in the gut, making him refocus. He didn't want to anger Tenan any further.

"Are you the man that they call Blessed?" Desmurose asked.

"Who is asking?" the man replied.

"We were sent here by our friend, Menzuo. He told us to find Blessed in Jerusalem. He said that you would know why we are here and would be able to help us."

Blessed and Rekluse now stood just a few feet away. Tenan and Slaycick stood in position directly behind them, ready to attack if they felt a threat of an impending battle.

"How do I know that your energy is good?" Blessed asked.

Desmurose looked to Allucio. "We have to show them."

Allucio nodded. In an instant, the two warriors transformed into their power suits. Their energy levels shot up, making the Majesties step back. "We honestly mean no harm or disrespect to you all," Allucio said. "We just really want to know why we need to find you." He turned to Tenan. "I am sorry for the tension that I caused. I tend to joke around too much, and I kind of lose it around pretty girls."

Tenan didn't break a smile. "Don't let it happen again. Apology accepted."

Allucio turned back to Blessed and Rekluse. "You are beautiful, Ms. Rekluse, but it's not my place to push. I am sorry for disrespecting you."

"It's no problem at all. I must say thank you, because it actually woke Tenan up a bit," Rekluse said. She heard Tenan sigh as his jealousy slowly digressed.

Blessed stepped forward. "I am the one you are looking for. I have to tell you, we do not know of your friend, Menzuo, or what our purpose could possibly be in helping you both out. Where is your friend? Why didn't he come?"

Desmurose sighed. "Menzuo is on a personal journey at the moment. Not too long ago, we were battling a very powerful Pirate Warrior, and a lot has changed for the rest of our team and us. We're called the Solar Warriors."

"You mean there are more of you?" Rekluse asked.

"Yes, but we are spread throughout the universe at the moment. The other warriors are on their home planets to keep them protected," Allucio replied. "There is a serious threat coming, and we have to be ready for it."

"Hmm," Slaycick said. "There seems to be more than one threat coming our way."

"Slaycick, you're right," Blessed said. "These battles we're fighting are just pieces of the war that we'll be facing. We will surely have our hands full. Not to mention what else could be out in this universe. We must strategize and figure this out."

"We didn't know that there was so much evil coming at us. I hope our travels to find you and the Majesties are an answer to all this unrest," Desmurose said.

Blessed started to walk back to the building. "Follow me. We can sit and talk strategy. We need to know what the Solar Warriors are facing, and we can tell you both everything that the Majesties are up against. From there, we can talk about everything that is centered in Hero City and what we know so far. We can also figure out how your friend Menzuo has us all tied together. I may have an idea as to why you both are here, so your journey may not be as strange as you think."

Everyone followed Blessed back into the building, ready to put everything on the table about their past battles and what the future may hold.

CHAPTER 4

SOMETHING BAD IS UPON US

"In about an hour, we will be entering the Earth's atmosphere," Judge Amaruk said. "Make sure our artillery is prepared and command our aeronauts to put us in cloak mode. Scramble all satellite frequencies so we can't be detected. We will strike without warning and put the inhabitants of Earth on their heels with no time to react."

"At once, sir," General Swadin said as he made his way toward the flight deck.

Judge Amaruk turned his attention towards Natas and the two giants.

"And for you three, it's best if you stay together," Judge Amaruk said. "They say a threefold cord is not quickly broken. Even I must agree that, in unity, the three of you will be more powerful than what any army can throw at you."

"When we arrive, I will retrieve Dr. Samir and Dr. Bernstein," Natas said. "I will lay waste to The Majesties' headquarters and kill all of them. Afterward, I will begin my reign as the new emperor of Earth."

"Spoken like a true antichrist figurehead," Judge Amaruk said. "However, there is one more cog in this engine – an uncalculated move that I've kept close to the vest until now."

"What is this cog you speak of?" Natas bellowed.

"A space pirate named Stratus. His relevance in our mission is paramount and will require your patience, Natas."

"You can bring anyone you want to join as long as they don't interfere with my plans. I have two objectives: kill the Majesties and put the entire world under my command with the new world order agenda I have been planning from the start. Anyone who tries to hinder me from doing so will be killed immediately."

"You're heard loud and clear, Natas," Judge Amaruk said. "Just keep something in mind. Don't allow the fury that drives your mission to blind you from the support that is given to you from those who are noble to your cause. If it wasn't for me, you and your colossal comrades would be dead right now. There would be no mission. With that said, I'll leave you three to discuss your strategies and devices concerning Earth."

Judge Amaruk left the weapons deck where he and the giants had been talking.

"Grrrrrr. Father, I have a bad feeling about him," Gath growled. "I don't trust him."

"That's a good thing, son," Natas said to the giant. "Everyone in our line of work has a self-motivated agenda. Assume no one as a friend. In the meantime, we'll play nice. He did reel us in from certain death had we remained in space. If he crosses us, we'll deal with him accordingly."

"I hope he does cross us," Siph said. "I still owe him for what he did to us during training. This time I'll smash him for real."

The two brothers high-fived each other and listened to Natas as he laid out his plan for their return to Earth.

***

Judge Amaruk approached a door that opened automatically. He stepped inside and sat down at a black desk with a square silver box on top of it. He picked it up and opened it. A bright purple glow illuminated his face as he smirked with a menacing grin.

"I'm learning your ways," he whispered softly. "Soon, I will be able to manipulate you for my purpose, which is the greater good for all galaxies."

He closed the box and pressed a red button that was installed on his desk. An image appeared on the large screen. He gazed in amazement as the partial silhouette of a shadowy figure, draped in a long-robed hoodie with cut-off sleeves, sat motionlessly. The person had massively huge arms that likened him to a tremendous Greek sculpture etched out of stone. A hood covered the face, and nothing could be seen in the darkness except two glowing green eyes.

"I take it, you have good news for me," said the dark figure.

"I do, Lord Stratus," Judge Amaruk said. "I'm proud to report that everything has been set in motion. The antichrist figure is set on his vendetta to destroy the Majesties and the other Super-Normals who partner with them, clearing the path for your reign."

"In your estimation, Amaruk, is Natas someone who will be on board when he realizes that my plans for Earth are not the same as his?"

"Truth be told, Lord Stratus, Natas is one of great pride. He has already made it plain that he would kill anyone that gets in the way of his plans. We should put a contingency plan in place in the event that he does not cooperate."

"Duly noted," Stratus said. "Any weaknesses?"

"Natas and the giants are of great size, and I have reconstructed their new suits with Sinathyst. Nonetheless, they are still not as powerful as you. Your ability to manipulate both Oramite and Sinathyst makes you the most powerful being in all of the galaxies. If Natas and the giants do decide to challenge you, you will have full control and power over them."

"Very good! You have done us well," Stratus said.

"If I may inquire, Lord Stratus, you made a promise to me that you would make me ruler over this galaxy if I assisted you on your quest. I have been nothing but cooperative and loyal. Do you plan on honoring your word?"

"We'll cross that bridge when we get to it, Amaruk. Remember, I spared your life because you had a special skill set that I admired. I even spared your comrade at your request. I made you captain of this vessel. I gave you crew members from other planets whom I showed mercy to, and I placed them under your command. I didn't have to do any of that. That in itself should be enough for you to be grateful towards me."

"And I am, Lord Stratus. Please don't think that I'm not. I just know that General Swadin and I would be able to carry out these tasks more efficiently if we had more help. Please don't take my questioning as an offense, sir."

"Carry out your directives," Stratus said. "If everything goes according to plan and we are victorious, you and I will have that discussion. Until then, let's stay focused and execute our duties. My World Harvesters are gearing up for their raid on planet Earth, and your role is imperative to its success."

"Understood, Lord Stratus."

The screen went black, and Judge Amaruk leaned back in his chair. He sighed deeply and closed his eyes as a somber flashback replayed in his mind. He stood atop a balcony overlooking a courtyard filled with dead bodies, laid waste in the wake of Stratus' vengeful path of death and destruction. The entire nation of his homeworld was pillaged and destroyed as Stratus and his World Harvesters arrived and drained the life out every living being. Judge Amaruk, the only survivor along with General Swadin, battled back against the World Harvesters using his gift of necromancy, telekinesis, flight, speed, and hand-to-hand combat.

He recalled being overpowered by Stratus and the World Harvesters. Just as he was about to surrender his life to them, Stratus unexpectedly extended a hand of mercy on the condition that Judge Amaruk would serve him. Judge Amaruk agreed while pleading over the life of a nearly dead General Swadin. His reason for agreeing to the terms was simple: he and General Swadin were the last of the Necromenian race.

The planet Necrom was a world full of terrestrial beings who practiced mysticism, magic, supernatural spells, charms, and making their bodies as strong and agile as possible. They were one of the most powerful planets in all the galaxies until they were overtaken by Stratus and the World Harvesters.

Judge Amaruk was one of the most powerful of the Necromenians. He learned how to reverse the power of telekinesis on himself, lifting his own body and maneuvering it wherever he wanted to. To those who witnessed it, they would call it flying. He studied the darkest depths of mysticism, making him one of the most powerful enchanters in existence.

Judge Amaruk became so skilled that he taught himself how to travel by spirit throughout the galaxies, yielding him access to find such elements as Oramite and Sinathyst. It was a skill that even Stratus did not know he possessed. Yet, he still was not strong enough to defeat Stratus or the World Harvesters on his own.

As he sat, the door slid open and in walked General Swadin.

"Sir, our pilots are ready, and we're already in cloak mode."

"Thank you, General Swadin," Judge Amaruk said with a perplexed look on his face.

"Is everything okay, sir?" General Swadin asked.

"No, everything is not okay. Stratus speaks to me as if I should be thankful to him for sparing our lives after killing off our entire planet. I'm tired of being controlled by him. All this talk of giants, the antichrist, and killing people just so he can exalt himself has become tiring. We've done this for centuries, and for what?"

"Sir, you said yourself that he hears from Lucifer. Should we not be thankful? Stratus asserted you as the one who makes the way for the galactical antichrist figureheads. You were looking for a place in his kingdom with all of your studies into the dark arts. Consider this a righteous fate."

"Are you siding with him, General Swadin?!" Judge Amaruk shouted with a scowl on his face. "He killed off our planet and would have left you for dead had I not pleaded for your life! We are Necromenians – a powerful species. We are not made to be servants or pawns!"

"Sir, look at me," General Swadin said calmly. "Whenever you're ready to make a move, I'm moving with you. I have not forgotten what Stratus did to our planet and our loved ones, but you and I are alive for a reason. Let's use that advantage and be ready when fate turns her favor to us again. Come and let us eat. You and I can discuss our plan over a hot meal."

Judge Amaruk took a deep breath and rose from his seat. He followed General Swadin out of the room as they began to deliberate their own scheme.

***

Blessed, Slaycick, Tenan, and Rekluse walked into their headquarters located in the Israeli Prime Minister's house. They were followed by Allucio and Desmurose. Several government officials and military security guards greeted them as they walked through the large estate. They entered into an office where Aganathin sat conversing with K'nia and Kasitia.

"Boss, how's it going?" Aganathin said. "And who are these two with you?"

"Allucio and Desmurose, meet Aganathin, K'nia, and Kasitia," Blessed said, pointing his finger back and forth between the new associates. "Aganathin, K'nia, and Kasitia, this is Allucio and Desmoruse. They're Solar Warriors from another planet."

"Well, we actually live in America, but our birthright is from planet Yardania, which is located in the outer realm of our solar system," Desmurose said.

Aganathin chuckled, "Oh boy, this plot just gets thicker and thicker. How did you run into these two?"

"We actually found them," Desmurose interjected. "We were sent here by our friend, Menzuo. He told us to find Blessed in Jerusalem and that he would know the purpose behind our joining forces."

"What do you got so far, big guy?" K'nia asked.

"I'm not so sure just yet," Blessed replied. "These two have revealed their gifts and, from what they've shared with us, I believe them. With the number of Super-Normals, good and bad, surfacing across the globe, I can't help but to discern that something greater is behind this. Perhaps a puppet master playing Geppetto."

"I'm not sure I get it," Allucio said.

"It's a reference to a famous novel about a woodcarver who creates a wooden puppet that comes to life," Tenan said. "Blessed is saying that there may be a bigger force out there beyond our realm that triggered the occurrence which transformed ordinary people into people with super abilities."

"Ahhh, I got it," Allucio said, "Pinocchio! I loved that story as a kid. Very interesting analogy, Blessed."

"But if that's the case, how do we find the people or aliens that are behind this?" Kasitia asked.

"That's what we have to figure out," Blessed said as he nodded toward a muted flat screen mounted on the wall. "But I don't think it will be hard."

"Yo, isn't that Blurr on the TV?" Slaycick asked as he pointed to the screen.

The news footage showed Blurr, along with Thief and Paladin, fighting off soldiers and militia groups. The drone video captured her darting from spot to spot like a jumping spider as flashes of her speed literally looked like a blur.

"Turn that up," Slaycick said.

"The story continues to develop revolving around the Q-18 meteor that landed in the North Pole just about a month ago," the reporter on the screen said. "Key members of The United Nations are connecting the meteor to a deliberate scheme from possible alien life forms from other planets to draw out the Super-Normals. We'll have more on that developing story as we get more detail."

"Aaagh," Tenan yelled as he grabbed his head and crouched.

"Baby, what's wrong?" Rekluse asked as she rushed to Tenan's side.

Tenan immediately stood up, and his eyes were white. His body became tense as he gritted his teeth.

"Baby!" Rekluse screamed.

"Tenan!" Blessed yelled as he ran to his friend's aid.

The rest of the Majesties and the Solar Warriors looked on with concern as Tenan shook with pain. After a few seconds, he came to, and his eyes returned to their normal color.

"Something is coming," Tenan said, breathing heavily. "I saw a vision: a large ship traveling towards Earth. I'll be right back."

A portal opened in front of him, and he stepped into the cusp of space just outside the Earth's atmosphere. The portal closed behind him. He touched his collar and a thin black mask constructed around his face. He floated aimlessly, looking around for the ship that he saw in his vision, but he saw nothing except stars. Confused, Tenan searched some more, opening another portal leading him further into the depths of space, but nothing was there. He turned around, eyeing the endless canvas of blackness and stars, suspended by the gravity-less pull of space as it slowly drew him closer into its darkness. He admired the beauty of the blue and green planet before him. From this distance, Earth never seemed so stunning. Still, there was no ship in sight.

He opened another portal and returned to the Prime Minister's house. The others stood before him, looking even more disturbed.

"I didn't see anything," Tenan said, "But something is definitely coming to Earth."

"What did you see, babe? Where did you go? You're putting me on edge," Rekluse said.

"I saw a ship with the giants on it," Tenan said. "There were two other figures who I couldn't make out. The vessel was large and it was close to Earth. I went into space to get a closer look, but did not see anything. Yet, there is this feeling in me that something is upon us."

"I've sensed the same thing for a while now," Blessed said. "Slaycick, can you get a hold of Blurr?"

"Sure thing, big man."

"I have a feeling that the meteor she and The Capes found in the North Pole has something to do with Tenan's vision," Blessed said. "Let's start putting our battle plan together now. Something is on the brink, and the clues are right in front of us. I can't shake the feeling that our meeting Allucio and Desmurose, the Meteor the Capes found, and Tenan's vision just now are all correlated. We need to be ready before the fireworks start."

The Majesties and the two Solar Warriors made their way to an elevator within the Prime Minister's house and descended below.

CHAPTER 5

ACCOMMODATIONS

Karla sat up on the side of the bed. The light from the Moon slashed in through a slit in the curtains dangling from the rods of her and Sebastian's bedroom window. Her forehead was littered with beads of sweat. She closed her eyes and breathed slowly, trying desperately to slow her heartbeat. It was all she could do to make another attempt o fall back to sleep.

Over the past two days, sleep was at a premium. Ever since the last vision following her alter ego, Blurr's failed attempt to apprehend Slingblade, waking from sleep in a cold sweat, had become the norm. Sebastian turned over and joined her at the side of the bed; his hands found her shoulders. "You okay, baby?" She shrugged and gave a slight nod. "Dumb question, I know. But I still have to check on you."

"I know, doll. But there's nothing you can do right now. It seems that this is something that I'm going to have to tackle on my own."

"Never!" Sebastian said, his voice heavy and intense. "You won't ever have to face anything alone. Not as long as I have breath in my lungs." He reached around and lifted her chin with his finger. Their eyes met. "You hear?"

A slight smile broke across Karla's face. "I do," she replied mildly.

"Together, we are going to get to the bottom of this, once and for all. Tell me about your visions and dreams again."

"They're both very different. Which one do you want to start with?"

"How about the visions? Starting from day one."

"Like, day one from before the last one with Slingblade?"

"Yes, that day. We need to look at everything. The answers have to be here somewhere, hidden in the minutia of the details."

"The *min-u-what*?"

Sebastian shook his head slightly. "It's the crux of the details."

"Oh, got it." Karla straightened. "But I'd rather begin with the dreams, since they're the most recent."

"Okay, shoot."

"Well, remember I told you before that I see things?"

"Yeah. You told me that you see fluctuations in time. Images. People. Places."

"Right. Some seem familiar, like you, Alice, and Lydia. Well, it's not like that anymore. Everything is different now. It's all unfamiliar. I don't recognize anything."

"Aliens? Like the visions I had of you being taken away?"

"No, not like that. There isn't any aggression. Just people surrounding me and touching my skin. Little kids and elderly women. They don't talk, just smile, but I can hear their voices. You know."

"Like telepathic communication. That's typical of dreams."

"Nothing typical at all about these."

"Everything sounds real peaceful. So what's with the cold sweats?"

"After the peace comes the war. I feel an intense sense of danger wash over me. Like, there's a powerful presence threatening to harm the women and the children."

"Can you see it?"

"No. It's nothing I can point to. Just a strong feeling." Karla shook her head in frustration. "It's hard to explain."

"Try harder, Karla," Sebastian said softly, taking her by the hand. "Look, I took a meditation class once in college. I can walk you through it."

"You're always so high-strung. I didn't take you for the mellow type."

"Well, I don't know what that's supposed to mean, but yeah, I did take it, thank you very much."

"It must've been an easy elective."

"Really, Karla? I can chill out too, you know."

Karla pointed at him. "See, right there, you tell on yourself."

"Would you just listen, please?"

"Alright, alright," Karla said shrugging.

"And for your information, it was an easy elective, but that's beside the point. Now, close your eyes and focus only on the sound of my voice." Karla followed his cue and closed her eyes. "Now, breathe in slow and deep. Let your mind drift off for second, only to a place of serenity and bliss. Maybe like a beach or a mountain top. Do you see it?"

Karla nodded. "Yes, I'm there."

"Great. That's your perfect place. Your special place. The place where you are safe and nothing can harm you."

"I'm there. I can see it. It's all so beautiful."

"Am I there, too?" Sebastian asked, somewhat concerned.

'No!"

"No?"

"I said no. It's my place, Sebas."

"Alright, alright. If this place was so special, I just thought I'd be there, that's all," Sebastian mumbled.

Karla opened her eyes. "This isn't working."

"Sorry, sorry. My bad. Close your eyes again," Sebastian insisted. Karla listened and followed his instructions. "Now, try to think back to the most recent vision. What can you recall?"

"Not much. It's all a little hazy."

"Think of objects that may stand out to you. Something significant that you may remember. Weapons, lights, or maybe the ships. The large ships. Are they there too?"

"Kinda. But remember the ships you described when you said they took me away?"

"Yes."

"Well, I can see them. But like I said, everything is bigger now. Massive in size, scope, and technology. There are beings of indescribable authority. It's like I'm envisioning some super advanced alien race."

"Are the dreams and the visions one?"

"No. The dreams are calm, with the exception of the creeper evil feeling washing over me, while the visions are the exact opposite. They're filled with a sense of overwhelming power that matches the scope of the images."

"You said before that you felt like you know them. Is that feeling the same now?" Sebastian asked.

"No. These beings are nothing like those before. Where the previous ones felt like they came to save me, these desire to hurt me. I feel a strong sense of separation. As if they mean to divide us."

"You mean me and you?"

"I'm not sure. Maybe the whole of us. Thief…me…you." Karla shook her head and opened her eyes. She gazed at Sebastian with tears slowly beginning to form. "I'm so frustrated, Sebastian. Am I losing my mind?"

Sebastian reached out and pulled Karla close to him, wrapping his arms around her shoulders and giving her a firm squeeze. "No, baby. You're fine and you're going to be fine. We are going to get through this together. No matter what. I think it's the speed power playing tricks on you. Were you able to ask Slaycick anything when you were with him?"

"It totally slipped my mind. I was worried about the mission at hand."

"Well, I'm going to see if we can reach out to them and get some more insight. Hopefully he can be of some help." Sebastian pulled back and planted a string of soft kisses on Karla's forehead. When she finally looked up at him, he finished it all with one long soft kiss on her lips, before pulling away.

Karla's eyes were still closed. "Hmm, that was wonderful," she whispered. "What did I do to ever deserve you?"

"You're just you. And I love everything about you, dream girl." Sebastian looked over at the curtains. The light from the moon had dimmed. "Looks like the moon is finally beginning to fade. Won't be long until the sun comes up. I think I'm gonna shoot down and whip up something to eat. You game for some old fashioned strawberry pancakes?"

"Your pancakes? The kind with the fluffy edges and warm syrup?"

"The one and only."

"All day, every day."

"Great, I'll race you down."

Karla tilted he head at him. "Seriously, fly guy? Not without your super suit. I'd whip you without using my speed." Karla's eyes beat up and down his body. She pointed at him. "Besides, you need to put some clothes on first. Don't think Lydia would appreciate your perfect bottom as much as I do."

Sebastian blushed and turned to look at his backside. "Is it really that perfect?"

"Perfect enough to balance a coffee cup on. If I drank coffee."

"If you say so."

Karla slapped him on the rear. "I know so."

***

Following breakfast, Sebastian took to the laboratory, busily flipping through multiple computer screens as he mulled over some final designs for an upgrade to the S4.

"You're totally obsessed, you know," B.R.A.I.N. observed.

"I'm not," Sebastian barked. "I'm just…I don't know. I feel like I always need to be ready for the next thing, that's all."

"Next what?" B.R.A.I.N. asked.

"It's all coming to a head. Karla's been really stressed out over these dreams and visions. They seem to be advancing in scale and scope. I can't shake my visions. It can't be coincidence. And then there's that time with Zenith."

"There's always a time with him," B.R.A.I.N. said.

"And it's never smooth sailing." Sebastian straightened. "That vortex he took us into."

"Oh, you mean The Orchid characters?"

"Yep. Calling me the Lightning Rod, Karla the Queen, and hinting at seeing the smoke of Autumn's veil. All riddles. It only adds to the already convulted state of confusion. What do you think it all means?"

"I agree."

"What? I asked what you think it all means and you say 'I agree?'"

"I do agree with you. I think it means you need to keep working on that S4 upgrade after all. I like being in The Beacon and I'd like to continue to exist as one with this fabulous structure. It's a magnificent upgrade to that drab pad you had before. So yes, I have no desire for aliens bombarding the planet and destroying any of us."

"Wow, B.R.A.I.N., you have such a way with words."

"It's as sweet as I come, Sebastian," B.R.A.I.N. said mockingly.

"Projection," Sebastian said aloud. At once, a green wire-frame skeleton of the S4 appeared above him, turning slowly as the lights dimmed overhead. Sebastian stroked his chin. "Like what I did with it?"

"Smooth lines. Elegant design."

"You make it sound like a fancy foreign car," Sebastian said.

"I notice you finally removed the breastplate."

"Yeah, with the full integration of the telepathic communication interface, it wasn't necessary. The S4 can almost anticipate my next move. It's pretty amazing, if I do say so myself."

"Don't stroke your ego too much, smart guy. I'll one up you," B.R.A.I.N. said.

Sebastian folded his arms across his chest. "How so?"

"I've been working on a final modulation code for the S4. Once I integrate it, the S4 won't only be able to anticipate your next move, it will make it for you."

"What?"

"I call it A.I.M. Artificial Intuitive Movement. Once you master learning how to let go – something you clearly struggle with – your performance proficiency in the field will increase some one hundred to one thousand fold."

Sebastian's eyes widened. "No way."

"Yes way. If I had eyes, I'd wink."

Sebastian looked out the window and walked over to it. "But you do have E.I.E.s, B.R.A.I.N." A drone passed by the glass, sailing across the city. "How are they running nowadays, ever since Big Brother got involved with their intel gathering?"

"Oh, you mean the Electronic Investigative Eyewitnesses? They're fine. They'll continue to record the daily activities of the Super-Normals."

"The Nightwatch's ratings are down again."

"Not much activity since Caine bit the dust and Dame Lightning went bye-bye at the North Pole," B.R.A.I.N. said.

"It's all for the better, right? Don't need the government prying into our business anymore than they already do."

"Well, we only show them what we want them to see and hear. I still instituted that lockout protocol on the E.I.E.s – giving us the final say on what is newsworthy. Just like you instructed."

"Sweet."

"You can thank me now."

"For the E.I.E.s protocols?"

"No, for A.I.M.," B.R.A.I.N. said.

"Funny, I thought I did."

"He never does," Lydia said, entering the room.

"Really, cousin?" Sebastian asked.

"You owe me about a thousand, but who's counting," Lydia said, throwing a pair of underwear at him. The lights turned back on and the image of the S4 faded.

Sebastian caught them. "Hey, what are these?"

"Your dirty undies. Found them in the kitchen and please don't try to explain, 'cause I'm doing my best to block out any imagery of you and Karla waxing the counters."

"Well –"

"I said no!" Lydia said.

"So, what's on tap for you today, cuz?" Sebastian asked.

"Did you not read your email I sent?" Lydia asked.

"I was pre-occupied. What happened?" Sebastian asked.

Lydia pulled out a small device resembling a sleek cell phone from her coat pocket. She tapped on the screen and held it up to him to see. "Check it out."

Sebastian began to read aloud, slowly. "From the Pentagon. Hello Sebastian Teleford, we would like to extend another hearty thank –"

Lydia snatched it back. "Blah, blah, blah."

"Hey, I was reading that. It looked like it might have been important."

"Less important and more like cool. I'll give you the Cliff Notes. Remember that whole *Infinity* team name you guys were bouncing around before you packed up Q-18?"

"Yeah," Sebastian said.

Lydia tapped the screen again and turned it around. A logo of an Infinity sign gleamed on the screen. "Well, Uncle Sam wants to be the first to make suits for you guys. Courtesy of the good ole U-S of A."

CHAPTER 6

BEGINNING OF THE REIGN OF TERROR

"I can feel the presence of your return, my son!" Lord Fetid said, looking into the dark sky of planet Exervo as he sat on the balcony of his castle, as his Drones trained in battle with his newest developing Pirate Drone. "Your energy has risen. Your strength has almost become unmatched…your father is almost impressed."

The Drone in training, who had risen to the ranks to become the next released Pirate, made his way up the stairs to meet Lord Fetid. He knelt in front of him. "Master, what do you wish of me? I have killed hundreds of the Drones in training. My energy is growing within me. How close am I to completing my development?"

Lord Fetid directed his attention to the Pirate Drone. "Havoc, your development is complete, but your purpose won't be what you expect moving forward. There has been a great change in my plans for this universe."

"My Lord, I only exist to serve you in any way that you deem fit," Havoc said. "My purpose is to serve the all mighty Lord of Exervo."

Lord Fetid nodded. "Rise, my Pirate Drone and look into the sky."

"What am I looking for, Master?" Havoc asked.

"Do you feel that energy? Do you sense the immense strength that has entered our galaxy?" Lord Fetid said.

"Is it the strength of Menzuo that I am searching for, my Lord? I know that the young Prince has protected the universe in his battles against us. Is this something that should bring us worry?"

Anger started to rise within Lord Fetid as he stared into Havoc's eyes. "Menzuo? Why the hell would I be worried about that meaningless warrior? He and that sorry team of fighters that he has by his side are nothing. With the return of my son into our galaxy,

Menzuo and his Solar Warriors have just become a non-issue for Exervo."

The Pirate Drone redirected his attention to Lord Fetid. "Are you saying that Prince Stratus is alive and has returned? But I thought you had your son killed in the Traingulum Galaxy after the birth of the World Harvesters?"

"So I thought as well," Lord Fetid said. "But it seems that Stratus has not only survived, but has become a true terror. I can tell by the energy that I can feel within him. His resiliency to survive has intrigued me. The return of Stratus can be my victory to the takeover of this galaxy."

"My Lord, if Stratus has returned, should it lead you to believe that he will now be a threat to you and Exervo?"

"I have no threat!" Lord Fetid shouted, making all of the Drones below stop from fighting each other. He looked at his hands as he continued. "I am the ultimate being. With the defeat of Queen Eaziah in her battle against Menzuo on planet Earth, my body and most of my strength were returned to me. She drained enough energy from that planet and it fed us all. My Queen's sacrifice has damn near made me invincible. With my son's return, I will be unstoppable."

Havoc took a knee before Lord Fetid again. "I mean no disrespect to you, my Lord, but it may take some serious convincing to get Stratus on our side. Do you think he remembers that you tried to have him killed?"

"I pray that he does," Lord Fetid said. "I hope that death has motivated him to become the strong Pirate Warrior that I expected him to be. Leaving him for dead was part of my plan to develop a monster that would kill anything that tries to protect this galaxy."

"But don't you think that he'll try and kill you?" Havoc asked.

A smile fell upon Lord Fetid's face. "I wouldn't doubt it one bit. If I know my bloodline, I know that Stratus will take no mercy on me and I love it. He is exactly what I need to conquer this universe."

"My Lord, what will my purpose be?" Havoc asked.

"I need you to die by the hands of Stratus," Lord Fetid said. "You will be my greatest sacrifice and you will be responsible for returning my son under my reign."

Havoc bowed. "As you wish, my Lord. Please let me know of my mission at hand. I am ready."

Lord Fetid sat back in his chair and looked into the sky. He took in a deep breath then let it out slowly. "I will let you know very soon. For now, return to your training with the Drones. Become as strong as you can as you prepare to die."

"Yes, my Lord," Havoc said. He walked back down to the flood of Drones, killing as many of them he could, filled with vengeance and rage.

***

The Majesties and the Solar Warriors sat around the table, analyzing the recordings from the Quintillion asteroid. The sound of a faint signal grabbed Allucio's attention. "Do you guys hear that?"

"What is it?" Blessed asked.

"Play it back," Allucio said. "I can hear numbers under the white noise."

Blessed started the recordings over and turned the volume up. Everyone leaned in closer, focusing as hard as they could. They all listened for a few minutes.

"I can hear it now, but it's faint," Desmurose said. "I think that it is a sequence of numbers and I think it's repeating."

"Yes, it is," Allucio said. "I can hear it clearly for some reason."

"I still can't hear it," Blessed said. "What numbers do you hear?"

Rekluse grabbed a pen and paper, preparing to write the numbers down. "Can you repeat them, Allucio?"

As the numbers started over, Allucio sounded off. "Okay, here they are. 9-1-9-2-2-2-3-1-4…there is a pause and here comes the second set of numbers."

"I'm ready," Rekluse said.

Allucio nodded then continued. "2-6-9-4-7-8-7-0-5, that's it."

"Great work, Allucio," Blessed said. "Now we need to figure out what these numbers mean."

"I'm thinking that if these numbers are coming from the Quintillion asteroid, then this must be some type of coordinates from space. These numbers must lead us somewhere," Tenan said.

"Where did the Quintillion asteroid come from?" Slaycick asked.

"From the Titan moon of Jupiter," Blessed stated.

"Babe, can I have that paper?" Tenan asked Rekluse.

"Of course," Rekluse said. "What are you thinking?"

"I'm thinking that these numbers are leading us to Titan. If I can decipher the coordinates, then I can open a portal to take a peek at this moon."

"That's a great idea," Slaycick said as he went over to the computer. "Shoot me those numbers, Tenan."

Tenan read the numbers off as Slaycick typed them in. "You got them?"

Slaycick nodded. "You were right, my friends, there are the coordinates for Titan."

"That is amazing work, everyone," Blessed said. "Tenan, you have your location. Check it out."

"Be right back," Tenan said before quickly opening a portal. He stepped through it and it closed behind him.

"That is the coolest thing that I have ever seen," Desmurose said. "He can portal jump."

"Yeah, it's cool for him, but I haven't forgotten how he put me in that damn fish tank," Allucio said.

"He had good reason to do so," Desmurose said. "But it's all good now. We're all on the same team."

"I still owe him one," Allucio said, not letting it go.

Rekluse smiled. "He's very protective of me. Please don't hold it against him."

Allucio sighed. "I'll try not to, but that was embarrassing."

Before another word was said, the portal opened back up and Tenan returned to the room. "There is a ship on Titan, but I couldn't tell if anyone was on it. It looks like it crashed there. The strange thing about Titan is that there is oxygen there and the gravity is normal."

"This is very interesting," Blessed said. "The signal from the Quintillion asteroid has led us to Titan. We have to figure out the meaning of this."

"Well, Allucio and I are willing to travel there to check it out. I mean, we do have some experience with space travel," Desmurose said.

"But we don't have a ship anymore, remember?" Allucio said. "That thing disintegrated during our last trip. We're lucky we're alive."

"I can get you both there," Tenan said.

"Oh no! Hell no!" Allucio shouted. "Portal travel is out of the question for me. Won't we be stuck there if we go through that portal? How will we return?"

"I can always open another portal for you both to return. And don't disrespect my skill. I never miss my mark with my portals."

"Whoa, so testy!" Allucio said. "I'm just saying, that's a little risky."

"It's only risky if Tenan wants to dispose of you," Blessed said. "But since we are on the same team, he will keep your travels safe."

Desmurose put his hand onto Allucio's shoulder. "C'mon, you can't be that worried after all that we've been through? This is just recon. We go in, get the information that we need and head back through the portal."

"Wait a minute," Allucio said, thinking quick on his feet. "Isn't there another ship that your father has that we can use?"

Desmurose's eyes widened. "The ship that's stuck in the river near our house? That thing can't fly."

Allucio smiled. "Yes, it can. Your dad fixed it for us, just in case we needed to use it."

"Then it's settled," Tenan said. "I can bring you into your ship back in America."

"I like that idea much better," Allucio said.

"Once you all return, we can meet to discuss your findings," Blessed said.

"How will we be able to contact you?" Desmurose asked.

"Slaycick, give them one of our mobile coms," Blessed said. "Once you return to Earth, you can reach us through this."

Slaycick handed Desmurose the portable com. "Keep this close. The range is unbelievable. We can reach you from anywhere in this atmosphere."

"Your technology is sick!" Allucio said. "I think we're ready to go."

"Good luck, Solar Warriors. We're counting on you to bring us great information," Blessed said.

"We hope we can find out what's on that ship," Allucio said. "Hopefully we will see you all soon."

"C'mon, let's get you both home," Tenan said, He opened a portal that led back to Springfield, Massachusetts.

"Man, I wish we knew you before we flew all the way here. Just walk through a dang on portal and poof, we're home," Desmurose said. "This saves us so much time."

"It's the gift that I have," Tenan said. He looked at Allucio, tight-lipped and still a little ticked at him for hitting on his girl. "Let's go."

Allucio turned his nose up at him, fuming from what Tenan did to him. "See you soon, buddy," he said sarcastically.

Desmurose pushed him in the back, through the portal. "Get a move on, man!"

Allucio turned back and locked eyes on Rekluse and winked at her, making Tenan's grit his teeth. "Boy, you want to disappear into a black hole? I can put you there!"

"Sheesh! I was just playing. So damn sensitive!" Allucio said. "See you guys later and be safe."

"See you all soon," Desmurose said. They both walked through the portal, back to their home city.

As the portal closed, Aganathin turned to Blessed. "Hey, big guy, do you trust those two?"

"You know my trust is thin with new people, but I don't see a reason to think otherwise. Believe that I am weary of their motives, but hopefully what we have learned will strengthen us. If they were evil, I believe we would've figured them out by now. I just don't know their importance."

"I guess we'll soon see," Rekluse said. "I can tell you one thing, they are interesting characters."

"Yes, they are," Slaycick said. "But I'm curious to meet their friend, Menzuo. There seems to be more to his importance that we will find out very soon. A universal protector… hmm. That sounds powerful."

"It does," Blessed said. "We just have to allow time to play out."

The Majesties returned their focus back on the signals coming from the Quintillion asteroid, hoping to find any other hidden clues.

***

Allucio and Desmurose situated themselves in the spaceship hidden on the bottom of the Connecticut River. Desmurose powered it up and looked over to Allucio. "You have the coordinates to Titan?"

Allucio nodded. "Sure do. Are you ready for another adventure?"

"Of course. Let's go!" Desmurose shouted. "We'll be there in no time."

"Time for some action!" Allucio shouted.

Desmurose activated the cloaking mechanism and the ship completely disappeared from sight. He yoked the throttle forward, lifting the ship from the bottom of the river and catapulting it into the sky. The invisible vessel shot through the sky and broke through the clouds in a matter of seconds. With heavy anticipation of what was awaiting them on Titan, The Solar Warriors set a course to the moon of Jupiter with the hopes of solving the elusive mission at hand.

CHAPTER 7

SOW THE WIND

Night fell upon Hero City. Blurr and Paladin slowed to a brisk jog as they raced across one last rooftop, passing over a dark alleyway below. "So what do you think tonight, the Docks, or are we slumming it?" Paladin asked, gazing out over the lip of the building, eyeing the streets beneath them.

"Uh, I'm a little too tired to deal with Mob Bosses tonight. I say it's time for finger-licking, trigger-happy goons from the Slums," Blurr said, wrapping her flowing black hair in a long ponytail.

"It never gets old to me," Paladin said.

"What, beating up goons?"

"No, taking in your beauty."

A crimson tinge exploded across Blurr's cheeks. "You always know just the right things to say to make a girl smile, don't you?"

Paladin's helmet retracted backwards from his face. "Of course. Just to see you smile," he said, flashing all of his pearly whites and pointing at his cheeks.

"Wow, another new feature of the S4, huh?"

"Oh, you mean this," Paladin said as the helmet protracted back around, covering his face as before. "Yeah, just another one of the niceties of being a world class Super-Normal."

"That's what they're calling us now, world class?"

"Well, not exactly. It's what *I'm* calling us now." Paladin paused and flexed one of his biceps. The S4 tensed around his arms. "We're all over the news and it's not like anyone else is saving the world, you know?"

"There is the one group called The Majesties of Canaan, you know. I think they'd have something to say about it," Blurr teased.

"Well, it's seven of them and only two of us. And I didn't see the United States calling them to protect Q-18."

Blurr winked at him. "Ahh, don't go defending your ground, lover boy. I know you're a stud. They ain't got nothing on you, baby," she said in a soft, singsong voice.

Paladin shook his head. "So, are we good for Slums or nah?"

Blurr looked over the side of the building. Just as she was about to answer, an explosion ripped through the base of the building and the sound of hurricane force winds swirled about. The building began to disintegrate on top of itself. Paladin reacted, snatching Blurr from the edge and leaping from the side of it. He turned his back to the streets below as they plummeted some twenty stories down. They landed on the ground with a loud thud, and Paladin cradled Blurr in his arms to shield her from the debris and the collision. As the dust rose around them, Blurr sat up, straddling Paladin for the moment as she shook off the daze. "You okay?" Paladin asked.

"I'm fine. How about you? You took the brunt of the impact, didn't you?" she asked.

Paladin flashed the OK sign. "Seriously. S4, baby."

"You could've warned me, you know."

"Yeah, but I think it adds to my heroic flare, you know, world class hero stuff."

"Well it ain't world class if no one is here to see it," Blurr said, standing.

Paladin pointed at the sky. "Oh, I think they did." A pair of E.I.E.s zoomed by and hovered above them, just short of another building. "See, everyone will be talking about the scene of the Capes and a crumbling skyscraper on the Night Watch later on."

Blurr pulled Paladin to his feet and the two turned to observe what remained of the building as it toppled over upon itself. "How did happen? Who runs demolitions at night?" she asked.

"This building was brand new. I hope no one was in there," Paladin said.

"Two and thirty," a voice bellowed from behind.

Paladin and Blurr turned around to find a bald old man sporting a pair of dark shades and a fisherman hat. He wore a full length, white lab coat that covered a tight-fitted dark unitard costume that revealed way too much.

"Excuse me?" Paladin asked.

"I was answering your questions kids. Two and thirty. As in two people run demolitions, and thirty people were in that building when it crumbled. Two Super-Normals and thirty victims."

Paladin's hands fisted at his sides. "What the hell kind of game is this? You just killed thirty innocents!"

"Thirty Normals, son. And none of them were innocent. We've all sinned and fallen short of the glory of God," the old man joked.

"This look like some kind of game, old fart?" Blurr asked, stepping in front of Paladin.

"I'm too old to plan games, girl," the old man replied waving a finger at her.

Blurr shook her head. "Well, Mr. Age-inappropriate fashion-nova, you're gonna have to pay for that. You better hope there are survivors."

Another explosion ripped from behind Paladin and Blurr as a hulking man garbed in a full suit of sheet metal walked from the debris of the fallen building. He dusted off his hands. "Nah, I can vouch for the fact that there aren't. They're Normals darling, unlike us," he said sarcastically in a thick Italian accent.

"Well, since we don't have time for formalities," the old man began to circle Paladin and Blurr as the larger man slowly closed in. "I say we just get into it. I'm Whirlwind and that towering, ten-foot force to be reckoned with is Demonnition. You see, you two were the targets of that devastating demonstration, but you proved to be a little more elusive than we expected. Admittedly, I'm equally as disappointed as I am impressed."

Paladin gnashed his teeth. "Well, prepare to be even more amazed!" He leapt in Whirlwind's direction but was met by a backhand of wind that seemed to project from the old man's fists, repelling Paladin back in the direction of Demonnition, who snatched Paladin out of the air with one hand.

Demonnition held Paladin by his waist with both hands and gazed into his mask as if he could see right through it. "Come on out and play," he said, as he slammed Paladin with a head butt that sent Paladin into a daze.

The sound of cracking metal sent a shriek down Blurr's back. "No!" she screamed as she dashed into action and performed a series of uppercut and jab combos that quickly persuaded the brute to release his grip on Paladin, dropping him to the floor.

Paladin shook his head to realign his focus. Inside his helmet, the HUD waned between double, triple and single images. It was all he could to do to line them all up. But before he could, he was lifted into the sky by a torrential gust of rain and wind that tossed him clear across three city blocks and crashing through two more buildings in the process.

Demonnition swung at Blurr, who was preoccupied by trying to ascertain what happened to Paladin, and connected a backhand of his own to the side of her face, sending her reeling into to spin that flattened her to the gritty city street. Demonnition stepped over her and raised his fists overhead. With a roar he swung down in her direction, but before he could connect, Blurr had already sped around him and was now standing in his back as his fists pounding the city pavement. "Looking for me?" Blurr asked while performing stampede of sorts along Demonnition's back and head, before somersaulting away from him and landing atop a nearby parked car.

Demonnition faltered, dropping to one knee. He expelled a large bolus of blood from his mouth and stood, wiping the remnants from his jaw. He pointed at Blurr with his other hand. "Stand still so I can give it to you, whore. Don't make me beg!"

"Another limp idiot making promises," Blurr joked.

"Super-sonic speed!" another voice echoed in the distance, as a flash of purple raced in Blurr's direction. Before she could react, someone grabbed her by the arms and raced into the night sky. The two engaged in a barrage of punches and slaps while simultaneously running through the air, Blurr backpedaling and the purple foe sprinting forward. It was a young male, no older than his early twenties, sporting a backwards hat, dark goggles and pair of four finger rings on both hands.

"Who… the … hell…are you?" Blurr asked.

"I, I, I am just an Icon living!" Icon replied.

"Oh, please," Blurr grunted.

On the street below, Paladin returned, his body easily four times his original size as the S4 bloomed into strength mode. Demonnition wasn't impressed. "My, how you've grown since the last time. Are those 'roids in your pocket, or are you just happy to see me?" he joked.

Whirlwind stepped forward. "Let me blast him back to size." Gail-force winds streamed from Whirlwind's hands and pounded Paladin. But this time, to their surprise, he didn't flinch. "What?"

"Hit 'em again!" Demonnition cried.

Whirlwind collected himself and shook his hands at his sides. After rubbing them briskly together, he tried again, this time shouting, "Reap the Whirlwind!" All matter of free standing objects around Paladin lifted into the sky like tissue paper. Buses, cars, light poles and chunks of concrete and asphalt tore away and scattered. Paladin stopped and leaned forward, his feet slowly digging into the ground beneath him. Seconds passed and the wind finally broke as the old man fatigued of his unsuccessful efforts. Whirlwind dropped to the ground, gasping. "That's impossible. It can't be. How?"

"Tropical breezes in Chi-Town and it isn't even summer yet," Paladin joked.

"Don't worry," Demonnition said, slamming his fist into his opposite hand. "Nobody can resist these hammers."

Demonnition attacked, swinging uncontrollably at Paladin, who had already switched to the speed variant of the S4 and slipped around each punch and countered with blows of his own which strategically began to pierce weak points of Demonnition's armor.

"One last point, cousin," Lydia said over the IEPCS.

Paladin ducked and landed one more punch under Demonnition's armpit that split the entire armored suit in half. Paladin sped away as the protective shell peeled from Demonnition's body with a loud clang, leaving him half naked with only a pair of underwear covering his groin.

Demonnition's eyes widened. "What?"

"I know, it can't be, right?" Paladin asked, just before turning invisible, the last variant of the S4.

Demonnition looked around, twisting about in an attempt to find Paladin. When his eyes landed on Whirlwind – who was back on his feet – it was too late. Paladin materialized behind the old man, larger than before, and chopped Whirlwind in the back of the neck. The old man dropped to the ground instantly.

"Father!" Demonnition screamed, as he railed in Paladin's direction.

Paladin set his feet, took a protective stance and cocked back his fist one final time. Demonnition carelessly attempted a double fisted punch, but missed as Paladin easily dodged it and parried his attack with a jab that smashed Demonnition's breastbone and stopped his heart. The mammoth of a man slumped to the ground in a snap. Paladin turned his attention to the dark sky above. All he could make out were streams of baby-blue, gold, and purple lights flashing against the black background. After what seemed like an eternity, one final color bloomed in the distance – red, as a single purple flare rocketed to back to Earth.

"Miss me, love?" Blurr asked from behind Paladin.

Paladin turned around as his helmet began to retract. "Damn, you're fast."

Blurr looked around observing Paladin's hand-work. "Damn, you're strong."

He leaned in and gave Blurr a kiss, his hands slowly running along her back and waist. They were interrupted by a swift breeze closing in around them. "Pause," Paladin said, as his helmet protracted and the two of them turned to face the source of the wind. A portal appeared as Blessed and the rest of The Majesties exited.

"Paladin," Blessed said. "I hope we weren't disturbing you two?"

CHAPTER 8

THREAT ON TITAN MOON

"You see that light just over that mountain ridge?" Allucio said as he pointed to his right.

"Yeah, I see it," Desmurose answered. "Do you think that's the spaceship that we're looking for?"

Allucio looked at the directions that he typed into the ship's navigation system. He nodded. "I believe that it is. Tenan said that the atmosphere here is similar to Earth's, so we can fly there if need be. Let's park the ship at a safe distance. We don't know what we'll find."

"Good idea," Desmurose said as he turned the spaceship to the left. "I'll land the ship in the crater over here. It looks like we're just a few miles away."

Desmurose guided the space ship down into one of the moon's craters. Shutting down the engines, they both unbuckled their seatbelts and walked to the back hatchway.

"Keep your eyes open and your guard up," Allucio said. "We have no clue as to what we might find, or even if this is a setup."

"A setup?" Desmurose said. "You don't trust what we found with the Majesties?"

"It's not that I don't trust them or what we found, but they didn't offer to come with us. It's just a little strange to me," Allucio replied.

"You have to remember two things. They have never traveled to outer space, other than Tenan. He used his ability to portal jump to space, and Blessed did mention some type of potential threat coming to Earth. I know for sure that, as a leader, he wouldn't think that it would be wise to put all of their resources on this mission. Plus, I don't think they fully trust us either, I mean…we did just show up out of nowhere, looking for them."

"Then, the feeling is mutual. Trust has to be earned. Menzuo sent us searching for a needle in a haystack, and we found it. Now we're on a moon that floats around a different planet, searching for another needle in a haystack. I feel like I'm in a role-play videogame."

Desmurose chuckled. "You've got to admit this is a little cool."

Allucio nodded with a half-smile. "It is...okay, let's get to that ship."

Desmurose hit the button to open the hatchway. As the door slowly exposed them to Titan, the temperature plummeted, as a windy shrill skipped along his skin. "Wow, that drop in degrees is crazy!" Desmurose said. "Feels close to freezing out here."

"Good thing I packed our jackets," Allucio said. "My mom trained me well. Can't ever be over prepared."

They both put on leather jackets that were designed with similar insignias that their power suits had. As they moved their arms, they tightened their muscles to test the flexibility of the jackets just in case they ever needed to fight in them. It was easy to see that they fit perfectly.

"Are you ready?" Desmurose asked.

"Yup, let's go," Allucio said.

They both flew off, flying low to the ground and over the barren mountains. Both of them did their best to keep their energy levels hidden, just in case they were not the only ones on Titan. As they continued to fly over the highest mountain peak, a blinking light caught their attention. It was coming from a crashed space ship.

"There it is," Allucio said. He and Desmurose scanned the sky and the ground as they flew closer. "I don't see or sense any strong life out here, but it feels eerily strange."

"It does feel strange. We have to be prepared for anything. Let's get close to the ship and go from there." Desmurose said.

They both sped up, within a few minutes, they landed on a mountain just a few hundred yards from the ship. Crouching down, they scanned the area a little longer as well as studied the ship. "I don't sense any movement from the spaceship or anything around it," Allucio said.

Desmurose looked at the ground, noticing a long skid mark that the space ship left as it crashed. He could tell that the back end of the ship had exploded. He figured that it was from the impact of the landing. "There is no energy that resembles life coming from the ship. It looks safe, but I can't be sure."

"Me either, but we can't be sure about anything from here, so I guess we should just get to it," Allucio said.

They both jumped down from the mountain, landing on the ground. The two warriors started to walk towards the ship.

As they continued on, Allucio and Desmurose scanned the area on Titan with caution. Within moments, they were both upon the ship and noticed that the ladder leading to the hatchway was down. There was a large hole in the windshield where the pilot would sit, and the cracks on the gaping hole were filled with blood.

"This doesn't look good at all," Allucio said.

"Looks like the impact of the crash was terrible for whoever was flying this ship," Desmurose added.

Allucio studied the entrance. As he did, something felt off. "I don't think that we should both go on the ship to check it out. It feels eerie out here. I'm not sure that we're alone."

Desmurose looked back over his left shoulder, peeking back at the mountains in the distance. "I think you're right. I don't feel good about this journey. It almost feels like a setup."

"I knew you didn't trust those Majesties! You think they set us up, don't you?"

Desmurose shook his head. "No, I don't. I didn't get that vibe from them. I don't think the Majesties are mischievous like that. It's something else here that's very strange. Focus on it."

Allucio looked down to the ground. After a few moments, his head popped up. "I can feel it, too. It feels like…death."

"I'll stay out here and keep watch," Desmurose said. "We have to stay cautious."

"Got you," Allucio said. "If you see or hear anything –"

Desmurose nodded as he cut his friend off. "Don't worry. I'll make sure that I alert you. Just be careful, and you do the same if you find anything."

They shook hands, then Allucio walked up the ladder and into the opened hatchway of the spaceship.

As he got to the top, the stench of decaying flesh rushed to his senses. "Man, that smell is unreal. Something has been dead a long time in here."

As they investigated the vessel, Allucio noticed that every door was open. A faint ticking sound from the pilot's cabin quickly grabbed his attention. He moved closer to the sound but could not see entirely inside the cabin as the door was blocked by a metal cabinet that had fallen over. "Damn, that's strong," he said to himself. He tried to focus on the noise to distract himself from the overpowering odor. Allucio leaned in closer. In actuality, it was not just a ticking noise at all, but a series of counting numbers indicating the coordinates of the spaceship's location.

The young warrior tried to peek over the fallen cabinet, but could not see anything. He decided to lift it out of the way so that he could get in. After moving the cabinet, Allucio could now see a figure slumped over in the pilot's seat. Blood had covered the right side of the figure's body and a dark liquid was dripping from his head. He walked closer to get a better look at things.

Allucio finally covered his nose, blocking the intense smell of the dead pilot. He looked at the person, noting severe injuries, possibly from the impact of the crash. A strange metal collar was strapped to the neck. "There's nothing that I can do for this guy. Sorry, buddy."

"Is everything okay up there?" Desmurose shouted from the outside of the ship. "Do you see anything?"

"Yeah, a dead guy!" Allucio shouted back. There was a blinking light to the left of the pilot. "Wait a minute! I think I found something else. There's a recording on the captain's log." Allucio pushed the red button on the dashboard, and the audio file started to play.

"This is captain Sans of Necrom," the voice shouted. The audio was loud enough from Desmurose to hear from the outside of the ship. Both warriors focused on what was said as the captain continued. "The Necromanian people on my home planet have been wiped out. Our planet has been completely drained of all energy and resources. There was no way that we could save our people or our home from that monster and its beasts. I don't know who he was, but I have never faced fear and death like this in all my life. I heard someone call him 'Lord,' but my findings of this man are incomplete. He entered our planet with these…these huge monsters…these things that he controls called World Harvesters. They have fed plentifully on the souls of every Necromanian. To see the spirits of my friends taken from their bodies is an unimaginable death to witness. These World Harvesters continued to grow as they destroyed everything in their wake." The captain was breathing heavily as he continued. "I barely made it off of the planet alive, but I feel that I'm not alone. I think I'm being followed."

The audio file started to break up as the sound of an explosion filled the background. "This doesn't sound good!" Allucio shouted to his friend.

"I think we know what made the ship crash," Desmurose shouted back. "Someone or something attacked it."

The captain's audio came back on clearly. "I've been hit! I've been hit! The ship has taken critical damage. I may not survive this! I'm going to make a landing on this planet's moon. I have to send my coordinates to Earth in hopes that this galaxy's saviors can locate it. If this message reaches you…take the halo spheres to Earth. They…they are the key to stopping these World Harvesters." The audio started to break up as the ship descended from the sky. "They must be activated with…with the serum of the dark…dark…dark…" Captain Sans' audio file ended abruptly as the spaceship crashed onto Titan.

"Mixed with what?" Desmurose shouted.

Before Allucio could respond, something latched onto his neck. "What the…" he shouted. The young warrior could hear a rumbling coming from behind him. Quickly turning around, he was stunned by a sonic wave blast, which knocked his equilibrium off and instantly blurred his vision. "What's happening?"

The sound of the sonic wave caught Desmurose's attention. "Allucio, what's happening up there?"

Before an answer could be given, a loud bang shook the spaceship's inner core, and Allucio's body was shot right out of the broken windshield, shattering it into millions of pieces. As his body slammed into the ground, just a few feet from Desmurose, a collar tightened around his neck. "Aaah! What's happening to me?"

Desmurose quickly ran over to his friend. "What was that?" he asked. "What is that around your neck?"

Allucio slowly regained his vision. Just as he looked up, he saw a menacing figure closing in behind Desmurose. His eyes widen with fear. "Watch out!" Allucio shouted.

It was too late; the individual threw a collar directly at Desmurose, latching it right onto his neck.

"What?" Desmurose shouted as he grabbed hold of the collar. It tightened quickly, stunning him. He turned around to see man charging towards him, carrying a large sledgehammer. "I can't move!"

Before Desmurose could react, the man swung his weapon, connecting right in the middle of Desmurose's chest, sending him soaring backward, violently smashing into the side of the spaceship. His body went cleanly through it. He exited the other side of the spaceship and landed on the ground.

As Desmurose's body made impact, the other man blasted through the front of the ship, pointing his sonic wave gun directly at Allucio's chest. The force of the attack started to plant Allucio deeper into the ground. The man landed right next to his partner.

Desmurose picked his head up, clearing his vision. There were two men standing right over his friend. "Hey!" he shouted as he stood to his feet. "Who the hell are you two?" They didn't answer. Both men just stood motionless, looking forward as if they were statues. He brushed himself off and shouted out again. "I said, who the hell are you two?"

The man with the shiny sledgehammer turned to face the young warrior. Without hesitation, he charged right towards Desmurose with amazing speed. "Shut your damn mouth!" the man shouted.

"You want a fight, then you've got one!" Desmurose replied. He tried to power up, but couldn't. "What's happening to me?" He tried once more but was unsuccessful.

The man swung his weapon in an upward motion, connecting right on the bottom of Desmurose's chin. The impact sent the young warrior high into the sky. Just as Desmurose opened his eyes, he noticed the man floating right above him. "You two are going to be a great trade-in for that Oramite gold!" He lifted his hammer above his head then swung it violently into Desmurose's chest, stopping him from ascending higher into the sky.

The force of the blow shot Desmurose's body back towards the ground like a missile. Within a few seconds, he was right into the hole that Allucio was lying in. The unknown man landed back on the ground next to his partner and stood motionless once again.

"Man, get off of me!" Allucio shouted as he felt his friend on top of him. The dust cleared from the hole as they tried to collect themselves.

"I can't power up!" Desmurose said as he rolled over. "I think these collars can block our powers."

"That alien on the ship had one on, too," Allucio said. "I wonder who these guys are and what they want."

"I guess we need to find out!" Desmurose replied.

Both warriors quickly jumped out of the hole and landed on the opposite side of the two new threats on the Titan moon.

Brushing themselves off, Allucio and Desmurose stared the two men down. They stood about six feet tall, with very muscular builds, almost like heavyweight boxers. There were several scars covering their arms and faces. The unknown men's bodies were masked with different colorful tattoos, which painted a picture of death and carnage. Surely they were a force to be reckoned with.

"Who are you, and what do you want?" Allucio asked.

"We are here to collect the head of that Necromanian in that ship. You two can't claim it from us," one of the men shouted.

"That bounty is ours to keep," the other man shouted. "That is our kill and our prize, but you two will add to the bounty. Surely, you two have powers that will garnish us a hefty payday."

Allucio and Desmurose looked at each other confused. Their focus went back to the men. "Bounty Hunters?" Desmurose said with a very confused look on his face. "A Necromanian? What is that?"

"You two have no clue what's going on here, do you?" one of the men replied. "Let me make this easy for you. My name is Greavis, and this is my business associate Tearin. We are Bounty Hunters, and we're paid to collect the heads of any refugees that escape in any galaxy."

"And along the way," Tearin added. "If we so happen to find any special beings that will sweeten our payday, we collect them, as well."

"So you two think that you're going to sell our heads? To who?"

"Not your heads," Tearin replied. "Looks like you two are more valuable alive than dead. You both look like fighters. We can sell you on the open market in the gauntlet in one of the seven galaxies."

"Seven galaxies?" Desmurose said. "You mean there's more than the one we live in?"

Greavis sighed heavily while shaking his head. "I don't have time to explain these things to you, nor do I care to. Just shut up and come with us peacefully."

"Sorry, buddy, but we have to get back to Earth. We don't have time to mess with you, either," Desmurose said.

"And how do you think that you're going to get back to your planet?" Greavis asked.

"Duh, with our ship, of course," Desmurose answered.

Tearin raised his hand, letting Allucio and Desmurose see a trigger resting on his palm. He pushed the button. There was a loud explosion in the distance, and a mushroom cloud filled the Titan sky, right where their spaceship was parked.

"You mean, that ship?" Tearin said. "Too bad you now have no way home. We followed your every move once you broke through the moon's atmosphere. Such fools, leaving your only way home abandoned."

"What did you do?" Allucio shouted. "That's it! Powers or not, I'm going to rip you to pieces!"

Both Solar Warriors ran around the hole, bringing a fierce attack to the bounty hunters. Allucio and Desmurose punched and kicked Greavis and Tearin as violently as they could, but their attacks barely moved the bounty hunters back.

Allucio and Desmurose stopped their barrage of punches and kicks, noticing that it wasn't doing any damage.

"Are you serious?" Greavis said, questioning the young warrior's battle skills. "You have no powers to fight us. Just make this easy and give up."

"You have no idea who we are. We do not give up!" Desmurose shouted. "We will protect this universe until our dying breaths."

"Your dying breaths?" Greavis asked. "Then so be it...Die!" he shouted.

The bounty hunters wasted no time to attack the young warriors. Tearin hit them both with his sonic wave gun, completely stunning them. Allucio and Desmurose tried their best to stay on their feet as they covered their ears and struggled to regain their focus

Greavis spun his hammer above his head. "This is going to be fun!" Violently launching his attack, he slammed the head of the hammer into both of their chests with a combination of swings. The impact knocked the stunned protectors back a few hundred feet.

The Solar Warriors' bodies flew back, bouncing on the ground of the Titan moon, leaving deep body imprints every spot that they landed.

"This can't be happening!" Allucio shouted. He could feel his energy depleting. He wrestled to get the collar off of his neck.

"We have to try and fight!" Desmurose replied as he tried his best to release the grip from the collar.

Allucio slowly stood and controlled his breathing. He reached his hand out to pick up his friend. "Until our dying breath, brother."

Desmurose looked up, then grabbed Allucio's hand and lifted himself off of the ground with the needed assistance. He nodded. "Until our dying breath."

"Hmm, you both are tough," Tearin said. "Too bad we have to kill you. We could've made some great money off of you two as our slave fighters. Oh well, maybe we will find smarter warriors in this galaxy. Less stubborn ones."

The bounty hunters charged in as fast as they could, using their weapons to keep the Solar Warriors under their control. Their attacks were increasingly violent as the Solar Warriors' bodies were breaking down from the pain.

Over and over, Greavis and Tearin waged on without hesitation. Allucio and Desmurose were helpless and couldn't protect themselves from any punch, kick, or violent blow from the bounty hunters' weapons.

Slamming their bodies all through the Titan passage, the Solar Warriors did their best to protect themselves from the bounty hunters' attacks, knowing that they didn't have enough strength to fight back. One last blow to the bodies of the young warriors threw both of them to the ground.

Greavis and Tearin stopped their attacks, noticing that Allucio and Desmurose were hanging on by a thin thread of life.

Tearin stood over Allucio as he tried to open his eyes. "Please tell me that you want to live and be our slave fighters." Tearin said. "I'd rather not kill two warriors that can hold up against our vicious attacks."

Greavis stood next to Desmurose as he looked at Allucio. "Save your friend and say that you give in. I would hate to have to crush his skull right in front of you. There is no escaping this fate. There's only death or slavery."

Desmurose looked over to Allucio. “We choose death!” he shouted.

Greavis took in a deep breath then let it out slowly. “So be it!” He raised his hammer above his head, directing it right at Desmurose’s ear. “What a waste.”

As he started to swing his hammer downward, a flash of fire hit Greavis right in the back of his head, sending him bouncing across the ground and right into the mountainside in the distance.

The unknown attack caught Tearin off guard. “What was that?” he shouted.

A smile fell upon Allucio’s face as he chuckled. “Oooh, that means you’re in some serious trouble, buddy. Menzuo is here!”

“Who?” Tearin asked. He turned around. A hooded man in a black power suit, with a mask covering his eyes stood before him, a long black caped blowing in the wind. Tearin quickly raised his sonic gun and popped off a few rounds in Menzuo’s direction.

“Sensing Densor!” Menzuo shouted. As time stopped, he disappeared, quickly moving out of the way of the sonic wave and now was directly behind Tearin, just inches from his back. As time sped up again, the young protector formed a huge fireball in the palm of his hand. “Mega body attack!”

Without being able to react, Tearin was blasted out of the area, and into a mountain wall in the distance, right next to Greavis.

Menzuo stood in between both of his friends, shaking his head. “You two can’t stay out of trouble. I leave for a split second and look what happens. Can you do anything without me?”

“You can’t be serious!” Desmurose said as he rolled over to his back. “Please don’t forget who saved your butt on planet Bralose during your first battle against Hydrosion.”

“Someone is quick to forget that, I see,” Allucio followed. He grabbed hold of his ribs as he slowly crawled to his knees. “You owed us one, anyway.”

“I guess I did, but how did you guys end up like this?” Menzuo asked.

Desmurose pointed to his neck. "Those bounty hunters snuck up on us while we were searching that spaceship and got these power dampening collars on us. These things are unreal. We seriously have no powers to fight."

"That's not only it, Menzuo," Allucio said as he finally caught his breath. "These two bounty hunters are from another galaxy."

"Another galaxy? Are you serious?" Menzuo asked in confusion

"Very serious," Allucio replied. "And from what we found on that spaceship, I don't think they are lying."

Menzuo kneeled down and grabbed hold of the collar that was around Allucio's neck. He snapped it off with ease then helped his friend to his feet. "What did you find on that ship?" he asked. He made his way over to Desmurose and quickly snapped his collar off before helping him to his feet as well.

"We found an alien from a planet called Nercom," Allucio replied. "I seriously don't think that there is a hidden planet in this universe that we don't know about. Plus, this alien didn't look like anything we would recognize from our existing worlds."

"This is very interesting. Was there anything else on the ship that we could use?" Menzuo asked.

"We didn't have time to search it thoroughly," Desmurose said. "These bums jumped us quick. Honestly, we're lucky that you came."

"As a matter of fact, how did you get here?" Allucio asked.

Before Menzuo could speak, there was a rumbling coming from Greavis and Tearin's direction. "Give me a second. I need to take care of them first."

"Go ahead," Desmurose said, shooing him away. "I don't think we have enough energy to fight yet."

"Those collars did a real number on us, bro," Allucio added.

"No worries, I've got this," Menzuo replied. He turned and gazed in amazement as both of the bounty hunters flying in his direction. "Be right back…Sensing Densor!"

Time slowed once more. Menzuo darted over to Greavis and Tearin and grabbed them by their heads as time began to return. The bounty hunters could feel the pressure on their skulls increasing, blurring their vision.

"But…how?" Greavis asked with his eyes wide open from shock. He was unable to move his head at all.

"An unreal super-being!" Tearing added. "What a prize to behold."

"Just know that you're in my galaxy, and I am the universal protector," Menzuo replied. "Mega Body Attack!" he shouted. Three massive fireballs launched from his hands, directly hitting the bounty hunters in the head, thrusting them forward. Their bodies shot off like missiles, right back where Menzuo last put them. The impact of the bounty hunters' uncontrolled bodies from the universal protector's attack slammed them deep into the mountain, making it crumble on top of them.

Menzuo could feel their energy levels drop. As he turned to walk back to his friends, both of the crumbled mountains exploded. The bounty hunters shot up into the sky. "It's not worth it to fight this one!" Greavis shouted across to his partner.

"We will retrieve the Necromanian's head later," Tearin replied. "Our next mission is to capture these three and make some serious money in the gauntlet."

"See you soon, young warriors!" Greavis shouted as he shot up higher into the sky. Tearin followed. They both disappeared over another mountain top, vanishing from view.

Allucio and Desmurose had regained most of their energy and also their fighting spirit. They were both about ready to give chase, but Menzuo motioned to stop them. "Let them go. they are no threat to us anymore."

"We can't just let them get away," Allucio said. "They are monsters. What they did to us, oh, they need to pay!"

"We will deal with them at some point," Menzuo replied. "Something is telling me that we haven't seen the last of them."

"I hope that we do see them again," Desmurose followed. "We have a score to settle with them."

Menzuo's focus went back to the task at hand. "Let's get to why you both are here, what you found on that spaceship, and if it can be of any use to us."

Allucio sighed heavily as he tried to refocus on their recon mission. "Okay, just to let you know, we found that Majesty that you sent us looking for: the man known as Blessed, and he has a team with him. One of the girls on his team is fine as wine, but that's neither here nor there."

Desmurose rolled his eyes. "Can we just get to the point? I've got it from here," he said, cutting Allucio off. "So, after we found the Majesties, we went to their headquarters and studied the signal given off from the Quintillion asteroid. We came to find out that the signal was giving us the coordinates to come to Titan."

"That's when Desmurose and I volunteered to come here to find out what this was all about," Allucio added. "As we were getting through the captain's recording about how he ended up here, we were attacked. We figured that those bounty hunters killed him."

"That figures. So was there anything interesting on the captain's recordings?" Menzuo asked.

"Actually, yes," Desmurose said. "The captain spoke about something called World Harvesters and them being controlled by a mighty being. From what we gathered, he was able to escape from planet Necrom and was headed towards Earth to locate the saviors. If I'm correct, he was looking for us."

"Us and others," Menzuo added.

"Who, the Majesties?" Allucio asked.

"Not just them," Menzuo cautioned. "I believe there are more pieces to this puzzle. There are other Super-Normals that we have to meet."

"So we need to get what we found back to Earth," Desmurose said. "Let's see what else we can salvage before we head back."

"Speaking of heading back," Allucio said. He looked to Menzuo. "How did you get here to Titan? I know for a fact that there isn't another ship hidden on Earth, and last I checked, we can't breathe in outer-space."

Menzuo smiled. "Do you remember the space-gel that Scoop had us travel in when we flew from the moon to battle Queen Eaizah?"

"Yeah, I remember that," Allucio replied.

"Well, I figured out how to use it while I was away," Menzuo said. "I have a bit of the Walonokian magic within me. It was used to unlock the powers of the blue diamond, and once I absorbed it into my body, I inherited some of its powers. Luckily, that was one of them."

"So, we have a way home?" Desmurose asked, relieved.

"Absolutely. Now, let's get to that ship and get what we need," Menzuo said.

"I'm with that," Allucio added. "I really don't want to stay here any longer than needed. Not that I don't mind facing those fools again, but I kind of miss our home planet. It's my crazy normal place to be."

Menzuo shook his head as he chuckled. "Let's go guys. We don't have time to waste."

The three Solar Warriors headed back to the spaceship to gather what they could before heading to Earth. There they planned to meet the Majesties and discuss their findings.

CHAPTER 9

VISIONS, PROPHESIES & SUPERHEROES

"It's a pleasure to finally meet you, Blessed," Paladin said as he extended his hand to Blessed. The two connected on a firm, metallic handshake. "I feel like I already know you. Blurr filled me in on your battle in Syria. I knew our meeting was inevitable. And you must be Slaycick."

"Nice to finally meet you, Paladin," Slaycick said.

"Likewise," Paladin replied.

"This is the rest of us, Paladin," Blessed said pointing to the rest of the crew behind him. "Aganathin, Kasitia, Tenan, Rekluse, and K'nia."

Paladin shook hands and made his acquaintance with the rest of the Majesties.

"Hey, sis! It's good to see you again," Kasitia said as she walked towards Blurr and gave her a tight embrace. Rekluse and K'nia followed suit.

"It's good to see you ladies again, too," Blurr said. "I wish you all had gotten here about ten minutes ago."

"What the hell happened here?" Slaycick asked looking at the rubble around them from the collapsed building. "Were you just in a fight?"

"Yes!" Blurr replied. "Three evil Super-Normals just tried to take us out. They killed thirty-two people in the process. They even bragged how Paladin and I were the initial targets."

"Where are these Super-Normals now?" Aganathin asked.

"They're no longer with us," Paladin said.

"May they rest in hell," K'nia said as she brushed some dust from the debris off of Blurr's shoulder. "Are you okay, girl?"

"Yeah. You already know how I get down," Blurr replied. "The bad thing is, there are a bunch of these Super-Normals popping up all over the place. These idiots find out they have new abilities and some power, and the first thing they want to do is take advantage of others. Thirty-two people dead just like that."

"We're afraid that more bodies may drop," Tenan said. "Something bigger is headed this way that's not a part of this universe."

"I know," Blurr said. "I've been having these visions lately."

"You too?" Tenan asked. "That means all of this stuff is indeed connected."

"That's why I had Slaycick reach out to you, Blurr," Blessed said. "We believe that the Q-18 meteor that you all defended in the North Pole is linked to the visions that you and Tenan have been experiencing. We wanted to come to talk with you all to see what they might mean and to put a fight plan together."

"That is a good idea. We can head back to The Beacon and talk there," Blurr said. "The authorities are on their way to deal with this wreckage, but we can assist them by removing the bodies from the rubble before we go. Slaycick, you mind giving me a hand, big bro?"

"Let's do it."

Immediately, Slaycick and Blurr began darting amongst the rubble. They moved so fast it looked as if they were disappearing from one spot and reappearing in another. When they found a body, they would pick it up and lay it out on the sidewalk so the paramedics and police officers would have an easier task of trying to identify the victims.

"It never ceases to amaze me how fast those two are," Aganathin said, shaking his head left and right in amusement.

The Majesties and Paladin made their way over and began assisting the two speedsters. Blessed and Aganathin began moving the big chunks of brick out of the way with ease as the others looked for bodies. Once all the bodies were discovered, they stayed around to give their statement to law enforcement before making their way back to headquarters.

***

"So let me get this straight," Paladin said as he handed out bottles of water to his guests. "You sent two teenagers with powers to the Titan moon of Jupiter to look for a signal that you believed was traced from the Q-18 meteor?"

"We didn't send them," Tenan said. "They are from a planet called Yardenia…which I believe is located in the outer realm of our galaxy. They do live on this planet, though, right here in America; Springfield, Massachusetts, to be exact. These young guys seem to be very comfortable with intergalactic travel. They are going to contact us with any info they retrieve. Said they were sent here by some character named Menzuo, who is also gifted."

"Okay, but in the meantime, we need to prepare ourselves for any potential danger," Paladin said. "Baby, why don't you explain your visions to Tenan? Let's see if there is any correlation in your description."

Blurr took a sip of her water and let out a sigh. She bit her bottom lip as she tried to gather her thoughts. Shaking her head she said, "It's death…it's harm, it's chaos. I have seen images of a large black vessel carrying three figures whom I can't make out. They're huge like the giants we fought in Jableh, but they're much more dangerous, more powerful."

"Did you say a large black vessel?" Tenan asked. "I saw a large black vessel in my vision also. I couldn't see any figures in the vessel, but my intuition told me it was a great deal of evil coming towards Earth. When I opened a portal just above the Earth's stratosphere, I didn't see anything. Then I went deeper into space and saw nothing but the stars."

"It's a possibility that they could have been cloaked," Paladin said. "If something is coming for us, and they know that there are people here of our caliber protecting Earth, then it's possible they want to take us by surprise."

"We want to prevent that if possible, Paladin," Blessed said. "Do you have any tech that would be able to locate a cloaked ship? Perhaps we can stop them before they reach Earth."

"Not at the moment, but give me a day to see if I can come up with something. I'm sure B.R.A.I.N. and I can come up with something. In the meantime, let's prepare as if they're coming here."

"If they come here to Earth, we'll have the advantage," Rekluse said. "But we have to think about where the enemy is most likely to strike."

"Hero City seems to be the place where all the Super-Normals are popping up," K'nia said. "My guess is that this would be a primary location. Natas came here all the way from Syria. My thoughts were he had plans to link up with the Super-Normals who would back his mission."

"I think we have to assume that our enemy can strike in any location," Aganathin said. "The Middle East is just as susceptible. Remember we found Paraflyte and the Four Horsemen there in Egypt? Hero City is not the only place with Super-Normals with bad agendas."

"Paladin, we have reason to believe that the enemy is a cosmic being who purposely caused the inflation of Super-Normals," Blessed said.

"Were you all affected by the storm too?" Paladin asked.

"No," Blessed replied. "We came about our gifts another way. A celestial being named Titus gave us access to an element called Oramite. The Oramite became infused in us and gave us all different abilities. We stumbled into a deeper world of evil and unnatural beasts back when we were assigned to snuff out Tanwar Terah. Come to find out Tanwar was just a pawn of a demonic figure named Natas Selur – the one whom we battled and killed in Jableh."

"And you're sure he's dead?" Paladin asked.

"Slaycick and I dismantled his arms and stuck a sword through his chest before Paraflyte tossed him into Tenan's portal which led to deep space. There's no way he survived."

"Babe, unless he was already dead when you threw him in the portal we have to assume the worst-case scenario."

"I do remember his words," Tenan said. "He thanked me and told me he would see me soon; that he would be bringing death and hell back to Earth when he returns."

Tenan had a somber look on his face as if the possibility had just hit him that Natas could have been telling the truth. Paladin turned his attention toward Tenan and studied him closely.

"And do you believe his prophecy, or do you believe he's truly dead? If I were a betting man, Tenan, I would say that your gut is telling you the former."

"If he somehow survived that thrashing we handed them, then the next time we meet I'll make sure that I introduce my axe to his head," Aganathin bellowed.

"Pardon me, you all, I have to use the ladies room," Blurr said as she politely excused herself and exited the room.

Paladin watched as his girl walked out of the room. Slaycick recognized the concern on his face.

"Hey," Slaycick said as Paladin turned to him. "How is she for real?"

"The battle in the North Pole took a toll on us," Paladin said as he let out a sigh. "Also, right before that, we experienced a very peculiar, supernatural experience with a Super-Normal named Zenith. He used a vortex to take us to another dimension where all this prophetic rhetoric was laid on us by some paranormal type creatures. They call themselves Orchid, purveyors of information. It was life-changing, and she hasn't been the same since. She's tough though, you know. She would never let anyone on to the possibility that something was bothering her. Thank you for accepting her, letting her join your mission, and looking out for her. She told me how bravely you all fought in Syria."

"It was an honor to fight by her side, Paladin, just as it will be to fight by yours."

"We still need to get answers," Blessed said. "I believe we have two culprits in custody who might be able to shed some more light on the elements that are responsible for the change in many of the Super-Normals."

“Who might that be?” asked Paladin.

“When we began tracking Natas, he made his way to Chicago with a man named Dr. Samir. Dr. Samir contacted a man named Dr. Albert Bernstein. Both of the men were with Natas when we fought in Syria. When we defeated Natas, we took Dr. Samir and Dr. Bernstein as prisoners. We questioned them, but both men swear they were coerced and threatened to carry out orders or their families would suffer death.”

“Wait! That’s impossible,” Paladin said.

“What’s impossible?”

“Dr. Albert Bernstein is dead. I watched him die,” Paladin said.

“You sure?” Kasitia asked. “Because this guy had all of his credentials and IDs that showed he was indeed Dr. Bernstein when we captured him.”

“I’m beyond sure. I’m positive. Dr. Bernstein was known as Caine, a.k.a. Mr. Magnificent. He was a Super-Normal in disguise. He definitely died during one of our battles here in Hero City. That I know for sure.”

“What?!” Blessed exclaimed, looking shocked and concern. “Well, if Dr. Bernstein is dead, then who is the man sitting in the jail cell in Jerusalem?”

“I’ll give you two guesses,” Kasitia said.

“I’ll only need one,” Paladin said. “And his name is Mystikal.”

CHAPTER 10

LOCKED-IN MODE

Blurr stood in front of the bathroom mirror. Her eyes slowly danced across the soft features of her face as she gazed at her reflection. She could just make out the hint of light brown in her pupils behind the grey tint of her racing goggles. There was something different in about her now, different from just a year ago. She were void of fear.

The girl she once knew who dreamt of the life she now lived was here, finally in the flesh, the exact opposite of the lifestyle she once lived. She had a man who worshipped the ground she walked on, superpowers, a steady flow of income, and a superhero moniker that any B-celebrity would die for. But still, something was amiss. How she could have almost everything she ever wanted and simultaneously have her life filled with so many unanswered questions was a mystery that stabbed at her brain.

The dreams – the visions of unfamiliar people, places and times – were perplexing, but they were not the root of the problem. It was the unshakable fear of the unknown that cost her hours of restful sleep every night.

"Come on, girl," Blurr whispered to herself as she turned on the faucet and ran cold water over her fingertips. After wetting her hands, she patted her face and allowed the wetness to soak into her skin – her failed attempt to wash away her anxiety. She turned to exit the bathroom but was startled to find none other than Zenith standing before her.

"Can't a girl have any privacy?"

"What privacy? You weren't naked or using the toilet. I thought it was sufficient to enter," Zenith said.

"I don't need to be using the bathroom to have privacy," she replied, shaking her head. "But I'm not telling you something you don't already know, am I?" Zenith remained silent, staring at her. Blurr crossed her arms. "And for the record, you didn't enter the bathroom. That would require you to open the door and to walk in. What you did was poof your way inside."

"I entered this dimension."

"No, you didn't, you *poofed.* Totally different."

"I may not have used your traditional door to enter as you would, but I merely utilized a vortex to do the exact same thing –"

Blurr held up a hand and cut him off. "Please, spare me right now. I don't need a technical lecture."

"I can apologize nonetheless," Zenith said.

"Not necessary. You're here now, which means it must be important. Paladin's out front and the Majesties are with him, so whatever you have to report, you can share with the entire group. Come on," Blurr said as she made for the door.

Zenith grabbed her arm. "What I have to share is not for their ears," he said in a grim tone.

Blurr turned to meet his gaze. "Go on."

"The Orchids, they have reached out to me once more. Said that there is great danger coming this way. You've sensed it as well; I take it?" Blurr remained silent, only nodding. "You haven't shared the full extent of your visions to Paladin, have you?"

"No. He…I wasn't sure if he could handle it. Plus, I'm not all that sure that I can handle it either. Half the time, I see things for a moment, and then just like that, they fade from my memory. It's like I can't hold on to them."

"Subconsciously, you're blocking them out. The Normal side of you is filtering out the things that your mind can't interpret because it is beyond mortal understanding. In order to ascertain the truth, you will need to tap more into the Super-Normal side of your existence. You must lose that thing that makes you human."

"How could I do something like that?"

"Focus."

'You don't think I tried?" Blurr asked, her voice rising. "This ain't Yoga class. This is real life, and beneath all this glossy Super-Normal façade, I'm still a human being, with real emotions, flaws, and concerns."

"Concerns, yes, but not for yourself. That is reserved for the one who holds your heart."

"Sebastian?"

Zenith nodded. "How long has it been since you began initiating your evolution?"

"What evolution? I have no idea what you're talking about."

"Oh, but I think you do. You've felt it, haven't you? The steady separation, the rise from basic genome to that of something…more. Pretty soon, that Earthling shell won't be enough to house what's coming."

Blurr peered down at her hands, staring. "Sometimes, I look at simple things like my fingers, without the gloves on. I take in every little detail like the wrinkles and the finger prints, wondering how it is that humanity fails to notice those simple things that make us so special from one another, yet so alike. I watch the second hand on a clock and appreciate the perfection of each tick as it makes its way around the face of the clock, designating the start of one thing and the beginning of the next. There's a perfect fragility to it all, and yet, it's wasted by almost every higher life form on the planet."

"Not everyone. There are some who share your admiration."

"I know," Blurr said softly. "But there's more who don't. You know, when I was a Call Girl, life seemed to be much simpler. No strings attached – no one to take care of – and I could come and go as I pleased, without being held accountable. And even back then, I couldn't see the world for what it was. I just thought that there was more good than evil, and I just happened to be on the bad side of things. But now, since moving into the lighter side I *know* that there is more evil than good."

"Se-crets," Zenith crooned dismissively. "Secrets that the Normals and most Super-Normals can never know."

"Why not?"

"Because they would lose the one thing that this world is starving for: hope. If they lose that, they will lose the will to fight. And without that, everything will be lost."

"And why can't we just go out there and tell Paladin and the Majesties all of this?"

"I'm not going to get into that now. Blurr, you are no longer seeing the same world that everyone else sees. It's changing right before your eyes in dramatic ways. There are shifts, fluctuations in time that are inversely proportional to one another. One second equals lightyears. One is equivalent to infinity. But currently, we are living in the beginning of the end times. Time, times, and half of time are all colliding together now. As the Conduit, you will need to evolve in order to maintain the breach between them and stabilize the peace of your world."

"What's all this evolution mumbo-jumbo, Zenith? Stop speaking in riddles. How do I do it, for Christ's sake? How do I evolve? I can just do it already and help everyone. If you have something to tell me, just spit it out already," Blurr hissed.

"I can't."

"You can't, or you won't?"

"Even I do not know the answer to that question. I desired to find answers, and I tried as hard as I could, searching the very recesses of my mind for clues. For the first time since becoming a Super-Normal, I am completely clueless. It's very frustrating. I have sat upon the peak of Mount Everest, meditating. I came to a place of perfect oneness with the universe, and as I contemplated the truth, my mind went blank. I realized that if I don't help, even time itself will cease to exist."

"And so now what? I'm supposed to be able to help you? Are you saying that you came here to get answers from me?"

"No, I came here to tell you that you must get answers from yourself. And when the time is right, you will contact me. Hopefully, before the Travelers arrive. That is when you will come into your own, and it will be a very satisfying day for me indeed. Because I will finally have the answers that I seek."

Blurr stepped to Zenith and took him by the hands, tears forming in the corner of her eyes. "And again, I beg of you, how do I do that?"

Zenith softly touched her cheek with one hand. "I didn't come to tell you how, but to merely tell you why. And now that you have that, you will come to know *who*. You only need to know where and when now. But now, I have said too much. With this conversation, you are locked in, and we are that much closer." Zenith pulled back, and a slight smile split the corner of his mouth. "So smile now. I am."

Before Blurr could speak, a vortex appeared behind Zenith. He slowly backed into it and waved as it closed again, leaving her all alone with her thoughts.

Just then, there was a knock at the door. "Baby?" Paladin's voice rang from the outside.

"Yes," Blurr replied.

"You okay in there?" he asked.

Blurr peeked at her reflection in the mirror once more, checking to make sure her eyes weren't red and full of tears. She fetched a few tissues and briskly dabbed at them with supersonic speed, instantly drying them. Satisfied, she turned and opened the door. "Yeah babe, what's up? I don't hear voices. Did the Majesties leave?"

"It's almost dusk. They went on the rooftop to get a good view of that fabulous Chicago Skyline. I told them I'd come and get you, and we'd join them."

"Uh, yeah. That sounds great," Blurr said.

Paladin could sense something was off. "What's really going on? I know you've been having the visions and dreams, but is there something else at play here? Something you're not telling me?"

"Something's coming, Sebas."

"Yeah, I know. Tenan said –"

"No, something beyond even what he can see. I…I, keep getting this feeling that I'm going to have to do something in the future, whether I want to or not, to save us all. And I'm not sure if it will be a good thing or not."

"Well, don't you think that if you have to do it, it will be for the good of everyone involved?"

"I'm not so sure."

Paladin took her by the hands. "Don't talk like that now. You've got to be optimistic. Hun. We have to think positively. And you know I've told you time and time again that you're not alone here. I'm with you, and I'm never going to leave your side. Ever!"

"Promise?" she asked faintly.

"Promise."

"I know. I just need one more promise."

"Anything, you name it."

"Remember our battle at the North Pole?"

"Right."

"When I went into Overdrive?'

"I do."

"I felt something that day. Something dark, something sinister within me. Uncontrollable. I was drifting away. The only thing that brought me back were thoughts of you."

Paladin's helmet retracted. "You won't lose control. You did it once. You'll do it again. You'll find a way. We both will."

"Well, I'm pretty sure that none of this is all a coincidence, nor are all these dreams and visions. I think that whatever is supposed to happen will center on me mastering my Overdrive powers. And, well, I'm going to need your help."

Paladin cupped her shoulders and squeezed. "I'm here for you."

"If and when I get out of control. I'm going to need you to kill me."

"What?"

"I couldn't live with myself if I begin to hurt other people…those I love. Especially you. Promise me that you won't let me do that."

"I…I don't know if I can do that."

"You must. Please, Sebas," Blurr pleaded as tears spilled over her cheeks.

"Let's just hope it doesn't come to that."

"But if it does –"

"I'll do it."

"Promise?"

Paladin hesitated, then finally spoke. "Promise."

"Thank you," she whispered.

"Hey, let's go get lost and grab some ice cream or something."

"What about the Majesties?"

"Ahh, they'll be all right. I'm sure they can take care of themselves until we get back." Paladin looked up. "B.R.A.I.N. –"

"Don't worry, I'll see to it that they find the remote controls to the television," B.R.A.I.N. replied, cutting him off.

CHAPTER 11

SOLAR WARRIORS ARRIVAL AT HERO CITY

Blessed and the rest of the Majesties stood on the balcony overlooking Hero City.

"It's still one of the best skylines in the world despite all the craziness that's going on here," K'nia said.

"I agree," Aganathin concurred.

"Hi, you all! You must be the Majesties of Canaan," a soft voice said from behind them.

All seven soldiers turned around to a beautiful, fair-skinned woman with long black hair.

"I'm Lydia," she said, holding a tray full of snacks and drinks. "I'm Sebastian's – excuse me – *Paladin's* cousin."

"Wait! Paladin's alias is Sebastian?" asked Slaycick with a chuckle. "Oh, I'm gonna have sooo much fun with him now. Tell me, Lydia, did he fall in love with *The Little Mermaid*?"

"Oh my God," Kasitia said, shaking her head at Slaycick's corny Disney reference. "Lydia, don't mind Slaycick. Nice to meet you, sweetie. I'm Kasitia."

"Hi, Kasitia," Lydia said. "Nice to meet you all. Paladin wanted me to make sure you all were comfortable. He and Blurr stepped out for some ice cream. They should be back momentarily."

"Thank you, Lydia," Blessed said.

The rest of the Majesties introduced themselves as they began to snack on the bowl of chips and dip that Lydia served them. The Majesties listened to Lydia as she explained all the capabilities of B.R.A.I.N. and the connection the intelligence network had with Paladin's suit. She bonded with the heroes that night as they spoke for the rest of the evening, waiting on Blurr and Paladin's return.

They were in the midst of conversation when, suddenly, a series of explosions began setting off in different parts of the downtown sector. From the balcony, The Majesties and Lydia could see the blasts detonating on both the east and west side. Two more blasts could be seen erupting further south.

"What the hell?" Rekluse exclaimed.

"That's got to be the work of villainous Super-Normals," Lydia said. "Their acts of terrorism have been escalating as of late, partly a ploy to draw out Paladin and Blurr or anyone else who challenges their authority."

"Well, they're gonna meet us today," Blessed said. "Tenan, you, Rekluse, and Aganathin take the west side of the city. Slaycick, you and Kasitia check out the south side, and me and K'nia will head to the east."

"I'm contacting Blurr and Paladin now!" Lydia said. "You all go!"

Three figures off in the distance caught Tenan's attention, landing on top buildings close to the carnage on the west side of the city. He opened three portals near each of the blasts. "Let's move. I don't know who they are, but I'm assuming those three over there might have something to do with the blasts. Everyone make sure they make it back in one piece."

The Majesties all jumped through their respective portals, which immediately closed behind them.

"Now that guy is cool," Lydia said to herself. She tapped her ear, accessing her IEPCS. "B.R.A.I.N., get a hold of Paladin and Blurr and give them coordinates to where the Majesties are going."

"Will do, Lydia," B.R.A.I.N. replied.

***

"Guys, we're here," Menzuo said as he landed on top of one of the buildings in Hero City. Allucio and Desmurose landed right next to him.

Desmurose took out the com that Slaycick gave him before they left for Titan. "Dammit! It's broken!"

"What is?" Menzuo asked.

"The mobile com that allows us to reach out to the Majesties when we got back. How the heck are we supposed to link up with them now?"

"We'll find a way," Allucio reassured him. "We found them once, so we will find them again."

"Right now, it's important that we find Paladin. He can get us in touch with them," Menzuo said.

"Okay, so where do we start?" Desmurose asked.

The Solar Warriors looked down, noting that the streets below were almost entirely covered in thick black smoke as many of the buildings were on fire. Several people were running frantically to get away from a visible threat that was rampaging the neighborhood that they were in.

"What is that down there?" Allucio asked. "The energy is quite disturbing."

Menzuo locked in on a couple of armored men running through the streets as he continued to look down from the building. He shook his head. "I'm not sure what or who they are, but they are powerful and very evil. This must be the effects of the Dark Spores Paladin mentioned in my dream. He wasn't lying when he said things were becoming uncontrollable. The increase in evil Super-Normals is a real threat."

A loud explosion rushed the sky to their left; it came from the other side of the building. They quickly ran across the roof to get a look at what was taking place. People ran, screaming as the fire continued to flood the street. Several were knocked unconscious and lying on the ground.

"This is pure madness!" Allucio said.

"We have to help them," Desmurose said as the anger swelled in his body.

"We can't go down there yet. We don't know what we are facing. We need to find Paladin," Menzuo replied.

The rage within Allucio and Desmurose was growing as they watched the unknown threat terrorize the city. Allucio shook his head in disapproval. “Menzuo, I’m sorry brother, we can’t just sit back and watch these monsters kill innocent people. I know we don’t know how powerful these men are, but we have a duty to protect the people down there, and as for Paladin, if he is here, we can leave him for you to find – that is, if he’s not dead already.”

Menzuo sighed heavily. “Okay, you two take care of the people down there and be careful. I’ll start my search for Paladin. If you guys need me –”

“We got this, brother,” Desmurose said, cutting him off as he and Allucio powered up. “We will meet up with you right after we handle this mess.” They both streaked down the street, ready to battle.

Menzuo powered up too and floated down to an empty street just a few blocks away from the violent battle that his friends had just entered. He scanned the area, hoping to be able to sense the same energy that Paladin was giving off while he visited him in his dream, but he couldn’t detect it. *I can feel three powerful sources around me*, Menzuo thought. His eyes darted between the cloudy sky and back down the street, scanning the areas between the buildings. “Whoever you are, a fight is not what you want!” he said aloud.

It was eerily quiet as Menzuo pressed forward. Many cars were still smoldering as the thick dark smoke billowed out of the broken windows.

“There he is,” Tenan said in a whisper. “Rekluse, move to the left and stay hidden. Get ready to attack. After I pull him through the portal, Aganathin, get ready to shove him into the side of the building. Once the bomb blasts this monster out of the sky, Rekluse, use your hypnotism on him. Make him think that he is in hell.”

Rekluse nodded. “I got it, babe. He won’t know where he is.”

Three drones sailed in nearby, focusing on the mysterious newcomer. “Looks like we have an audience,” Rekluse said, pointing at the drones.

"Well, let's give them a show. He's about to be in a lot of pain," Aganathin followed as he crouched down in a running stance. "I'm ready!"

"On my mark!" Tenan instructed.

Menzuo's muscles tensed. He could sense a wave energy increasing near him, so he prepared himself for an oncoming battle. Instantly the ground below his feet started to shake violently, almost as if an earthquake was approaching "This isn't natural!" he said.

As he tried to regain his balance, a portal opened up behind Menzuo. Before he could react, a hand reached out of it and pulled him in. "Now, Aganathin!" Tenan shouted. Another portal opened up right next to one of the fractured buildings to his right.

Menzuo was shoved out of the portal, right in front of an immensely large man holding a metallic axe. "What the…!" Menzuo shouted as he was caught off guard. He looked right into the man's eyes with confusion, wondering how he ended up in a different spot within the city streets.

"Allow me to introduce myself. I'm Aganathin!" the man shouted. Without hesitation, Aganathin shoved the head of his axe right into Menzuo's chest. The blunt impact propelled Menzuo forcefully into the side of the building. Another portal opened up behind Aganathin, and he slipped in it, disappearing instantly. Just as the young fighter's body slammed into the steel beams of the structure, a bomb exploded onto his back, launching him clear across the street and into one of the burning cars.

"Now, Rekluse!" Aganathin shouted.

Without hesitation, Rekluse grabbed hold of Menzuo's head, channeling her energy of hypnosis directly into his mind. "I've got you!" she said softly.

Menzuo opened his eyes. His vision was extremely blurry. He shook his head, taking in the image of a woman slowly backing away from him. Within seconds, she disappeared through a portal. "What's going on?" he asked.

"You're going to die!" Tenan shouted.

As Menzuo stood, he noticed the scenery around him changing. The city streets turned into a wooded forest, the leaves on the trees were covered in fire. The ground was made of moving sand, making his balance weak. He looked around cautiously. "This is unreal!"

"Come here!" Aganathin shouted, grabbing Menzuo's attention.

The young Prince looked down, noticing two arms made of sand reaching up and grabbing hold of his legs. "How is this possible?" Menzuo shouted as he was pulled into the depths of the sandy ground.

Menzuo wrestled Aganathin's grip as it got tighter the deeper he was pulled down. "No evil Super-Normal can defeat us!"

"What did you say?" Menzuo asked as he fought to free himself. "Enough of this!" he shouted. Powering up, he blasted Aganathin's strengthening grip from his shoulders. He shot up into the sky between the burning trees. His vision was still blurry. "Show yourselves!"

A ticking sound right next to both of his ears grabbed the young protector's attention. As he located the noise, two bombs exploded, blasting him back to the ground.

"That should do it," Tenan said. Rekluse and Aganithin walked over and stood next to him.

"That Super-Normal should be dead."

Menzuo slowly lifted his body from the ground. "I'm not dead…I'm pissed!" he shouted. Powering up again, Menzuo used a force-like wind to move the three Majesties back.

"This is impossible!" Aganathin shouted. "How is he this strong?"

"I've got this!" Rekluse said as she channeled into her hypnotism powers.

Menzuo shook his head as the waves of her attack increased in his mind. The young Prince was now seeing the burning trees melting right in front of him. His rage grew, but he knew that he had to control his stance. Menzuo closed his eyes, took a deep breath, refocusing on the battle. He slowly opened his eyes. "I can fight this! This is just a distraction. You've got to do better than that!"

“Let’s go!” Tenan shouted.

The three Majesties charged forward, ready to attack. “Bring it!” Menzuo shouted.

Just as Aganathin swung his axe at Menzuo’s head, the young prince floated back. A portal opened up just behind him. Tenan appeared out of it, swinging at the warrior’s head.

Menzuo could sense the Majesties’ powers from behind, quickly making him shout, “Sensing Densor!” Time was frozen. He could see the three fighters. He studied them quickly. “Who the hell are they?” Just as time was speeding up, the young Prince shouted out. “Sensing Densor!” Time froze once again.

He moved out of the way and stood directly behind Rekluse. Time sped up, having Aganathin swing his axe at thin air just as Tenan completed his punch, making it land against nothing. “Where did he go?” Tenan asked.

“Right here! Mega Body Attack!” Menzuo shouted, blasting Rekluse in her back, shooting her like a rocket right into Tenan, shoving them both through his portal.

As they disappeared, Rekluse’s powers faded, making her hypnotism spell break from Menzuo’s mind. The burning and melting trees with the sandy ground faded. The area went back to normal. He was now seeing the destruction of Hero City once again.

Aganathin charged without hesitation, swinging his axe violently, trying to chop the young Prince’s head off. Menzuo dodged and blocked every attack as he looked for an opening.

Just as Aganithin raised his weapon, Menzuo kicked him right under his left arm, launching the Majesty right into the building to his left.

Before he made an impact with the building, Aganathin’s body was absorbed into it without any sound being made. “You’ve got to be kidding me!” Menzuo said.

“Nope!” Tenan shouted as a portal opened up just above Menzuo’s head. Swinging his nunchucks, he smacked Menzuo right in his cheek, spinning his head violently to his left.

Rekluse flew out of the portal and drop-kicked Menzuo right in his chest, sending him back about fifty feet. "That's payback, baby!"

As Menzuo gathered himself, the building that Aganathin was absorbed in, fell on top of the masked warrior, crushing him in the middle of the street.

Aganathin appeared from the rubble, breathing heavily. "This man isn't normal!"

Tenan and Rekluse ran by his side as they studied the fallen building. "This battle isn't over!" Tenan shouted.

"Aah!" Menzuo shouted full of rage. His energy shot through his body immensely, making the crumbled building explode from the area. Menzuo walked forward with his eyes glowing. A smile fell across his face. He wiped the dirt from his cheek. "I'm going to make you all pay for that!"

"We're ready!" Rekluse shouted.

The young warrior and the three Majesties charged towards each other with reckless abandonment. A fierce hand-to-hand battle waged on in the streets of Hero City. Each punch and kick shook the ground and broke any remaining windows of the buildings around them.

"Hold this for me!" Tenan shouted as he opened a portal behind Menzuo. He landed a kick on his chest, moving him right in front of his portal.

Before Menzuo fell into it, he disappeared then reappeared to the left of Aganathin, punching him in the face and sending him right into the Portal.

Tenan's quick thinking caused him to open a portal next to Menzuo. Aganathin came charging out of it as he swung his ax right at Menzuo, just missing him in the stomach.

Rekluse charged forward with a violent round-house kick that Menzuo blocked, just as Tenan readied another portal above his head. Grabbing Rekluse by the leg, the universal protector tossed her into this sky.

As the portal opened, she was launched through it. Without hesitation, Menzuo punched Aganathin in the chest, knocking him off balance, then sped in front of Tenan. "Mega Body Attack!" Three bombs blasted him in the chest just as he was about to open a portal to bring Rekluse back.

Tenan's concentration was slightly broken, making him open a portal just above his own head. Rekluse fell through it, landing on Tenan's chest. "Sorry, baby," she said with a smile.

"It's okay. I'm glad I caught you," Tenan replied. "Let's finish this!"

"I'm right with you," Rekluse followed.

As they both stood, they watched as Menzuo was engaged with Aganathin. He was moving the Majesty back with ease.

Aganathin caught his two friends charging from behind, and then smiled. Menzuo noticed too, and his expression quickly changed. Aganathin dropped and disappeared into the ground.

"Now!" Rekluse shouted as she and Tenan sped up with flying drop-kicks aimed at Menzuo's head.

Without hesitation, Menzuo powered up. Rekluse and Tenan's came to a complete halt as his Energy Surge attack repelled their advance. They both back flipped but were able to balance themselves and land safely; Tenan on his feet and Rekluse on one knee.

Before Aganathin could form his body from beneath him, Menzuo shouted as he flew into the sky. "Mega Body Attack!" Three large bombs exploded into the street, making Aganathin reappear then roll out of the way of the attack. He stood to his feet, looking up as he gripped his ax tighter.

"He can't be a Super-Normal," Rekluse said. "Is he the threat that you and Blurr were mentioning?"

"I don't know," Tenan replied, "But his powers are unreal! He may well be who is coming for us."

Menzuo floated back to the middle of the street with Aganathin standing to the north and Rekluse and Tenan standing to the south. They were less than twenty yards from each other.

"This won't end well for you three," Menzuo said.

"We beg to differ," Aganathin replied.

Menzuo took a deep breath then tightened his muscles, ready to power up again. “Then I must end it now!”

Before Menzuo could attack, Paladin and Blurr sped into the area like a flash of lightning. “Wait! Stop this fight now!”

Menzuo directed his attention to the man in the metallic armored suit that was standing with a lady in a sleek, skin-tight baby-blue and gold suit. He looked to the man once again then relaxed his muscles. “Paladin, is that you?” Menzuo shouted. “It’s me, Menzuo…remember you visited me in my dream and told me to come find you here in Hero City?”

Tenan walked forward cautiously with his guard down. “Paladin, you know this guy?”

Paladin’s helmet retracted. A confused look was clearly shown on his face. “What? Who are you?”

Everyone stood in the middle of the street perplexed. As they all looked at each other, Allucio and Desmurose shot down from the sky and landed next to Menzuo. “Well hot damn. What in the world happened here?” Desmurose asked.

“Were you guys fighting?” Allucio said, pointing to the Majesties.

“You know this guy?” Tenan asked.

Allucio pointed right at Menzuo’s forehead. “This is Menzuo! Our friend we told you about? Did you guys try to kill him?”

“We thought he was a threat,” Aganathin said.

“A threat!” Desmurose shouted. “He’s one of us.”

“Did anyone bother to ask him who he was?” Allucio said, looking directly at Tenan. “I bet you didn’t. You probably saw him and just went into warrior mode; he had you all bugging out!”

“Young boy, I do not play when it comes to unknown threats,” Tenan replied. “We couldn’t just walk up to him with all of this madness happening in this city.”

Rekluse stepped forward, looking Menzuo in the eyes. “We apologize for this. We did not know who you were.”

Menzuo nodded. “It’s alright. Plus, you three can really fight. You held your own.”

Aganathin stepped forward. “You did too. It seems like you can adapt to any form of battle. That’s impressive.”

Paladin stepped forward. “Enough of the pleasantries. You four destroyed half of downtown in Hero City, and these drones probably caught all of it on the worldwide network. By the looks of it, this was a battle of the ages.” He directed his attention back to Menzuo. “But…I still need to know who you are. You said that I visited you in a dream?”

Menzuo stood confused. “Yes, while I was on another planet, ready to head home after protecting it from a Pirate Warrior, you reached out to me and warned me of an oncoming threat. You mentioned some other fighters that we needed to link up with, you don’t remember?”

Blurr turned to Paladin. “Looks like someone else is having visions they can’t remember.”

Paladin nodded and focused back on Menzuo. “So you know something bad is coming?”

“Only from what you told me,” Menzuo replied, looking just as confused.

Desmurose stepped forward, breaking the awkward moment. “We recovered this recording from the alien ship on the Titan moon. It may need some tweaking to get it back working. The recording took a little damage during a fight that we had.” He handed it to Paladin.

Paladin studied it for a second, noticing a few dents in it. “We can get this back to the lab where Lydia can figure out the contents to get this working again.”

“And who is she?” Allucio asked.

“She’s family and the best technician on this planet,” Paladin answered. “Follow me. I’ll lead the way.” He took off down the street.

Everyone followed closely behind. Desmurose leaned into Menzuo’s ear. “I thought you said that he knows you?”

Menzuo shrugged his shoulders. “This is weird. We’ve met before, but he has no clue as to who I am. I don’t understand. I wish Solar was here to try and make things clearer.”

“We’ll figure it out together, bro,” Desmurose said. “Just give it some time.”

They all continued down the street. Tenan and Allucio locked eyes. Allucio shook his head. Tenan clenched his teeth. “Do we have a problem, young man?”

“I don’t know, do we?” Allucio replied.

“Will you two stop it?” Rekluse said quickly moving in between Tenan and Allucio.

Menzuo looked back at them then focused on his friend. “Why is he so mad at you?”

Desmurose shook his head with a chuckle. “Long story, but you know our boy. He’s all big mouth and googly eyes for the ladies.”

Menzuo shook his head. “Let me guess, he hit on his girl and almost started a fight with him.”

“Exactly,” Desmurose said.

“It wasn’t going to be a fight,” Allucio said. “I mean, I would’ve –”

“Would’ve what?” Tenan shouted as he overheard their conversation.

“Nothing!” Allucio shouted back. “Nothing, mean guy!”

“Would you please leave him alone,” Desmurose pleaded.

Allucio gave Tenan a mean look then continued down the street. “I swear…Imma kill that kid,” Tenan said.

Rekluse gently stroked Tenan’s chest. “Don’t lose your cool. I’m not going anywhere. Plus, I think the kid likes you as a friend.”

Tenan looked at her, confused. “Yeah right. He’s lost his damn mind messing with me.”

Rekluse sighed. “Let’s just get back and handle this recording with Lydia.”

Paladin touched the side of his helmet. “Lydia, we’re coming to The Beacon.”

***

Everyone followed Paladin inside. Lydia was sitting behind her work station, monitoring some type of configuration that was laid over three different monitors. "Whoa, this setup is amazing," Desmurose said.

Lydia turned around, seeing everyone behind Paladin. "What's up cousin, who's the crew with you?"

Allucio's mouth dropped as he gazed at Lydia's beauty. He walked over without hesitation. "Hey, I'm Allucio, but you can call me Michael. It's *extremely* nice to meet such a beautiful woman."

Lydia smiled with rosy cheeks. "Ooh, such a charmer this one is."

Desmurose smacked himself in the forehead. "Oh, Allucio, please shut up!"

"Does he do this with all women?" Tenan asked.

"Unfortunately, yes," Menzuo replied. "We're lucky he can fight."

Paladin stepped forward. "You already know Tenan, Rekluse, and Aganathin. This young man drooling over you is Allucio." He pointed at the other two. "That's Desmurose and Menzuo."

"Nice to meet you," Desmurose and Menzuo said simultaneously.

"Nice to meet you all too," Lydia replied.

"Blessed and the rest of our team will be here shortly," Tenan alerted the group. "We radioed them on the coms to let them know we were here."

Paladin nodded. He turned back to his cousin and held out the alien recording device. "These young men recovered this from a ship on the Titan moon. It's damaged, so I'm wondering if you can get it working again."

Lydia took it and analyzed the outside of it. Moving it around, she noted the scratches and dents along the exterior. "It shouldn't be a problem. Most technology has similar setups. It may take me a little while, but I'll figure out how to get it working."

Paladin gave her a pound. "You're the master. We'll leave you to it." He motioned everyone to follow him into the conference room, where they all sat down.

"So," Tenan said as he looked at the Solar Warriors. "Can you tell us what happened on the Titan moon and what you found?"

Allucio nodded with a very serious look on his face. "Luckily, we have the time to tell you all as Lydia figures out how to get that thing working again." Blessed and the rest of the Majesties walked into the room as he continued. "What we found and what happened to us was unreal. If this is the beginning of what we are all about to face, then we need to really tighten our bond, strap up our boots, and dig in. From what we heard, we're in some serious danger."

Everyone sat back, focusing on the Solar Warriors as they continued on with their discovery on the Titan moon.

CHAPTER 12

BY FAITH, NOT BY SIGHT

As the make-shift team of heroes retreated to the rooftop of The Beacon to take in some fresh air and clear their collective minds, The Majesties peered out over the city. They watched multiple fire trucks managing the fires started by their enemies.

"How are you holding up with all this alien mumbo-jumbo chief?" Aganathin asked Blessed.

"I'm not so sure," he replied, shaking his head. "We are soldiers, Aganathin. I'm used to war and military strategies. That story Allucio and Desmurose offered about their run-in with the Bounty Hunters on Titan was overwhelming."

"Yeah, it gives credence to the sinking feeling that things were truly escalating to a level beyond words and weapons," Tenan said, cutting in.

In a fight that was supposed to be against a common enemy, three of the Majesties found themselves fighting against Menzuo. Once tempers resided, the heroes came to an agreement that they would have to work as a team in order to defeat the approaching threat to the planet.

"Babe. Are you okay?" Rekluse asked as she softly rubbed Tenan back.

"I'm not, baby. Not until we get to the bottom of this and rid the world of all this evil."

"Glass half-full, baby. Remember? That's how you have to look at this. You see, we're not where we are by accident. Count it all joy, that God would choose us…us my dear…to be the ones to fight this battle on behalf of good and evil. For centuries, people wondered if there were other life forms out there; if there were other galaxies. Well, we finally got our answer. Come to find out, the battle of good and evil extends beyond multiple galaxies."

"I hear your optimism, sweetie, but there it's hard for me to view it that way."

"Really? Baby, how could you say such a thing? You were brought by God's grace into the Kingdom of Heaven. The only account we ever have of that ever happening is in the Bible with the prophet Isaiah and John the Revelator. Now, God has elected you. There is power and purpose connected to your being!"

"Babe, I was dropped from thousands of feet in the sky with the intent for me to die. I had to force myself to forgive Paraflyte because he was under the influence of madness. I'm not sure if I forgave him fully. Most times, I find myself wanting to call him up and really let him know that on some days, I want him dead."

Rekluse softly touched the side of his face. "Okay. I understand. It was a very traumatic experience. You have the right to feel a certain way. It's gonna take time, sweetie."

Tenan swatted her hand away. "Don't patronize me. I don't need that right now."

"Hey, I'm your girl! I'm not patronizing you. I'm trying to help you see the bigger picture here. Tell you what. I'm gonna head inside and let you get some alone time. I can tell you need it right now."

As Rekluse began to walk away, Tenan grabbed her by the arm and pulled her back gently. "Babe, I'm sorry. I'm sorry. I'm sorry," Tenan said as he pulled Rekluse in for a warm embrace. "I know you're helping. I'm just having a hard time wrapping my head around all of this. When I signed up for the military, I didn't know that I would be fighting demons, aliens, and villains with supernatural abilities. It's just a lot."

Rekluse's demeanor softened. "I understand, baby. Nonetheless, evil is evil, no matter what form it comes in. And because we have these amazing gifts and abilities, it is our job to fight against evil regardless of how it looks."

"You're right, baby. You're absolutely right." Tenan held his woman in his arms.

On another section of the roof, Slaycick stood talking to Blurr and Lydia as Blessed continued his conversation with Aganathin. Paladin joined them. The twin sisters, K'nia and Kasitia, were making themselves more acquainted with Allucio and Desmurose. Menzuo stood on the opposite side of the roof, looking into the sky as if he was in deep thought.

"Let's pull the gang inside, Blessed," Paladin said. "The devil is definitely turning up the heat, so it's time that we put our plan into play."

"Sure thing," Blessed agreed. "Everyone, let's head inside. We need to talk schematics before the next attack happens."

As everyone began making their way inside The Beacon, a cold front abruptly settled in. It was unnatural, and the heroes knew it as the temperatures were extremely warm that night.

"Whoa! Do you all feel that?" asked Lydia.

"Yeah," Tenan said. "Something is not right."

"Another Super-Normal perhaps," Blurr said. "Before you all arrived, Paladin wrestled with an old dude who called himself Whirlwind. He was literally able to create high-forced winds."

"It's not a Super-Normal," said Tenan as he fixed his eyes on the dark sky. He noticed the dark clouds coming closer together, but he did not see anything in the sky.

Lydia pulled out her vibrating phone from her pocket and scanned the message blistering across the screen. "You guys –"

"Ummm…it just looks like it's about to rain, dude," said Allucio. "You're sure you're not just overly paranoid?"

Desmurose cut a serious look over to his friend and stuck his hand out, signaling him to keep his mouth shut.

"I'm *not* paranoid," Tenan replied. "This is something else. I can feel it in my spirit." As he finished speaking, Tenan slumped over, holding his chest, writhing in pain, similar to how he did during his first vision. His eyes turned white, and he gnashed his teeth as his body tensed, arms and legs locking up. This time, his seizure-like episode was much more painful than the first.

Lydia began walking towards Paladin, still gazing at her phone. "Guys, I think you should –"

"Oh, my God!" Rekluse screamed. "It's happening again!" She knelt down and held him close, stroking his head. She and everyone looked on as Tenan's painful episode continued. After a few seconds, Tenan's eyes returned to normal, and his body relaxed. He began to breathe heavily.

"Uh, guys," Lydia said aloud.

"Baby, what is it?" Rekluse asked.

Tenan began to rouse and stood as his breathing steadied. As he started to contain his gasping, he looked into Rekluse's eyes with an expression of great concern. "I have to go somewhere."

Without further warning, he pushed Rekluse away just as a portal opened beneath his feet, and he slipped inside. The portal closed before Rekluse could react. "Baby! Wait!" she screamed, reaching out to him.

***

The large vessel hovered over Lake Michigan, still invisible to the unsuspecting inhabitants of the city below. The tide in the lake became more violent, as enormous waves crashed against the shore. Pedestrians looked up in the sky, taking in the dark clouds forming as if it were about to start thundering and lightning.

Aboard the craft, an argument was brewing amongst Judge Amaruk and Natas, with the giants firmly backing their leader. "This is not Jerusalem," Natas said sternly and disappointed.

"No, it is not," said Judge Amaruk calmly with his arms folded behind his back. "We are above Hero City, known formerly as Chicago."

"I made myself clear," Natas said. "I need to be in Jerusalem. My plan begins and ends with the deaths of the Majesties. The only one of importance to me is the portal dweller. I also told you that anyone who got my way or hindered me from executing my plan would face death."

"You dare threaten me aboard my ship?" Judge Amaruk said.

"Yes!" Natas shouted. His voice boomed, bellowing from his giant frame and reverberating throughout the vessel. "I do dare threaten you aboard your ship. And you can spare me the talk about how you saved me. You needed me alive to carry out the antichrist agenda. My purpose is connected to yours, and you know it. Now let's cut through the crap and take me where I need to be!"

"Father, let's just kill this ugly alien and go to Jerusalem on our own," Gath growled. "We're already back on Earth. We don't need him anymore."

"Silence, you impudent brute," snapped Judge Amaruk. "You're a five-month-old science project with an unnatural birth. Everything you know has been manually downloaded into you and your guileless brother. You haven't lived long enough to learn life lessons like humility, which let you know when to close your mouth. I've lived through centuries. Now shut your lips and let the ancient ones talk.

"I've lived long enough to know how to stomp you like an insect!" Gath said.

"Enough!" yelled Siph. He charged Judge Amaruk and cocked his fist back to deliver a blow. As he swung, Judge Amaruk stuck out his right hand, and Siph's punch was stopped in midair as if he hit an invisible wall.

His brother Gath joined in, charging at Judge Amaruk from the other side. Judge Amaruk raised his opposite hand and stopped the giant dead in his tracks. Neither one could penetrate nor break the psychokinetic hold Judge Amaruk had on them. With a quick flick of the wrist, Judge Amaruk sent the two behemoths flying to the other side of the room. He folded his arms behind his back once more.

Irritated, with one hand, Natas Selur grabbed Judge Amaruk by his neck and part of his face. He lifted him off the ground and held him up to his face, eye to eye. "I could kill you right now."

"No, you can't," Judge Amaruk said nonchalantly.

Within seconds, he vanished from Natas' grasp and reappeared behind him, floating in midair. Natas stared at his hand, opening and closing it in amazement. He turned around to see Judge Amaruk floating. Natas was slightly amused by the display of the extraterrestrial enchanter. "Impressive. But you think you can amuse me with your cheap tricks?" Natas said. "I'm not impressed. Do not forget that I have some unique abilities of my own."

The two giants picked themselves up from the ground as Judge Amaruk floated back down.

"Can you put aside your pride for a moment to listen?" Judge Amaruk asked. "Of course, you being alive benefits me. I would never deny that. And me fighting you does not make any sense either. Why would I destroy the body that I created? My best prototype at that. It wouldn't make sense. For the last time, we're on the same side. Now, regarding your other concern...we're in Hero City because the Majesties are here."

"Are you certain?" Natas asked, feeling somewhat at ease. "How do you know this?"

"Let's just say I'm *connected* to them," Judge Amaruk said as he walked out. "And by the way, keep those boys on a leash. You're important to this cause, Natas. But I have no problem eliminating them if they keep testing my patience."

***

Tenan stepped through the portal onto a road paved of platinum and gold. Above him, large cherubs flew to and from through the sky. A soft breeze carried a beautiful aroma combined with perfume notes, frankincense, and various flowers. Tenan walked down the road admiring the immense mansions on both sides of the roads. He studied the angels streaking across the sky above him before taking note of one, in particular, descending in his direction.

"Tenan, you heard my call, and you came," the angelic host said. "Bless you, courageous one."

Tenan recognized him. "Titus! Is that you?"

"Yes," he replied.

"You're the one who summoned me? I didn't even hear you. I just received a series of visions and knew to come here."

"Ever since your experience after your battle in Russia, Tenan, this gulf has been accessible to you. Nevertheless, you did not know the sacrifice it would take to come here regularly."

"I didn't know I was able…allowed to."

"No. You knew. You didn't think you were worthy. Your humility is often traded for guilt. Sometimes those lines become so blurred between the two, that you can't tell which is which. But, I'm here to reassure you that you are worthy."

"I thought this…this paradise was only accessible after death."

"There so much for you to learn, son. And you will, in due time. There is an enormous threat coming, one bigger than you can even imagine. You sense it already, don't you?" Tenan nodded. "You know it's there, but you can't see what it is, not fully at least. But you're not alone. There is another among you who can sense it as well."

"You're speaking in riddles Titus. Please clarify."

"There is a means to obtaining a faith so great that you would be able to see everything without being able to see anything at all."

"I'm not sure I follow, Titus. What does that mean?"

Titus held up a hand. "Let me ask you this way…What if God told you he would allow you to see everything, but first, you have to give up your sight. Would you trust him?"

"That's hard to say," Tenan said. "It's easier said than done, but you did say God would allow me to see everything, correct?"

"Correct," Titus said.

"You're asking me hypothetically?"

"Nothing is hypothetical when it comes to the Lord."

Titus' eyes remained fixed on Tenan, waiting for his reply. Tenan knew this was more than just a question, and depending on how he answered, his ideas would be challenged like never before.

He took a deep breath and finally spoke. "Titus, I'm not sure if I'm ready to lose my sight. Yet, if God is asking me to give up my sight for something better in return, then I guess there is no better testament of faith than trusting God with something you can't see or control."

"Correct," Titus said. "For you know that faith is the substance of things hoped for and the evidence of things not seen. But the reward that you will receive for this demonstration of faith is beyond description and can't be articulated with words. You have never experienced something like this before. Nonetheless, it is your choice, and regardless of your choice, you are still a beloved man of God."

Tenan thought back to the night he first received his abilities. His emotions were the same. Faced with a similar decision as the night he dipped himself into the liquid Oramite. He did it out of faith, not logic. He would now have to make a similar decision, except this one was tougher. Giving up his sight for something greater did not sound like a good idea. Especially when he couldn't know for sure precisely what "something greater" was until he relinquished his sight.

"If losing my sight is going to give me something that I can use to help save the world from the evil that's coming, then so be it," Tenan said. "The Lord gave his life for me, so I can give up my sight for him."

As he spoke, two more angels descended from above and landed on either side of him. They chanted words in a language he could not understand as they laid hands on his head.

"You have chosen well, Tenan," Titus said. "Of course, now your trust will be tested, and that test begins now." Without another word, Titus approached Tenan and touched his forehead. Immediately, Tenan's vision went dark. He could see nothing but utter blackness. He began to panic, touching his eyes as if it would return his sight. He reached out around him, trying to make contact with one of the angels.

"Because you have exemplified such a degree of faith like none other," Titus said, "nothing will be hidden from you. You will be able to see all things – past, present, and future. Your faith will now be your sight and guide you in all things."

"But, I can't see anything," Tenan said, his voice trembling. "I thought you said I would be able to see all things."

"And you will," Titus said. "Now, return and warn the others of the things you see."

Titus touched Tenan on the head once more, and he felt himself now sinking into the ground. As he drifted into the abyss, he knew he was no longer in Heaven. Without his sight, it was impossible to know his whereabouts. Tenan figured he was in space due to the absence of gravity.

Suddenly, an image formed in his mind just as his body locked up, and his eyes turned white. As he continued to drift in the dark chasm, all he could see in the recesses of his mind was the large black vessel from his previous vision as it hovered over the shoreline of Hero City's Lake Michigan. He could see the image as clearly as if it was showing on a monitor before him.

There were four figures aboard the vessel, two of which he recognized as the giants they battled in Syria while the other two were foreign to him. However, they were no longer the decimated beasts from before. They were slowly going through a regeneration process, with rejuvenated bodies.

A tall man, around the same height as the other two giants, stood next to the fourth person as although Tenan didn't recognize them at all, he could sense that both beings were full of power.

His mind drew him closer, and he studied the third giant. A vision of an armless, Natas Selur materialized. "It can't be," he whispered. His mind flashed to another scene where he witnessed all three giants stepping out of a regeneration pod, swathed in all black metallic-like suits. Immediately, Tenan's fears were confirmed. "Oh my God," he whispered. "It is him. Natas has been reborn and returned to Earth! How is this sorcery even possible? I have to get back and warn the others!"

All at once, Natas' words came back to Tenan. He recalled how he had told him he would return to Earth again one day and would be bringing death and destruction with him.

Panic rushed through him. In a hurry to get back to the others, Tenan opened a portal and ran into it. The vision in his mind quickly disappeared, and he went back to seeing nothing except complete darkness. Thinking the portal would lead him back to the others at The Beacon, Tenan fell and landed in what felt like sand. He scooped some of the substance up in his hand and gave it a whiff. "Sand," he whispered.

Judging from the heat beating on his neck, he supposed that he was in a desert. Filled with concern, he opened another portal and stepped through. A blast of cold wind slammed against his skin, sending chills along his body. Thousands of snow flurries swirled around him. He touched his neck, and his mask formed around his face to protect him from the cold. Frustration and panic rose within him. Again, he tried to picture The Beacon's balcony as he opened another portal. This time, his body plunged into a large body of water. Momentarily submerged, he swam to the top and broke the surface, slapping his fist in frustration. He kicked his feet and flailed his arms to tread water.

"Damn!" Tenan shouted. "What the hell is going on?"

He quickly opened another portal in front of him and swam into it. This time, his feet were met by smooth concrete as he dropped a short distance after entering the portal.

"Hello! Is anyone here?" he yelled out.

There was no reply.

"Hello!" he shouted again, but he was met by empty blackness all around him. Blind, angry and disgusted, Tenan couldn't figure out why he was missing his marks. Surely his powers weren't fleeing him, were they? But he couldn't deny the truth of his reality. His portals were leading him to random locations, and to make matters worse, he couldn't see where he was going or landing.

"Aaaaaaaaaah!" Tenan yelled, screaming at the top of his lungs. "Why would you do this to me, God? I trusted you. Your angel said I would be able to see all things. Instead, you cover my vision in darkness. You've betrayed me!"

Repeatedly, Tenan tried hundreds of more times – again and again, with similar results. After several more failed attempts and what felt like hours of trying to get home, he gave up. He opened one more portal and stepped in. From the feel of the ground and the smell of the pine trees, he was in a forest somewhere. But the truth was still very evident. He was lost, blind, and had no clue how to get back home.

He felt his way over to a large oak tree and sat down against it. Angry with God, Tenan's blind eyes now spilled tears, convinced that God had abandoned him. He felt like he had taken a raw deal, gotten duped in the process, and received the short end of the stick. He pulled his knees to his chest, dropped his head, and wept bitterly.

ACT II

CHAPTER 13

THE BIGGER THEY ARE…

"Open the containment unit and let me see my army," Judge Amaruk said to one of the armed guards that stood before him.

The guard, wearing all black with a red helmet that covered his face, turned and quickly punched in several numbers on a keypad. The large, metal door rose slowly, gradually revealing the over-sized legs, broad torso, and heads of tall, well-built soldiers resembling the race of Judge Amaruk and General Swadin. The bald, beige creatures stood roughly seven feet tall – the average height of the Necromenian species.

Several terrestrial beings of different intergalactic backgrounds were seen scattering abroad wearing white lab coats. A busty, purple-skinned female with orange hair approached Judge Amaruk.

"We're almost done. The last batch has roughly forty-five more minutes in the incubator," she said. "We've run tests on every single one of them. Their vitals are through the roof, and their immune systems are resisting every disease injected into them."

"Marvelous, Doctor! Thank you for the report." Judge Amaruk said with a wide smile across his face. "Our species will live again, and we will be superior…across all galaxies."

General Swadin slowly walked up behind Judge Amaruk, wearing a stunned expression; his mouth hung open in shock. "Sir! What…how is this possible? Are those what I think they are?"

"They are *us*. Behold," Judge Amaruk said with a sprawling wave of his hand, "our new family. Risen from the remains of the blood spilled by our own people."

Judge Amaruk walked among the rows of the newly cloned Necromenians who stood still in a catatonic state, waiting to be awakened by their creator. He touched their faces and squeezed their arms as he admired their defined muscle tone and flawless skin make-up.

"How were you able to accomplish such a miracle?" General Swadin asked.

"That disastrous day, when Stratus destroyed our planet, he made a mistake sparing my life. I begged him to allow me to give our people a proper burial. He agreed. Unaware that I was secretly collecting samples of blood among many of the fallen before putting them in their graves. Using a combination of magic and science, I was able to recreate our great nation all over again. These beautiful creatures are more than clones. Each one, when he or she awakens, will already be full of the knowledge of necromancy, magic, alchemy, and sorcery, just as our great ancestors had. They will be indestructible." He turned and smiled at the General with pride. "And you and I will lead them."

"Genius!" General Swadin exclaimed. "What of Stratus? Is he aware of this?"

"No. Neither should he be. He denied my request for an army when I asked for it, so I created one of our own. Besides, I was thinking ahead. My army is designed for a two-fold feat, General Swadin. I have earned a small fragment of Stratus' trust because he mistakes my submission as fear. We will continue to play our role. Like it or not, we *all* need each other to defeat those on Earth with abilities. Take no opponent for granted. That is the mistake that Stratus, Natas, and the idiotic goliaths have made with our kind."

"They are impulsive and reckless at best," General Swadin said. "You, however, are gifted at strategy and scheme. When do you plan on unleashing the army?"

"In due time, General. We're going to let the giants have their first swing at the heroes on Earth. Remember…*strategy* and *scheme*," Judge Amaruk said, tapping his finger against his own temple. "Let the eager and impulsive nature of Natas and his giants propel them to the front lines, as we allow both sides to weaken one other. Then we'll move in and bring the assault. Until then, let's continue to play our passive roles."

Judge Amaruk and General Swadin walked out of the containment unit together, but not before Judge Amaruk turned to the armed guard and gave him a final directive.

"Have your men clothe the Necromenian soldiers in the armor I prepared for them once the doctors and scientists are finished tinkering and evaluating them. Afterward, sit tight and wait for General Swadin's command."

The armed guard agreed and began barking orders over the intercom unit attached to his wrist. Judge Amaruk and General Swadin walked swiftly down a corridor leading to the hangar where Natas and the giants were deliberating on a strategy to take out the Majesties. They entered through a large door that slid up as they approached.

Natas, with two the giants behind him, approached the two Necromenians who were walking towards them. The two sides came face to face; Natas and the giants towered over the two seven-footers, making them look like dwarfs.

"You said the Majesties were here," Natas said. "I need you to point me to their exact location."

"There was activity a few hours ago in the downtown area," Judge Amaruk said in a sarcastic tone. "I'm not sure what their exact location is, but I'm sure you can draw them out by making a little noise. They respond to calamity very quickly."

Natas pointed at him. "Your lack of communication with me has put a stumbling block in my plans, Amaruk. Dr. Bernstein and Dr. Samir are important pieces to this puzzle. If I didn't know any better, I would think you were setting me up to be at a disadvantage when I finally came face to face with the Majesties. Would I be wrong?"

Judge Armaruk smirked, shooting an eye over at General Swadin. "I saved you and made you more powerful than you've ever been. I gave you a new body with technology that no one has ever known, and yet you still question me. Your pride and lack of gratitude are the reasons we can't work together. It's a shame because those two reasons will eventually lead to your downfall. You're equipped right now to destroy any being, super or normal, who stands in your way and you're still not satisfied. You said you wanted to rule Earth, right? Well, here we are. So go and rule it!"

"You fool!" Natas replied. "You knew I wanted to go to Jerusalem to rescue Dr. Bernstein because I said it to you clearly. You purposely ignored my request. You've been testing me and my patience from the moment I came out of that chamber. My patience, coupled with the fact that you revitalized me, is the only reason I haven't crushed *you* or your *General*. That's me showing you gratitude."

"That will be the last time you insult me on this vessel, Natas! I helped put you back together, but don't think for one moment that I can't take you apart like some scrawny puppet. I made a decision to help put you in a position to take out your enemies. Right now, nobody knows you're here, nor do they know the powers you possess. They think Natas is dead. The way I see it, you have a huge advantage!"

"Dr. Samir and Dr. Bernstein have a great deal of information that I need," Natas said as he took one step closer to Judge Amaruk. He looked down upon him with disdain. "They have information on other Super-Normals that are hell-bent on destroying the Majesties. I want them. So before I make a play on the Majesties, I'm going to make sure that Dr. Bernstein and Dr. Samir are with us to shore up our squad."

"Well, it looks like you should be on your way then," Judge Amaruk said slyly. "Jerusalem is a long way from Chicago, and my ship is staying right here."

"Grrrrrraaaaah! Father, let's crush him," Gath yelled.

"You two still haven't learned yet, huh?" Judge Amaruk said, taking a half step back in a defensive stance. "You took a shot at me once, and I let you off easy. If you come at me again, dumb brute, I will kill you."

As Gath lurched forward towards Judge Amaruk, Natas stuck a hand across the Giant's chest and stopped him. "Not now, son." He then redirected his attention back to Judge Amaruk and continued. "This is where we part ways, Amaruk, but I'm not going to

Jerusalem. I already have someone retrieving my doctors for me, despite your incompetence. However, I will have you know that my ambition will not be stopped. I have come to unite and rule over all the countries of Earth and fulfill the prophetic narrative of my calling. I know that you have a mission as well. With that said, I'm not forgetful of what you've done for my sons and me. I'm sparing the life of you and those on this craft because of that. However, if you interfere with me, I will kill you. It's the last time I'm going to say it."

"It's the last time I'm going to hear it, and it's the last time you're going to be on my ship," Judge Amaruk said. "And for your sake Natas, I hope that we don't cross paths again."

Judge Amaruk stretched forth his hand, and the back door of the hangar opened. Natas and the Giants looked outside. Dark clouds and rain filled the sky as the large vessel hung several thousand feet above Lake Michigan.

The cold air from the outside whistled as winds blew through the hangar. Natas and the Giants looked back at Judge Amaruk. "Have you lost your mind? You do plan on lowering your vessel right, Amaruk?" Natas said with a disconcerted look on his face.

"No," Amaruk said defiantly. "Lowering my vessel ruins the element of surprise. Besides, you're big, and I built your suits with shock absorption. When you hit the water, you won't even feel it."

"We're not jumping off of this craft," Siph grumbled.

"Yes, you are," Judge Amaruk said with a sneer. "Plus, your master has levitation abilities. He'll make sure you float safely to the bottom."

Without warning, Judge Amaruk waved his hands in their direction, as if he was shewing a fly. Siph and Gath toppled off the hangar, pushed out into the elements by an invisible force, which sent them plummeting thousands of feet to the waters below them.

Natas, unphased by Judge Amaruk's telekinetic thrust, held his ground, resisting his attack.

"You should go check on them and assure that they make it to the bottom safely," Judge Amaruk said sarcastically. "I didn't build their suits with flight technology."

"You dare taunt me!? We will have our day, Amaruk," Natas said. Awed and angered by Judge Amaruk's disrespect, Natas would have the last laugh before diving to bail out his Giants from their free fall. He quickly back-handed General Swadin and sent him hurling into the wall, rendering him unconscious. Before Judge Amaruk could react, Natas kicked him in his chest, thrusting the Necromenian leader into the large door from which they entered. The velocity and impact left a large indentation in it. Judge Amaruk pulled himself up and eyed the damage. "Get off my ship now before I destroy you!" he snarled.

Natas smiled, then sprinted towards the open hangar door as it slowly began to close. He dove and soared out the exit just in time to beat the door sealing tightly behind him. Natas barreled headfirst towards Gath and Siph, who were still plunging towards the waters below. Natas picked up speed as his momentum increased. Before long, he was neck and neck with the two Giants, and he reached out for both of them, taking Gath by the arm and Siph by the collar.

He focused his levitation powers and easily slowed their descent until all three of them were safely lowered into the water below. The rain continued its downpour, with pounding thunder and lighting decorating the Chicago skyline.

"Father, fly us back up there. Let's kill that punk-ass alien once and for all!" Gath yelled.

"No," Natas replied calmly. "Activate your suit's invisibility modes. I'm not ready for the Majesties to know we're here yet. We'll deal with Amaruk later. I have a plan for him. In the meantime, let's get to shore and find a place to lay low. Bernstein and Samir will be with us soon. I have a rescue plan already in the works."

CHAPTER 14

JUST A LITTLE MORE TIME

"Okay soooo…is he coming back anytime soon?" Allucio joked, but no one was laughing.

Rekluse knelt on the floor next to the last place Tenan's portal closed, sobbing. "Quiet, fool!" Desmurose said, nudging him in the arm.

"He's gone," Rekluse said softly.

Blessed came near and knelt down beside her. "Don't say that. Tenan will be back, I'm sure of it. Wherever he went, I'm certain that he needed to go."

Rekluse looked over at him. Her cheeks were stained with fresh tears. "How? How do you know?"

"Because he's a brother in arms. We never desert our team, and we never leave a man behind. Tenan is out there, and we'll find him. You have my word." Blessed stood and offered a hand to Rekluse. She took it, and he pulled her up. K'nia and Kasitia came over and gave her a group hug.

As the ladies wept together, Blurr stood next to Paladin and shook her head. "Things are going from bad to worse in a heartbeat."

"Agreed," Paladin said. "Another man down. Our numbers are starting to thin out. We don't even know where Thief is now. He should have reported back in days ago."

"Well, maybe he left us all to die," Blurr said, folding her arms across her chest. "Alice always had a way of knowing when to get out while he was ahead. I don't know why I thought any different of him. Same ole Alice. A leopard doesn't change its spots, Sebastian."

Paladin's helmet retracted. "But Cheetahs do, right?" Blurr sent him a daggering stare. Paladin raised his hands in an apologetic manner. "Hear me out, love. My Uncle Rooney taught me something when I was a kid: 'Good is fleeting, but evil is always near.' I took that message with me all my life, using it to remind me that, even in the presence of wickedness, I had a duty to find the good. It gave me hope."

"There you go with all that silver lining babble," Blurr said and walked off.

Slaycick called out to Paladin. "Everything good?"

Paladin nodded. "Yeah, don't worry about it," he snapped and quickly walked off after Blurr, who had already made her way inside The Beacon. Paladin called out to her as he skipped down the stairs. "Karla!"

Blurr hurried to their bedroom and Paladin followed, with Lydia in tow. "Sebas, wait up."

"Not now Lydia, can't you see I'm busy," Paladin demanded. As they both closed in on Sebastian's bedroom, they were met by an ashen glow, emanating from the door. As they stepped inside, they were amazed to see Zenith standing there talking with Blurr.

"Well, well, well," Paladin started, "if it isn't the Jolly *Sheen* Giant. Came to taunt us with some more riddles, Oh Great One?"

Zenith shot him a smoldering look with eyes narrowed to slits. "Oh, snap!" Lydia said, squeezing Paladin's arms. "Earth to Sebas. A word of advice. Don't make the powerful Super-Normal mad. Not when he's trying to help."

Paladin looked perplexed. "When he's trying to what?"

"That's what I was trying to tell you on the rooftop, cousin," Lydia said.

Blurr turned around. "He says he has information for us."

"Information?" Paladin asked.

"Yes! I got a news flash pinged to my phone. Apparently, he captured Slingblade," Lydia said, holding up her phone.

"To be exact, he turned himself in," Zenith said.

"What, you couldn't catch him? It would be against your *rules*," Paladin said, adding air quotes when he said the word rules.

Zenith's eyes narrowed even further. "See, that's the sign of pissivity swelling in the eyes of the most powerful Super-Normal known to man."

"I don't care. I'm tired of not having answers," Paladin said, stepping towards Zenith.

Lydia yoked him by his arm. "I'd like to take the time to suggest an alternative option," She said, grunting as she stepped in front of Paladin. "A more peaceful one…a wiser one."

"You know, ever since I met you on top of that building when you first donned the S3 suit, I must admit I was impressed," Zenith said, floating by Blurr and closing the distance between him and Paladin.

Paladin swallowed. "What, by my bravery?"

Zenith was now nose to nose with him. "No, by your blinding arrogance. It's both a hindrance and an asset."

"Please don't puff his head up anymore," Lydia said, stepping out of the way.

Zenith and Paladin glared at her. "Really, cousin?" Paladin asked.

"I second that," Blurr said.

"Really, babe?" Paladin asked.

Zenith turned back to him. "It pushes you to great feats of fantasticism."

Paladin held up a gentle finger. "Ugh, is that a word –"

"I've witnessed you take down Super-Normal tyrants, build a dazzling artificial intelligence computer –"

"He did say dazzling, right?" B.R.A.I.N. interjected over the intercom.

"Push back droves of military forces and even secure the woman of your dreams," Zenith continued. "And yet, you hearken to the mental capacity of a child when it comes to mere logic in dealing with something as simple as the theory of relativity."

Paladin shot a glance over to Lydia, who simply shrugged in return. He peered over to Blurr, who wore a smirk and shook her head. The only response to Zenith's narrative was obvious. "And…"

Zenith floated towards the ceiling. "My helping or perceivably not helping is only relative to your particular circumstances. If you look back at every interaction I've had with The Capes, I've only helped. It's only ended up for the good of the advancement of time."

"Of time?" Paladin asked.

"Yes, time. The one variable that is beyond any control or interference of man," Zenith said with finality.

"Is there a reason he's floating?" Blurr asked.

"Duh," Lydia stammered, "'cause it's cool as fu–"

She quickly shut her mouth as Zenith waved his hands the entire ceiling disintegrated, fading into a landscape of blackness and stars. "Time, times, and half of times. It is a parable of the present, future, and past. All linked together by relativity. I seek to move time forward, while Normals seek to both stop time and reverse time. To make up for past mistakes and prepare for future ones. By to perfect that which is lost, you need only look to the present."

"Here we go," Paladin mumbled.

The stars began to take shape as children playing in a field. As Zenith carried on, they slowly grew into adults and then finally crumbled into elderly people who morphed into skeletons who toppled into open graves. "We are all bound by time, and if we are careful not to take it for granted, we'll all attain that which we seek."

"We know what we want, Zenith, but what do you seek?" Blurr asked.

Zenith lowered back to the floor as the ceiling returned. He gently touched Blurr's chin. "Only answers, Conduit."

"Okay, okay, break it up," Paladin said, pushing Zenith's arm down and slipping in between them. "The arrogant one is here. Remember, they call me the Lightning Rod."

"Since you're in a talkative mood, Oh Beautiful One," Lydia said, eyeing Zenith like a piece of candy. "Can I have some answers, Zenith?"

"Proceed," Zenith replied.

"The evil Super-Normals. Over the past three weeks, since Q-18 plummeted to the North Pole, their activity has nearly quadrupled. We've had an impossible time keeping up with them. What gives? Were there no good Super-Normals that came from the storm?" Lydia asked.

"The Dark Spores are the answer. Those whose hearts are pure can resist the evil desires that stem from their poison. However, those of impure motives and intentions, it corrupts beyond measure," Zenith said mildly.

"But why?" Paladin asked.

"One must only look to the stars for further answers," Zenith said, pointing upwards.

"So did the Dark Spores corrupt Alice? Is that why he's been gone?" Lydia asked.

"No," Zenith said with a slight smile. "He is fighting with inner demons that have nothing to do with spores or you. When he has purged them, he will return."

"Well, hopefully, it will be in time to help sort out all this mess. Blurr's been dealing with quite a lot, and now it seems that even Tenan has gone AWOL. These visions they share are really driving them…" Paladin paused and looked at Blurr.

"Mad. You can say it," Blurr said. "But not crazy mad, just angry that I don't have answers."

"You're not angry that you don't have answers. You're upset because you know that you are the answer, aren't you?" Zenith asked.

There was a pregnant pause between the four of them, broken only by Blurr's answer. "Yes."

Zenith pointed at Blurr. "Se-Crets!" Paladin looked in Blurr's direction. "I told you that you could no longer function as a perfect unit if you keep secrets."

"When did you say that?" Paladin asked.

"Just now," Zenith replied.

"Of course, relativity," Paladin said.

"See, you're getting it," Zenith said.

"What secrets?" Paladin asked Blurr.

"My visions…they're telling me that…that I *may* be the answer to all of *this*," Blurr said softly.

"And what exactly did you see?" Paladin asked.

"I…I…don't want to talk about it right now," Blurr said with wet eyes.

"Honey, I…I didn't know. Why didn't you tell me?" Paladin asked.

"So, how do we stop the Dark Spores?" Blurr asked, changing the subject. "If this Super-Normal activity continues, they'll destroy the city and worse, maybe the world."

"The stars," Zenith said. "There is an alien artifact on another planet that can quell the effects of the Dark Spores in an adjacent Solar System. It is from the Traveler's home-world. But I cannot tell you the location."

"Q & A is officially over," Lydia said.

Blurr walked over and took Zenith by the hand. "How can we find it? You must tell us, Zenith."

"In time, my child. We still have a lot of time," Zenith said.

"What about Slingblade? Was he infected by the Spores?" Paladin asked.

"Yes, but he is recovering," Zenith said.

"How? He doesn't have the artifact," Lydia said.

Zenith held up a hand, shushing her. "Go to him. He is in military custody. He may not have the artifact, but he has something else entirely more valuable."

"What's that?" Blurr asked.

Zenith stepped away as the room began to shake. "Farewell," he said before vanishing.

CHAPTER 15

A NEW MISSION AT HAND

As everyone left the rooftop and made their way back inside The Beacon, Allucio and Demurose lagged behind, waiting on Menzuo. Menzuo noticed and motioned them to go ahead. "I'll catch up shortly. I need a minute," he said. His two friends nodded and left the balcony to catch up with their new team. Inside, they found Lydia over by her work station and began to assist her with the audio files that were collected on Titan.

***

Back outside, Menzuo took a moment to breathe, gazing up at the starts. He dropped to his knees and closed his eyes, focusing on his home planet of Yardania; searching for any signs to connect to Solar. After a few moments, he could feel the energy waves surging through his brother's body. He could tell that he was in training as there were spikes of power flowing all around him. "Solar, can you hear me? Solar, are you there?" Menzuo asked hoping to be able to reach him telepathically.

After a few moments of silence, Solar could hear a voice speaking to him in his mind. He ceased from his training and turned his attention to the voice. It was all too familiar to him. "Menzuo, is that you…but how?" Solar replied.

Menzuo focused a little harder and closed the connection between them. Solar's voice resonated in his mind. "Solar, yes, it's me. Thank God that I can reach finally reach you."

"How are you doing this?" Solar asked.

"I think that my powers are strengthening," Menzuo answered. "I've been trying to reach you for a while now. I think because things are so tense here on Earth, my focus has grown stronger." Menzuo paused as his energy levels diminished.

Solar could feel sorrow within his brother's heart as their connection strengthened. "Tensions on Earth? What's happening?"

"There is an unknown threat heading to our planet. Allucio, Desmurose, and I had to travel to the Titan moon of Jupiter to retrieve some information and were met by some very serious bounty hunters. We handled them, but they were not from this galaxy. I'm certain now that whatever is on its way is a threat that we may not be ready for."

"Then we all must stay on high alert," Solar replied. "Master Renzfly and I will notify the rest of our team so that they can be ready for anything or anyone who may enter their planets. I know that they will keep their homes safe."

"Good idea, Solar," Menzuo said. He paused for a minute to gather his next thoughts, then spoke. "But there is something else bothering me, Solar."

"Speak to me," Solar said.

"I feel another growing threat," Menzuo said. "A threat that is directly connected to the energy of all good and evil. It may be the fear that Lord Fetid tried to place within my head when his ghost tried to take over my mind, but I feel his presence strengthening."

"I figured that would happen to you," Solar replied. "Upon my return home with Master Renzfly, we have kept a careful eye on the action brewing on planet Excervo. Lord Fetid is definitely getting stronger, and so is his planet. I assume he may be planning an attack."

"That's not good. Not good at all. How am I going to be prepared to face him and this unknown threat coming to Earth?"

"You won't be alone," Solar said.

Menzuo smiled. "You're right. Now we have a strong team of fighters with us," Menzuo replied.

"What warriors have you, Allucio and Desmurose connected with?"

"Where do I start? There are many with us here on Earth."

"Tell me about them," Solar said.

"Do you remember that man Paladin reaching out to me in my dreams? Well, Allucio, Desmurose, and I have found him. We also teamed up with the Majesties of Canaan."

"That is good news. It sounds like you have a very strong team, indeed. And that's a great thing," Solar said.

"They are strong fighters, but I fear there is still something seriously off," Menzuo replied. He took a deep breath, let it out slowly then continued. "When I finally met up with Paladin here in Hero City, he had no clue as to who I was. While I was telling him everything that he said to me in my dream, it was as if it was the first time that he heard it."

"That is strange. Do you think that your dream was an illusion?"

"You tell me," Menzuo retorted. "You were with me in that dream. Did it seem like an illusion to you?"

"No, not at all," Solar said. "It was clear as day, but I do wonder where the break in contact is."

Anger began to grow within the young warrior. "I wish you were here to help me figure this out, Solar. But whatever comes my way, I'm going to destroy it before it knows what hit it," Menzuo said.

Menzuo could hear Solar sigh heavily. "I wish I could be there as well, my young brother," Solar said. "But this is the time where you, as our Universal Protector, must become that true leader. The wisdom to figure out how to lead others and protect everyone within this universe while also making the right decisions for the greater good; all lies on your shoulders. You cannot be irrational, cocky, and arrogant as a true protector. The weight that you must carry while trying to become that wise warrior is not easy to uphold."

"How can I search for wisdom when my brother and my master are back home on Yardania?" Menzuo asked. "I have no clue what evil has entered our universe and will be coming to Earth, and now with Lord Fetid getting stronger, I have to go on instinct, and that is to fight hard against all evil. There is no one here to guide me to that realm of wisdom."

"Remember the promise we both made to Master Kane on Legerdamien?" Solar asked. "I believe that once you figure out what needs to be done to protect Earth from these unknown threats, we have to honor that promise."

Menzuo nodded in agreement, eyes closed. "I guess this is what Master Kane said when he told us we would know when it would be time to see him again."

"So now you know what you must do, right?" Solar asked.

"Yes…protect this universe and survive," Menzuo answered.

"Correct," Solar replied. "Just remember that no matter what happens, I believe in you, and I will always be here for you. This journey that you are on at the moment is yours to face without me. We will see each other very soon, little brother."

"Yes, we will, Solar, and thank you for the talk," Menzuo said. "We will talk again very soon."

"I cannot wait. Goodbye and stay focused," Solar said as he disconnected from their telepathic conversation.

Menzuo opened his eyes, then relaxed his muscles. As soon as he did, Allucio returned to the balcony and came by his side. "Hey, bro, Lydia fixed the audio files. She's ready to play them for us."

"Coming," Menzuo said as he stood and began to follow Allucio back inside The Beacon.

The two of them found Lydia diligently finishing up the last of her tinkering at her work station. She held up the audio file and waved everyone over. "We got it, guys. I'm ready to play it."

"Great job, cousin," Paladin said, as he and Blurr joined her. "We're ready."

Lydia plugged the audio file into her computer and pressed play. A video popped up on the screen. It was the Captain, repeating the message that Allucio and Desmurose heard on the Titan moon. Everyone in the room focused their attention on the Captain's every word.

The explosion in the background shook the pilot's nerves as he shouted. *"If this message reaches you…take the Halo Spheres to Earth. They…they are the key to stop…stopping these World*

Harv...esters. They must be activated with...with the serum of the Dark...Dark...Dark..." Captain Sans' video ended, and the screen turned to white noise.

"That was the last of the audio we heard right before being attacked by those bounty hunters," Allucio said. He gently rubbed his neck, reliving the moment when the power restraining collar was once there.

"Halo Spheres? What are those?" Blessed asked.

Desmurose shrugged. "Not sure, but the Captain seemed up in arms about them."

"Can we trust them?' I mean, we don't even know how to use them. They could be some alien tech with negative side effects on humans," K'nia said.

"Most likely not," Lydia interjected. "Recall Dr. Everson's work on biomass molecules?" Everyone stared at her with empty doll's eyes. "Okay, wrong audience. In his book 'The Molecular Man' Everson theorized that all organic life-forms in the universe seem to be constructed from similar DNA."

"I recall some of his work in college, but most experts regarded him as a quack; especially since he later turned into a Super-Normal after the storm," Paladin said.

"Right, but we've later come to find out that there's an agenda to undermined and discredit Super-Normals; just like they've tried to do us in the past. It wasn't until Overdrive that we were able to garner a little respect."

"Saving the world will do that," Blurr said.

"Okay, so we're on board with using these things, so that only leaves one question," Paladin said as he turned back to Allucio and Desmurose. "Did you guys ever grab the Halo Spheres?"

Allucio patted the pockets of his jacket, feeling several round objects. He reached inside of his left one and pulled them out. "I completely forgot that I grabbed these things. I mean, with all of that confusion out there, how could I remember?"

Menzuo moved closer. “The Captain said they could be activated with the serum of the Dark –”

Paladin jumped in the finish Menzuo’s sentence. “The Dark Spores serum?”

“Cool, you know what it is,” Desmurose said. “So, where do we get it?”

Paladin’s muscles tensed as he was about to speak. “No, I was asking, not telling,” Paladin replied.

“Oh, right, asking,” Demurose said sarcastically.

“Yeah, dummy,” Allucio joked.

“Shut it!” Desmurose said. “I know what he meant, fool.”

“B.R.A.I.N., any idea where we might be able to locate some kind of serum of the Dark Spores?”

“Paladin, there might be only one place to retrieve such a serum,” B.R.A.I.N. said.

“And that is?” Paladin asked impatiently.

“Where the Dark Spores were originally released, of course. Dr. Bernstein’s old laboratory. But that place is in ruins now, and that portion of land is extremely unstable. I must insist that you all stay clear of that area.”

“I knew it,” Paladin said. “Nothing is ever easy.”

“If you haven’t been keeping up with current events, oh fabulous A.I. one,” Allucio said with a hand gesture, “we’re kind of amazing. Just point us to this laboratory. We’ll get it back for you, no sweat.” He looked over to Desmurose. “Right, Dez?”

Desmurose nodded. “Right.”

“Still, Dr. Bernstein was no slouch, you guys. He was also known as Mr. Magnificent or Caine. I’m sure that place is booby-trapped on top of booby-trapped,” Blurr said.

“Yeah, it already imploded upon itself after his death,” Lydia said.

“But if Captain Sans believes that this is the only way to stop these World Harvester things, I think we need to take the risk,” Allucio said. “I honestly don’t want to see what these things can do up close and personal. That Captain said they obliterated all life on his home planet. We may not have a choice."

"Allucio is right," Menzuo followed. "The threats that we may be facing are many. We have to be as prepared as possible for what is coming."

"That's not a smart idea to go to the heart of Dr. Bernstein's lab," Paladin said. "That place is probably crawling with defenses, much less more loose spores. We have no clue as to what more harm they may do to a person, Super-Normal or not. That place is volatile. Besides, isn't that place just a pile of rubble?"

"Actually, Dr. Bernstein's old lab was built on the foundation of the original Trenton tower. It was rumored that there was a basements sub-floor used for military training. I pulled up the schematics, and they show that there is a chance that it was kept intact," B.R.A.I.N. said.

"Then, I will go it alone!" Menzuo barked.

"No way," Desmurose warned. "You're not going anywhere else alone. We're a team."

"That's right," Allucio added. "We all go together. This bond cannot be broken."

"You don't even know what you're looking for," Paladin said.

"Then you and your team will show us," Menzuo insisted.

"Hell no!" Paladin shot back.

Menzuo stepped towards Paladin aggressively. "What's with you? You don't trust me? You are the one who called me here!"

Paladin's hands fisted at his sides as his helmet protracted around his face. "I still don't know what you're talking about, nor do I know you, so how can I trust you? Plus, there is no chance of you returning to that area, so you need to relax yourself."

"Relax myself?" Menzuo said with anger. "You have no damn idea what's going on or what's coming. You act all high and mighty, but you're clueless!"

"*I'm* clueless? Young man, you're the one who doesn't have a clue. Being in the belly of the beast with possibly a pure form of the

Dark Spores? They can destroy a person on contact," Paladin said. "We cannot risk it."

Blurr jumped in between her man and the young protector. "Guys, we are on the same side," she said then turned to Paladin. "Even if you cannot remember speaking to him, I don't think he's lying or a threat to us. Things haven't been exactly normal around here lately. Who knows what this all means?"

Paladin calmed as he listened to Blurr. His helmet retracted. "It's just not a safe idea."

"But what if there was a way to get down there safely?" Lydia said over the crowd.

Paladin directed his attention towards her. "How so?"

Lydia stepped forward, holding a tablet in her hand, fingering the screen. "I think that if they stay in the side corridors of the stairs leading down to where the Dark Spores are, they can stay unaffected. Plus it is probably freezing in there now with all the power offline."

"You mean, the cold protects us from any type of infection?" Allucio asked.

Lydia shook her head. "No, it won't protect you from an infection. It will slow the Dark Spores' mist down, which should make it harder to be absorbed into your bodies."

"I know we can make it down there," Menzuo said.

"I'm just not sure we can risk it," Paladin said.

Menzuo changed his tone, knowing that his anger wasn't breaking him down. "We are in uncertain times, and whatever these World Harvesters are, I don't think we can chance it. As warriors, we risk our lives to save others. This is part of our task. I overheard you say that we are losing people left and right, well, let's not lose anyone else by not trying to stay ahead of an oncoming threat."

"Listen to him, honey," Blurr said, trying her best to keep Paladin calm.

"Let me prove to you why you called me here," Menzuo said. "Hopefully, you can see why I trust you as much as I would like you to trust me."

Paladin sighed as he looked Menzuo in the eyes and then spoke over everyone. "Lydia, provide the safest way down there and make sure these boys back in one piece."

"You got it, Captain!" Lydia said.

Menzuo nodded with respect, then walked back over towards Allucio and Desmurose. Paladin turned back to Blurr. "Why do you always make me see things clearly?"

"That's what love does, baby," Blurr said and then placed a soft peck on his cheek.

"Are you sure about this, Menzuo?" Desmurose asked. "Being ripped apart by some Dark Spore mist sounds painful."

"Can't be worse than facing the Naleezar on planet Walonoke," Menzuo replied. "Plus, this time, I have my boys with me. It'll be a breeze."

"I'm kind of rethinking what I said," Allucio added. "Do we really have to go wherever you go? I think that I can find a nice seat right next to Lydia." He shot her a wink.

"She'd be annoyed with you like every other woman," Menzuo snapped. "And yes, you're coming."

"Well, I guess if this is how I go out, then I'll do it with pride," Allucio replied.

"You're too damn silly," Desmurose said.

"Once Lydia triangulates the route, we have to hurry," Menzuo warned. "We don't know how much time we have left."

"Understood," Desmurose said.

"Got it," Allucio added.

Paladin stepped to Menzuo and offered a hand. "Good luck Menzuo."

Menzuo took Paladin's hand and gave it a shake. "Thanks. Something tells me that we'll need it."

CHAPTER 16

IN A MIND'S EYE

Tenan raised his head up and wiped the tears from his eyes. He sat a few moments longer under the pine tree, trying his hardest to pull himself together. When he opened his eyes, the world around him was still enveloped in darkness. He nodded in acceptance of his present circumstances and began to pray.

"Okay, Lord. There is something you want me to learn in the midst of this. What is it that you want me to see? I know that you're with me despite the tribulation that I am enduring physically. I know because of the remembrance I have with all the things you have done for me...and for everything you have allowed me to see and experience. Forgive me for my lack of faith and for lashing out at you. You are God and God alone. Now, with your loving kindness and power that surpasses all, help me to conquer this darkness that has befallen me. I pray these things in your powerful name. Amen."

Tenan stood and brushed himself off. He sniffed the air and slowly turned around in a circle, giving his senses a chance to pick up any clues as to where he might be. He took a few steps and noticed his body drifting sideways. He was definitely on uneven ground. He assumed he was in a forest from the heavy scent of pine and the feeling of tall grass touching his knee, but where exactly, he had no clue.

He headed towards the higher part of the ground, keeping his arms stretched out so he would not run into anything. Every so often, he would touch shrubs or another pine tree and safely move around it. In the distance, he could hear the sounds of wolves howling and tell by the sounds of crickets that it was night time. The incline became steeper with every step, and Tenan could feel gravity weighing on his chest and legs.

As he continued his arduous trek up the beastly, forested mountain, it took him about an hour to finally clear the trees. He was now walking along an uneven path of rocks. He could feel and hear the snow crunching underneath his feet. After a few slower, cautious steps, he put his right foot forward and caught himself abruptly as he realized there was nothing under his foot except air. He was standing at a cliff's edges, and the bottom was most likely a fall he didn't want to take.

Tenan gasped as his heart raced in excitement. Immediately, a familiar scent filled his nostrils, and he knew exactly where he was. The fragrance was all around him and calmed his nerves. It was Mount Kumgang, a place his father used to take him as a child. The beautiful mountains located in the Northeast of Korea is where the young Tenan learned many life lessons.

One time when he was fourteen, his father challenged him with the task of climbing to the top of the mountain on his own. His task was to retrieve a certain type of granite rock that could only be found at the cusp of the mountain. That would be his only proof that he was successful. Tenan remembered the fear that flooded him back then. He relived the memory of how he fought past his own trepidations as he traveled through that dark forest alone; to over the odds and retrieve the rock despite the elements and the dangerous wild life that roamed the area.

Of course, he thought to himself. "The Lord brought me here to recall the days of my youth and how I attained the faith to overcome my biggest fears," he said in a whisper.

Tenan bent over and touched the rocks and the snow beneath his feet. He felt the granite stones at his fingertips and picked up a few of them. After running his fingers over them, he rolled them around in his palms and smiled. "Thank you, Lord. I appreciate the reminder."

It was at that same moment that Tenan considered how that journey as a teenager required him to use faith to overcome his circumstances, despite the unseen and the unknown surrounding him. The same scenario was now before him, but on a much larger scale. "I may have lost my physical sight, but I've gained something far more powerful," he whispered. His faith strengthened as he continued to tap into those memories, reminding him of who he was;

a warrior and a soldier with a lion's heart who was no stranger to adversity. His impaired vision was just another obstacle he would have to overcome.

"Lord," Tenan said as he closed his eyes in prayer. "You know that I read your Word daily. I'm reminded of an account of Elisha's servant and how he couldn't see the protection you had encompassed around him because of his lack of faith. When Elisha prayed, you opened the spiritual eyes of his servant, and he was able to see a host of heavenly angels around him. Though my vision is gone, allow my faith to remain intact and give me the sight that only you can, so that I can see all things in the spirit."

Without hesitation, Tenan leaped from the cliff and swan-dived head first towards the bottom. As his body plunged, images materialized in his mind. Flashes of the familiar faces of his team and the looming threat that was already upon planet Earth blazed in his head. Not only did he see the people in the images, but he was also able to see their spirits, good and bad. It was almost as if he was able to see life in a new code. He saw the past, the future, angels, and demons. Darkness no longer confounded his vision. He could see everything, and he understood the visions in his head, the clearer his mind became.

As he continued to plummet, he could see the team and the new allies scattered throughout The Beacon preparing for war. He saw his woman Rekluse, with a look of concern plastered across her face. He had to get back to her. "Come on Tenan, focus," he said to himself. As he calmed his mind and spirit, he could feel the power resonating at his finger tips. His hands began to heat despite the cool air, and the muscles in his arms tightened. He no longer had panic in his heart. Faith filled him as fear, worry, and anxiety drifted away. He was unknowingly only moments away from crashing into the ground below. Nonetheless, he still clung to the confidence that everything would be fine.

Suddenly, a portal opened before him and Tenan smiled. He slipped inside just before hitting the ground. Tenan tucked himself into a ball and somersaulted through the portal before entering The

Beacon. He landed with an Olympic-like flip, sticking a perfect landing just behind his team. Everyone turned around weapons and powers activated, startled by his unexpected arrival.

"What the hell!" Allucio stammered as he nearly jumped out of his uniform.

The other heroes crouched in a fighting stance until they realized that their missing comrade had returned.

"Whoa, Tenan!" Slaycick shouted with his hands on his sheathed swords. "Bruh, you can't come flying in like that! Do you know how close you were to getting your head chopped off?"

"Baby! You're back!" Rekluse said as she ran to hug her man.

She was surprised to see that his pupils were no longer there, replaced by a cloudy white color. She kissed his face numerous times as the others began to relax one by one, disengaging from their fighting stances. The team gathered around the couple as they embraced. Rekluse held Tenan's face and instantly became worried. "Baby, what's wrong with your eyes?" she asked. "What happened? Where did you go?"

"Sh-sh-sh-shhhh," Tenan said as he tried to get Rekluse to calm down. "Baby, I'm okay. My sight is gone, but I can see so much more than ever before, and I've gained so much more faith because of it. I can't describe it, but my faith has become my sight and my guide."

"Brother, how did this happen?" Blessed asked as he put his hand on Tenan's shoulder. "Who did this to you?"

"I'm fine, boss. I'm not impaired. I'm actually more powerful than I was before I left. This was a choice given to me by Titus," Tenan said.

"Wait! What? Titus did this to you?" Rekluse asked, perplexed. "Why would he do this?"

"Baby, calm down. I know it sounds crazy to our finite minds, but there is a much bigger picture at stake. I know who the threat is. Natas Selur is back."

"Natas?" Reklused asked. "But how?"

"Yes, he's back, and he's a lot bigger and much more powerful," Tenan said. "The two giants are with him as well, and they are not alone. They were brought back here by another cosmic entity. I don't know his name. I do know for certain that our fight is no longer just against other Super-Normals, but other beings beyond this galaxy."

"You learned all of this at the cost of losing your sight?" Paladin asked. "This Titus guy couldn't have just told you."

"No," Tenan said. "I've gained a greater power beyond sight. It's accompanied with wisdom, knowledge, and understanding."

"Baby, you're talking crazy," Rekluse said with tears running down her face. "First, you run out of here through one of your portals without explaining where you're going, then you come back here blind as a bat and speaking in riddles like you've been hanging out with Socrates. What the hell! Talk to me…talk to *us* in plain language."

Tenan caressed Rekluse's hands and took her by the wrists. "Before things went crazy in the Middle East last month, you challenged me to expand my gifts, and you taught me not to limit myself. Because of that, I was able to take you to Mars by way of my portals. You opened my mind, and my powers increased. Tonight, God challenged me in a similar fashion, and I became even more powerful. I now have access to the heavens and other realms unknown to man. In addition to that, I can see events before they play out…and…and my confidence has grown exponentially. There is so much more I can do. I will explain it in more detail to you all in due time, but as of right now, we have a massive world-wide war that's getting ready to take place here on Earth with Super-Normals, cosmic beings, and invaders the likes we've not yet seen. We need to be focused on that whole-heartedly."

"Celestials, maybe?" Desmurose asked, looking at Menzuo.

"Celestials?" K'nia asked.

"Beings of great power that rarely interfere in the affairs of less powerful life-forms unless deemed absolutely necessary," Menzuo said.

“Tenan, we’re glad to have you back,” Kasitia said in an attempt to lighten the mood. “All of us are being stretched right now in unimaginable ways, and I’m sure there are going to be a lot more inexplicable challenges that will present themselves to us individually and collaboratively. I agree with you. It’s time to start focusing on the war that’s coming.”

“She’s right,” Rekluse said, wiping the tears from her eyes. “We’ll talk about your travels later. Tell us about the threat,” she hissed.

“As I was saying, Natas is here,” Tenan said. “He’s been reconstructed with a new body, one as big as the giants with him. I’m sure his powers have increased. I could sense it in my mind. They are already here in Hero City, along with another enemy. We have to locate and kill them.”

“Lydia was able to decode the files,” Desmurose said. “We learned that there might be a key element into stopping these enemies that you speak of. Once we get the coordinates of where we can find these Dark Spores, Menzuo, Allucio, and I will be on our way to retrieve it.”

Tenan nodded. “Whatever advantages we can find will help us. And make no mistake about it- victory will require the sum total of all of us.”

“Agreed,” Blessed said. “There’s something else. We need to get back to Jerusalem. We fear that the man we captured, known as Dr. Bernstein may not be whom he says he is. We need to pay him a visit ASAP.”

“I’ll create a portal back to the Prime Minister’s house and let him know we’re on the way,” Tenan replied.

“Tenan, hang back on this one,” Blessed replied. “I want you, Slaycick, Rekluse, and Kasitia to remain here with Paladin and Blurr in case the giants reveal themselves. Aganathin and K’nia will come with me to retrieve Dr. Bernstein. We’ll bring him back here so he can answer to all of us.”

“Sure thing,” Tenan said as he opened the portal for the three. “Be safe, boss.”

As the three soldiers walked through the portal, Tenan closed it and made a call to one of the Prime Minister's staff. He notified them that three of the Majesties were on their way to pick up Dr. Bernstein. Rekluse turned to him with a slight smile. She touched his face before walking off.

Tenan watched her as she left. He could sense a wave of emotion overcoming her and a wall of tension between them. She was hurt, and the "tough girl" persona would be her defense mechanism. Tenan thought about chasing her down to explain everything, but he stayed put, thinking it best to let her have some time to reflect alone. She had to clear her mind and be focused for the oncoming danger.

"Tenan," Allucio said as he approached the blind hero. "Listen, I know we got off on the wrong foot, and that's my fault. I can't even imagine losing my sight. You're handling it with such maturity; something I haven't been. I pray that you forgive me and just know that anything you need from me, I got you."

Allucio stuck out his hand, forgetting that Tenan was now blind. Despite his impairment, Tenan grabbed Allucio's hand and gave it a firm shake. Allucio wore a look of confusion. "Hey, how–"

"I know, I know," Tenan said. "Don't look so alarmed, young man. Like I said before. I now have something far greater than sight, which I consider an upgrade. I can see emotions, intuitions…even you're spirit. It's all there, even moments before they happen. My intuition and senses have heightened during my encounter with Titus, …and yes, I accept your apology."

Allucio continued to shake Tenan's hand as the befuddled look on his face slowly disapeared. "Oooookaaay," Allucio replied. "Who is Titus?"

"He's the angel responsible for introducing us to Oramite, which gave us our powers," Tenan said as he pulled his hand away and tapped Allucio on the shoulder. "If we survive this, I'm sure you'll meet him soon enough."

Tenan walked off, leaving the young warrior confounded by his thoughts. "Angels and Oramite," Allucio whispered. "Hmm…interesting. Very interesting."

CHAPTER 17

THE ESCAPE OF THE GOOD DOCTOR

Aganathin, Blessed, and K'nia stepped out of the portal and right into the Prime Minister's livingroom. Two armed soldiers saluted the three Majesties, and the Majesties returned the gesture.

"Good to see you, Blessed," said one of the soldiers. "Follow me. The Prime Minister is expecting you."

The soldier led them to the Prime Minister's office, where he greeted them happily. "Majesties! Always a pleasure seeing you guys," he said passionately.

"Prime Minister Mashol, it is good to see you, sir," said Aganathin.

"Thank you," the Prime Minister replied. "I just sent two of the soldiers downstairs to our jail detainment unit where we're holding the doctors. They'll be bringing them up for you."

"If it's okay with you, Prime Minister, do you mind allowing us to go down there?" Blessed asked. "We have reason to believe that one of the doctors down there is an impersonator. If that's the case, there is no telling what he could be holding up his sleeve."

"Sure, follow me," Prime Minister Mashol said. The Majesties accompanied the Prime Minister on to the elevator.

The elevator descended and opened on a basement sub-level of the Prime Minister's home. It was a long hallway with jail cells on both sides opposite one another. It was a place where they only detained high-level terrorists. One of the two soldiers closed the cell door as the elevator opened. Dr. Bernstein and Dr. Samir were already standing in the hallway. Blessed noticed that the two doctors weren't handcuffed, which was protocol.

"Soldiers, you should've handcuffed those two men before letting them out!" Blessed shouted as he stormed down the corridor. "They are prisoners and should be treated as such. We'll take it from here. Step aside."

"I'm afraid we can't do that," said a full-bearded soldier wearing brown army fatigues as he locked the cell door. He was burly with a Middle-Eastern complexion. The other soldier pulled out his firearm and aimed it at Blessed, anticipating resistance. "We have orders. These two soldiers are coming with us."

Blessed pulled up short, hands fisted. "I'm not asking. Step aside. I won't say it again."

"I authorized no such thing!" the Prime Minister added as he walked besides Blessed. "Soldier, I gave you orders to put restraints on the doctors and bring them upstairs."

Unexpectedly, the Prime Minister's house shook with what sounded like explosions. Small debris fell from the ceiling. Right before their eyes, the big, bearded soldier shape-shifted into a six-foot-tall black man with dreadlocks.

"The name is Mystikal," the black man said in a thick Creole accent. "And we really don't want this to get messy, so for the sake of your own health, please stand down."

"He's a Super-Normal!" K'nia exclaimed.

"Exactly," said Mystikal. "And there are others on the way, so again, for your own sake, please stand down. I don't want to have to kill any of you unnecessarily."

"Ha, you puny turd," Aganathin scoffed. "You're not the only one with gifts. We've been putting you Super-Normal suckas' to sleep ever since you reared your evil heads. So, for the last time, step aside...as my brother told you to do."

Mystikal pointed his gun at them. Dr. Bernstein and Dr. Samir backed up behind Mystikal.

"Those weapons won't prosper against us," K'nia said as four Oramite stars slowly protruded from slits in her opened palms as he held them by her waist.

"Dr. Bernstein and Dr. Samir, please don't make us go through this again," Blessed said. "Come over here and stand behind us. If you go with these clowns, I can't promise you that you'll survive."

"We'll take our chances," Dr. Bernstein said. "You have no idea what's coming. We're going to be on the right side of this thing when it all goes down."

"My master has returned," Dr. Samir said. "Natas Selur has sent for us, and he's bringing wrath and a vengeance that will eclipse what Hitler did with Germany."

"He's going to die," K'nia said. "And you will too if you stay with them."

"My choice is made, woman," Dr. Samir snapped.

"Enough of this," said the soldier who accompanied Mystikal. He ripped off a barrage of bullets from his semi-automatic machine gun in the direction of the Majesties.

Blessed crossed his arm in front of his face, forming an "X", as he stepped in front of the hurling bullets. Each one bounced off of his Oramite platted forearms as the Prime Minister's house shook violently with explosions and gunfire that could be heard upstairs.

"K'nia, get the Prime Minister out of here!" Blessed yelled as he continued to repel more bullets with his forearms.

K'nia retracted the stars back inside her palms, grabbed the Prime Minister, and ran with him back towards the elevator. Aganathin joined Blessed as Mystikal began firing as well.

Aganathin's entire body morphed into one solid metallic material as the bullets ricocheted from him. The two continued to press forward, deflecting the shots. Blessed was finally within arms-reach of the soldier and snatched the gun from him. He bent the nozzle and tossed it away

Before the soldier could run, Blessed grabbed him and punched him in the face. His Oramite fists rendered the soldier unconscious. Blessed dropped him on the floor and snatched Dr. Bernstein by the collar, who was wearing grey prison rags issued to him by the Israeli government. Blessed looked behind him and saw K'nia getting on the elevator with the Prime Minister. "K'nia! Catch!" Blessed yelled as he threw Dr. Bernstein down the hall as if he were a rag doll.

Dr. Bernstein slid down the hallway floor into the elevator and slammed against the back wall, just as the door closed.

K'nia pulled a gun out of her holster with one hand while still holding on to the Prime Minister. She pointed the gun at Dr. Bernstein, who remained on the floor, writhing in pain. "Now stay, little doggy," she said as Dr. Bernstein held his hands up in surrender as the doors closed and the elevator rose.

Aganathin was now upon Mystikal, who continued to unsuccessfully fire his gun until his magazine clip emptied.

"Are you finished yet?" Aganthin asked sarcastically, unfazed by the bullets and shell casings that now laid at his feet. Mystikal looked up at the Angolan giant who towered over him by eight inches. He was stunned and nervous at the same time.

"Awww, dayumm!" Mystikal said. "What the hell are you?"

"I'm the man that knocked your ass out," Aganathin said as he cocked back and delivered a blow to Mystikal's nose that sent him sliding across the floor. Aganathin grabbed Dr. Samir by the neck. The doctor was now cowering with his hands over his head.

"Please don't hurt me," Dr. Samir said. "Pleeease!"

"Man, shut up and stop crying," Aganathin said. "You're coming back to Jerusalem with us to answer some questions. If Natas wants to see you, he's going to have to come see us. And I promise you, this time, he will die."

At that moment, the Prime Minister's house rattled violently from another explosion. "Let's get back to the top," Blessed said. "K'nia and the Prime Minister will need our assistance."

"What do you want to do about the shape-shifter and the soldier?" Aganathin asked as he pointed to the two who were still lying on the ground, unconscious.

"Leave them. They're not of importance to us at the moment. There's a melee going on upstairs that needs our attention."

As they were walking back down the hallway towards the elevator, the ceiling crashed down before them. Three Super-Normals dropped down in front of them.

"Yeah, we thought reinforcements would be needed for this mission," said a young, blonde-haired, baby-faced male Caucasian teenager. She was wearing red leather pants with a matching jacket and a black shirt underneath. "You must be Dr. Samir, I take it?"

"Yeah, it is," Aganathin said. "He's coming with us, kid. Now please step aside. We don't kill kids, but with the type of day I'm having, I wouldn't be surprised at what rules I break."

Behind the blonde-haired teen, were two others: a Latina girl with long black hair wearing a dark-blue jumpsuit and a short, bald, muscular black teen wearing blue jeans and a yellow T-shirt with two cartoon-looking speakers drawn on the front.

"My name is Flame," said the teen who seemed to be the leader of the trio. "This is my home-girl Arctic and my brother Decibel."

"Oh boy," sighed Aganathin, as he shook his head in disappointment. "People get some new abilities, and then they want to start nicknaming themselves with some dumb-ass hero or villain names. Why? You know what, don't even answer that. It was a rhetorical question. Let me guess," he said as he pointed to one of them. "You piss fire from your little pecker, she makes snow cones, and mighty mouse here who is too big for his extra-*smedium* shirt, sings like a lil' bitch. Did I get it, right?" The teens sneered at him in disgust. "Dude, get the hell out of our way before we hurt you. I'm losing my patience."

"Says the big, bad black man," Flame snarled with a grimace on his face. "You some kind of comedian or something? I'll bake your ass right now!"

Flame opened his hands, and they became engulfed in flames. Small fireballs formed in his palms before growing to the size of bowling balls.

"Listen, kid. This is not a laughing matter," Blessed warned as he clenched his fists, cautiously looking at the balls of fire Flame was controlling. "I'm guessing that was you three up there causing all the commotion, right?"

"Yeah, that's right," Flame said. "I took out all of those armed soldiers upstairs by myself, and you're about to be next if you don't hand over the doctor." He gazed over Blessed's shoulder and noticed Mystikal and the soldier laying on the ground. He smirked. "I see you took out Mystikal and the soldier."

"They're sleeping it off," said Blessed. "Who sent you, kid?"

"I came with them," he answered, pointing to the two unconscious figures on the floor.

"Okay. And who was it that sent them?" Blessed asked.

"None of your business," Flame said. "We were paid a hefty amount of money by some very powerful people to see this mission through, and hot damn are we gonna see it through! We were the clean-up team in case things got out of hand, and so well, since they have, we're here to clean-up."

"Typical teenagers," Aganathin said. "To busy selfishly carrying about themselves and other irrelevant garbage to see what's going on."

"Keep talking, Mohawk, and I promise I'm gonna barbecue your black ass!" Flame said.

Aganathin still held Dr. Samir in his right hand, but reached around with his left and pulled out his Oramite plaited ax.

"Whoa," Blessed said as he put his hands up. "Kid, nobody needs to get hurt here. There's a war coming that's bigger than all of us, and I'm sure that whoever sent you is on the wrong side of that war. If you knew the extent of what's coming, you wouldn't be here."

"On the contrary, soldier. I know exactly why I'm here and who I'm fighting for. You see, we're Satanist, and the time of the Antichrist, Natas Selur is here!"

Abruptly, Flame hurled a fireball at Blessed. The fireball hit his chest and sent him hurling backwards to the other end of the corridor. Aganathin reacted quickly and threw Dr. Samir out of the way. He leaped at Flame and grabbed him by the neck, lifting him up off the ground. Flame's entire body ignited as he tried to burn Aganathin's hands.

"Little boy, please stop," Aganathin said nonchalantly as his body transformed and became metalic, making him impervious to fire. "I'm Aganathin, master of the elements. I can fight fire with fire."

Suddenly, Aganathin's body and axe were engulfed in an inferno of rage. He squeezed Flame's neck until his fire was extinguished. The teenager gagged for air with his feet dangling in the air.

Decibel let out a scream, "Aaaaaaaaaaaaaaaaaaaaah!" Aganathin was forced to drop both Flame and his axe while he covered his ears. Decibel held the scream, making Aganathin to the floor. His high-powered sound waves were too much for anyone to endure.

Arctic chuckled and pointed to his ears. "Good thing we have these little babies," he said, referring to a pair of special hearing devices that dampened the high-frequency sound blasts of Decibel. Aganathin writhed in pain and changed him back to his normal self.

Arctic walked over to Aganathin, who was now on his knees and covering his ears. She touched his arm. "You need to chill, big boy," she said slyly.

Aganathin's body turned white and became covered with tiny ice sickles. Paralyzed by her icy touch, Aganathin now looked like a kneeling frozen statue.

"Let's hurry," Flame said rubbing his neck. "Grab Mystikal and the soldier and let's get out of here."

Decibel ran down to the end of the hallway where Mystikal laid semi-unconscious. He slapped him on the face a few times. "Mystikal, get up," Decibel said. "I can't carry both of you."

Mystikal grumbled a little bit until he finally came to. "I think that bastard broke my nose," he said.

Decibel picked the other unconscious soldier up, put him over his shoulder and ran back down the hallway with Mystikal in tow. Arctic jumped through the hole in the ceiling. Decibel followed right behind her, tossed the unconscious soldier up first, and then climbed up afterward.

Mystikal held out his hand to Flame in gratitude. His nose was still bleeding from Aganathin's punch to the face.

"Thank you for coming through, youngster," Mystikal said. "You saved our asses!"

"Nothing to it," Flame said as he looked down disgustedly at the frozen statue of Aganathin. "Master of the elements my ass."

Flame kicked Aganathin's left shoulder as the frozen flesh cracked, and his arm broke off in pieces. He scoffed at his handy work and spit on the frozen sculpture of Aganathin. Flame and Mystikal jumped up through the hole and assisted Dr. Samir through as well.

Moments later, the elevator door opened at the bottom of the jail corridor, and K'nia walked out to a devastating sight. She gasped. "Oh no!" Blessed was still unconscious, with smoke rising from his body as small flames danced on his shirt.

K'nia ran over to Aganathin. "Oh my God!" she said as she knelt beside him. "Who did this?"

Blessed began to stir. She quickly ran back over to him, calling his name. She beat her hands across his body to muffle the remaining flames. She pressed her com-link button to radio Tenan. "Tenan," she said weeping. "Please track my coordinates and open a portal. I need help. Blessed and Aganathin are down. We have Dr. Bernstein, but this is bad."

Blessed finally began to come around. His fatigues were charred, and he could barely stand. His face was covered in black soot from the heat. A portal opened before them. Slaycick with Tenan, Rekluse, Kasitia, Paladin, and Blurr stepped out.

"Sister!" Kasitia yelled. "Oh my God! What happened?"

"I don't know!" K'nia said. "I didn't see! We came down here with the Prime Minister, and two soldiers were trying to free the two doctors. One of the soldiers was a shape-shifter."

"Damnit!" Paladin said. "That must've been Mystikal!"

"That's him," said K'nia. "He told us his name. He disguised himself as a soldier and then shifted right in front of us. They started shooting at us. Blessed told me to get the Prime Minister to safety. He was able to capture Bernstein and put him on the elevator with me as he and Aganathin battled the Super-Normal and the other soldier. Dr. Samir was still down here with them. The Prime Minister and Bernstein are upstairs in a hidden location. Bernstein is tied up. When I got to the top, all of the guards and soldiers were dead. It had to be the work other Super-Normals."

"Where are Mystikal, Dr. Samir, and the other soldier now?" Paladin asked.

"I'm not sure," K'nia said. "When I came back down to help, Blessed was unconscious, and Aganathin was…" K'nia paused and pointed to Aganathin just a few feet away, frozen and missing an arm. The others walked over to him.

"Christ," Slaycick said. "Who in the hell did this to my friend?"

Blessed pulled himself up and limped over to the others as K'nia and Kasitia helped him. Tenan put his hands on Aganathin and rubbed them across his head and Torso. "He's not dead. His life will be preserved. His spirit has not yet left his body," Tenan said. "We are fortunate. But we must get him back home now and begin work on him right away."

"Let's grab the Prime Minister and Bernstein and get back," said Blessed. "It's not safe here. Plus, I'm sure those other Super-Normals are going to be persistent in trying to find Dr. Bernstein."

"Maybe not…they already have Dr. Samir," said Kasitia. "Either way, we need to bleed Bernstein for all the information he's got."

The Majesties, along with Paladin and Blurr, secured the Prime Minister and Dr. Bernstein. Blessed carefully picked up Aganathin and carried him with the help of Slaycick. Tenan opened a portal, and the heroes stepped in, making their way back to The Beacon.

***

As they stepped through the portal, Rekluse tossed Dr. Bernstein on the couch with his hands still handcuffed behind his back.

"Talk!" she screamed. "People are dying and getting permanently injured because of this bullshit! You have information as to what's going on. If you don't tell me what we need to hear, I'm putting bullet holes in different parts of your body until you break."

Rekluse cocked the slide to her gun and pointed it at Dr. Bernstein's knee. Dr. Bernstein began laughing as he slowly transformed into an Iraqi soldier wearing military fatigues.

"What?" Rekluse exclaimed. "Who the hell are you? Another shape-shifter?"

"My God," Paladin said. "He's not a shape-shifter. That's the work of Mirage. Another Super-Normal. His powers were on display at the Prime Minister's house. It's almost like a spell. He can make you see things that are not real."

Rekluse quickly turned towards Paladin. "So what, the explosions, everything? Was it all a lie?" she asked. "Aganathin?" she asked weakly this time.

"No, I think most of it was all real. Just not everything," Blurr said.

"So he essentially can do the same thing as me," Rekluse said. "I wonder can he fight like me. Because when I see him, I'm gonna break my foot off in his ass and let him tell me whether the pain he feels is an allusion or not."

Frustrated, Rekluse slid the barrel of the gun from the soldier's knee to his head. "Tell me what you know, scum," she continued. "And don't feed me the "they don't tell me anything" garbage because I swear I'll empty these bullets into that skull of yours, and you really won't know squat after that."

"Baby, please! Calm yourself," Tenan said as he rushed over to calm Rekluse down. He pushed her arm away. "Don't let your anger make you forget what your gifts are. You can make him talk another way, babe. Remember?"

Rekluse took a deep breath and exhaled. She holstered her weapon, put her hand on the soldier's head, and looked into his pupils. Both of their eyes turned white as snow as she took control of his mind and sense of will.

"Tell me who you are?" Rekluse commanded.

"I am Ramaad Shahir. A soldier of the Iraqi government," soldier replied.

Rekluse continued. "Who sent you, and where's the real Dr. Bernstein?"

"I was summoned by Mystikal, who said he had a message for me from Natas Selur. He said Natas had a place for me in his ranks if I helped him. Before you all got downstairs to the detainment unit, Mystikal morphed into a soldier on the Prime Minister's staff. He killed the original and disposed of the body. Mirage, who has been pretending to be Dr. Bernstein this whole time, made himself appear as a soldier. They anticipated that you all would be coming, so Mirage used his spell and made me appear as Dr. Bernstein. That way if you all came, you would grab the wrong one. Mirage and Mystikal both escaped with the others. You played right into their plan," the soldier said.

"You've got to be kidding me," Blurr said.

"Where are they heading?" Rekluse asked.

"I'm not sure," soldier replied. "They wouldn't tell me. They counted on me getting caught."

"How did Mystikal contact you?" Rekluse asked.

"He called me on my cellphone one day from an untraceable location. He said he had an offer I couldn't refuse," the soldier said.

Rekluse continued. "Where's your cellphone, Ramaad."

"In my vest, left side pocket," the soldier replied.

Rekluse reached in the soldier's bullet-proof vest pouch and pulled out the cell phone. Rekluse rolled the soldier over and used his thumb to unlock it. "Soldier, when I snap my fingers, you are going to go into a deep sleep until I tell you to wake up."

"Yes," said Ramaad. "I will go into a deep sleep until you tell me to wake up."

Rekluse snapped her finger, and the soldier shut down like he was a robot that had just been turned off. Rekluse tossed the phone to Lydia, who was standing next to Allucio and Desmurose watching everything since the team returned. "Lydia, if you don't mind, can you run those numbers on the phone for me? See if you can trace where those incoming calls came from. Once you have them, we can start shaking down the spots. Natas is out there somewhere plotting an attack against our world, and I want to eliminate him before he even has a chance to begin."

"Sure thing," Lydia replied.

"Wow," Allucio whispered under his breath to Desmurose. "I am soooo glad she rejected me. Could you imagine having a girlfriend like that? All up in your head and shit. You can't even lie to her."

"You're an idiot," Desmurose said, shaking his head.

"What? I'm just saying."

Rekluse walked out of the room as Tenan reached out for her. "Babe." She gently brushed his hand away and kept walking.

Slaycick approached Tenan to comfort him. "Give her some time, friend. She's dealing with this the best way she knows how. It's a lot for her to see you like this."

Tenan nodded and took a seat on the couch. Paladin and Blurr approached the Israeli Prime Minister and assured him of their support. "Prime Minister, I'm sorry about the attack on your headquarters," Paladin said. "I know you have to get back to your people, but for the time being, why don't you rest here for tonight until we sort out which of us can head back to Jerusalem with you? We have to keep you safe."

"Thank you, Paladin. I'm contacting some of my personnel back in Israel right now to let them know of my whereabouts. I need to warn them to stay safe. Tomorrow, I will need to get out in front of this."

"You won't be alone, sir," Blurr said.

Menzuo helped Blessed walk Aganathin over to a clear area and gently placed him down. His friend was still frozen. Blessed placed one hand on Aganathin's head and another on his shoulder where his arm used to be. He closed his eyes as Paladin, Blurr, and Menzuo watched intently. Kasitia and K'nia stood off in a corner and watched as their leader tried to perform another miracle.

Blessed's hands reddened, and Aganthin's color began to return. As Aganathin started to thaw, the frost disappeared, and his body became limp. He could barely open his eyes. The wound on his shoulder sealed as his body slumped over. Blessed caught him. "Easy, big fella. I got you. You need to get some rest." He allowed his incoherent friend to rest on him for a bit before standing him up.

"Take him to my bed," Paladin said.

"Thanks, Paladin," Blessed replied. "Slaycick, give me a hand, please."

The two men helped Aganathin to the room and laid him down. Kasitia and K'nia helped wrap him in blankets to keep his body warm. When they were all finished, they returned to the living room where everyone was quiet. Emotions were all over the place, and Blessed could sense the overwhelming flood of sadness in the room.

"Tonight, I almost lost my friend," Blessed said solemnly. "And I almost lost my life. A young group of Super-Normals did that to him, very powerful ones led by one named Flame. They are Satanists summoned by Natas. Whatever he's planning is big, and if we're not careful, it may cost us our lives. There is no reasoning with these kids. I tried to talk them down, and the kid, Flame, wasn't hearing it. He hit me with a fireball so strong it would've killed the average man. So, if you cross them, use your God-given abilities to put them down. Kid or no kid, I'm done negotiating."

The team nodded in agreement. "Blessed, Aganathin lost a limb tonight," Paladin said. "I know you have healing capabilities as you have demonstrated, but are you sure you don't want me to have him transported to the hospital? He needs around the clock care. I have friends who can help us get him there inconspicuously."

"I appreciate it, Paladin," Blessed said. "I have a plan for his arm. I'm putting a call into a friend that owes us a favor." Blessed walked out onto the balcony and pulled his cell phone from his back pocket. After dialing the numbers, someone answered on the other end. "D'mitri, it's Blessed. We need you, buddy."

CHAPTER 18

INTO THE DEPTHS

"Well, I don't know about all of you, but I'm spent. This has been a long day. Traveling through space, fighting people, watching gorgeous women walk in and out of my life," Allucio said, eying Lydia as she passed by. "My heart can't take much more," he said with a smile, gently patting his chest.

"Knock it off Allucio," Paladin said. "She's taken."

"Taken, by who?" Allucio asked.

A gust of wind sailed in from behind the group, catching everyone's attention. Before them stood Thief, fully clothed in his costume, minus his cowl, that was pulled down, draping over his back. "By me," he mumbled.

"Alice!" Lydia screamed. She dropped the tablet she was holding in her hand and Blurr zipped in to grab it before it hit the ground. Lydia ran to Thief and wrapped her arms around his neck in relief, giving him a firm hug. Thief hugged back, his arms tensing around her. They shared a moment of silence.

After a few seconds, Allucio spoke up. "Ugh, anyone else feel like talking? 'Cause I feel very uncomfortable right now."

Desmurose elbowed him. "Knock it off."

Lydia pulled back and gazed into Thief's eyes. "You…you were gone so long. I only thought the worst."

"I know and I'm sorry," Thief said.

"What happened to you? I mean, if you don't want to be with me, I get it. But just tell me so that I don't keep going on worrying about you," Lydia said.

Thief shook his head. "It's not that, Lydia, I –"

Lydia dropped her arms from around him and folded them across her chest. "I mean, really, it's no big deal. Like I said, I get it. I go through these phases, you know. I fall for a hot guy, I get clingy…I press too hard. I get it. I push guys away…I mean, not to say that I'm pushing you away, because I hope that I'm not, but I'm just saying that *if* I was pushing you away, I get it. I just don't want –"

Before she could muster another word, Thief grabbed Lydia by the waist and pulled her close, landing a warm kiss on her lips. Lydia tensed and then slowly melted in his grasp.

"See, I told you," Allucio said, elbowing Desmurose back. "Uncomfortable."

"Yeah, I kinda agree with him now," Paladin said, speaking up. "Hey Alice, I hate to break this up, but I need a word with you," Paladin said as he walked by, heading for his room.

Thief pulled away and smiled at Lydia. "I'll be back." He followed after Paladin.

Lydia stood motionless, eyes closed. "I'll be here waiting," she whispered.

"Snap out of it and get those coordinates for Menzuo, will ya?" Blurr joked as she slapped the tablet back in Lydia's hand and processed to walk away and join Thief and Paladin.

Lydia opened her eyes and turned away. Desmurose, Allucio, and Menzuo gazed at her shyly. "What?" Lydia exclaimed.

The three of them broke into a sea of murmurs to play off their staring. Menzuo's voice rose amongst the trio. "The coordinates. Whenever you…recover," he joked.

Lydia rolled her eyes and walked to her work station. "Right."

***

Inside Paladin's room, Thief, Paladin, and Blurr settled into an open space as Blurr shut the door behind them.

"What gives, Alice?" Paladin asked as his helmet retracted from his face. "I thought you were supposed to cleaning out your old place. Doesn't take two to three weeks to do that, last I checked. And we couldn't reach you anywhere. And please don't hand us any of that dossier B.S. again either."

"First of all, you're getting way too comfortable using my real name, and second, you'll be very interested in what I was doing this entire time. Trust me, I have a good explanation," Thief said.

"Well, chat it up, Alice," Blurr said, emphasizing his real name, "'cause Sebastian isn't wrong for questioning you. You had us worried, and you put this entire team's safety at risk. For all we know, you could be Mystikal or Mirage."

"Yeah, why don't you say something to prove who you are? Something only the real Thief would know," Paladin said.

"Okay, how about five words? Saturday night, balcony, you two," Thief said.

Blurr's cheeks stained red. "Okay, it's Thief."

"So spill it," Paladin said.

"Remember that artifact that Slingblade had?" Thief asked.

"Yeah, the one we lifted from Titan that *supposedly* came from the Rothandians – mankind's deep-space alien step-cousins that can stand our guts – who now *supposedly* infiltrated our government? Yeah, we know it," Blurr said.

"Well, I got some more information on it," Thief said.

"Use that along with your black evidence kit from that crater left behind by Q-18?" Paladin asked.

"Not entirely," Thief said. "Those Dark Spores Super Samples we retrieved from the crash site were nothing like the ones on the blade artifact from that Super-Normal Titan."

"How so?" Blurr asked.

"I had a geek friend of mine analyze them," Thief said.

"Dossier time," Paladin murmured.

Thief rolled his eyes. "Their molecular structure was very erratic, unstable. The ones on the artifact seemed more 'organic' in nature while the ones from the fallen evil Super-Normals were more engineered, as if birthed in a lab," Thief said.

"Like a lab from our old pal Dr. Bernstein, a.k.a. Mr. Magnificent, slash Caine?" Blurr asked.

"Maybe, but I'm not quite sure," Thief said. "They just seemed strange."

"But wait a minute. Slingblade was just arrested. He turned himself into Zenith, but Zenith didn't mention anything about the artifact," Paladin said.

"Has the government reached out to you guys since Q-18?" Thief asked.

"They sent us an email one week after the event, asking us to come to Washington to talk about setting up that group Team Infinity. I've been holding off because we got a video mail from Slingblade warning us against it. I was hoping to catch him first and get some answers before I start chatting it up with Uncle Sam," Paladin said.

"Good, stay away for now," Thief said.

"Go back to the Dark Spore samples for a moment. So, we know that Bernstein took the Dark Spores and weaponized them into a mist so that they could be spread across Chicago during that storm to infect thousands of people," Paladin said.

"Right," Thief said, following.

"But the missing piece here is that from what we've gleaned of the Rothandians, Dark Spores also came from deep space, correct?" Paladin.

"So the last question remains is, where did Bernstein get his batch of Dark Spores?" Blurr interjected.

"That's precisely what I'm trying to tell you guys now," Thief said.

"Well, spit it out!" Blurr and Paladin said simultaneously.

"Se-Crets!" Zenith said from behind.

Paladin whirled around, stunned. "Again? Can you start knocking first or something? This is quite an invasion of privacy."

"Knock, knock," Zenith said.

"Zenith is here," B.R.A.I.N. said over the intercom.

"You're late!" Paladin said, looking skyward. He looked back over to Zenith. "This little disappear, reappear trick. I hope you don't do that when we're," Paladin paused, nodded towards Blurr and then back over to his bed. Zenith's white eyes narrowed, just as Paladin continued. "Better yet, don't answer."

Thief walked over to Paladin. "Zenith is right. No more secrets." He raised a hand and touched Paladin's temple.

Images flashed across Paladin's mind in a wave of scenes filled with people, places, space, and bright lights, none of which he recognized. It slipped by at what seemed like light speed, and when it was all over, Paladin dropped to one knee. Blurr caught him by the arm. "What gives?" she asked.

Paladin sat on the floor, shaken. "I saw it."

"Saw what?" Blurr asked.

"Everything," Paladin whispered.

Blurr turned back to Thief. "What did you do?"

"I used Zenith's telekinesis powers to share everything I learned from the time of joining up with you guys," Thief said. "The Darks Spores…technology…everything. Even what you refused to tell him."

"Why?" Blurr asked.

"Karla, he had to know," Thief said.

"No more Se-Crets, and everyone is empowered," Zenith said. "Even Alice's crush on you, all revealed."

"Past crush," Thief said.

"Yes, but even though his mind is linked to Lydia, his heart still has just enough room for you, Blurr," Zenith said. "But more like a –"

"Sister," Paladin said. Blurr helped him to stand. "You feel for her like a sister."

Thief nodded. "I realized that I did need to clean out my old place, along with my old feelings. But not just for Karla, those about my ex-wife and my kids. I needed to make things right with them. I spent a few days jockeying back and forth between Chicago and New York, helping them get settled. Their under FBI protection in fear that if anyone got a hold of my alias, their lives would be in danger. I even went to a few sessions of counseling on my own. I needed to cleanse my mind and body. When I did, I came to grips with my feelings of insecurity, and it allowed me to embrace my feelings for Lydia and compartmentalize those for Karla. As family, nothing more."

"Wow, that's pretty heavy," Blurr said.

"What about the flashes? All those people and places? The flashing lights? What does it all mean?" Paladin asked.

"The people are the Rothandians, and the place is their homeworld, not too far from here. Those flashing lights are the way we must travel to get there. The same way the Traveler got here. Through space and time itself," Thief asked.

"Can't we just use a portal from Tenan?" Paladin asked. "He's on some next level portal jumping now."

"You could try, but his powers are still very new to him. It could be risky to chance that he'd be able to get us to our destination successfully without imposing more risks," Zenith said.

"And we have to venture to a place outside of time. That's where the Rothandians live. They mastered this form of travel eons ago. We find their homeworld, and we'll find the artifacts we seek along with a whole bunch more answers, I assume," Thief said.

"How do you know all this?" Blurr asked.

"Let me guess, more *dossier* answers?" Paladin said.

"Actually, I paid Slingblade a visit, using a little ghosting juice I stole from another Super-Normal I met named Sight. She was a runaway, real sweet teen I met on the streets about three days ago. I set her up with a foster home, and when I heard the news about Slingblade being apprehended, I knew he had to have answers. He told me everything I needed to know."

"Willingly?" Paladin asked.

"No, I mind melded with him while he was asleep in his cell. I was able to glean as much as I could until I met back up with you guys, and actually, the answers didn't come to me until I linked with you in Blurr and Zenith's presence. It was like you three unlocked everything. Like some sort of crazy signal booster," Thief said.

"Is Slingblade on our side?" Paladin asked. "He warned that we shouldn't trust anyone, yet he's been running around from Blurr and me for the past couple of weeks."

"That depends on what side you're talking about. I know the U.S. can be quite elusive when it comes to sharing –"

"Se-Crets," Zenith interrupted.

"Do you just like saying that?" Paladin asked, annoyed.

"I like nothing," Zenith answered.

"Well, since you've been gone, Super-Normals have been coming out of the woodwork trying to kill us. Something about them being poisoned by the spores. How come you aren't affected by the Dark Spores?" Paladin asked Thief.

"Because his heart is pure," Blurr said.

"Naw, I can't take any credit for that love," Thief said with a smile. "I will say that my absorbing powers probably give me a large advantage over most Super-Normals and makes me immune to their infections. But keep an eye on you comrades out there. They need to be forewarned. These spores are nothing to mess with."

Paladin shook his head. "Yeah, if Menzuo and his team were to turn evil –"

"Well, one issue at a time," Blurr said, waving her hands. "My brain can't handle anymore. So, how do we travel to the homeworld of the Rothandians?"

"I was hoping Zenith could fill in the blanks there," Thief said.

"A Speed-Stream. Our universe is both created and controlled by time. There are streams of time that connect them, like railroads and expressways, woven together like clothing. If one could move fast enough, it is possible to skip from one stream to another and forgo real time itself. But the experience is very traumatizing and dangerous as the Normal mind cannot hold the pieces together." Zenith looked over at Blurr. "That's where I come in. Karla, you are the Conduit, the connection between the streams. Sebastian is the lightning rod, the thing that powers you and keeps you in our time. I will merely be the guidepost to keep everything in alignment so as to allow you to move without being ripped apart."

"Hey, I was with you all the way up until that ripped apart piece," Allucio's voice rang out.

Thief, Zenith, Blurr, and Paladin all turned around. Menzuo, Lydia, and the rest of the team, including the Majesties filled the doorway. "So, we're just going to skip the part about private conversations, right?"

Zenith raised a finger. "Se–"

"Crets!" Paladin said. "We know."

"Do not fear the ripping part. I will handle that," Zenith said.

"Got the coordinates," Lydia said, holding up the tablet. "Menzuo and his team are all set."

"So, deep space, huh?" Blurr asked. "I guess we'll need some sort of ship?"

"I think I know where we can get one," Paladin said. "Let's pay a visit to Washington, D. C."

CHAPTER 19

VISITING THE IMPACT ZONE

"Alright, guys," Lydia said as she kept her eyes on the tablet in her hand. "Dr. Bernstein's lab was right in the heart of the impact area where the last of the Dark Spores' mist was released. I have mapped out the safest route for you all to travel, but remember, there's a good chance that temperatures are extremely below freezing where you will be going."

"We can handle it," Menzuo said. "Our power suits are equipped to manage those types of temperatures."

"But what about the Dark Spores' mist mixing with the freezing temperatures?" Lydia asked, looking Menzuo in his eyes. "Super-Normal or not, I'm not sure that you all have ever faced anything this dangerous."

Allucio stroked his chin before he spoke. "Menzuo, do you think that the space-gel that we used to travel in would help keep us clear from the mist?"

Menzuo smiled. "For once, you show that you have a brain in that there head of yours," he joked. "That's actually a great idea. We can try that."

Desmurose looked over Lydia's shoulder to see the image of the impact area. "What are those red dots?"

"I believe those are heat signatures," Lydia answered. "There seem to be life signs down there, and I can guarantee you that whoever they are, they're unstable."

"And to think that this was going to be easy," Allucio said. "Of course, there's always a threat waiting for us."

"I'd suggest you three try your best to stay clear of any threats," Lydia said. "I'm not sure how stable that area is and if a battle were to break out while you all are down there –"

"Yes, we know," Menzuo interrupted her. "It may not end well."

Lydia handed Menzuo a spot locator that showed them the exact location of Dr. Bernstein's lab. "Make sure that you follow the directions I mapped out. This is the safest route to the bunker. You'll know that you're close when the temperature changes."

"Understood," Menzuo replied.

Paladin walked over to the three warriors. "You guys be very careful. No one knows the dangers that you will face down there."

Menzuo stepped forward. "We'll be cautious with this, Paladin. Our only mission is to recover the Dark Spores serum and return here so that we can prepare for the World Harvesters."

"We've been in sticky situations before, Paladin," Desmurose said. "We haven't failed yet, and we're not going to now."

"I like the confidence in you three," Paladin answered. "I'm sure that you all will be okay."

"Thank you for trusting us," Menzuo replied. He and Paladin shook hands.

"Remember to stay on the path I mapped out," Lydia reiterrated.

"We will," Allucio replied. He looked at his best friends. "It's showtime."

Menzuo, Allucio and Desmurose extended their right hands and placed each one on top of another, forming a triangle. They looked at each other and shouted, "Sensing Densor!" and then disappeared.

"Well," Zenith said. "Looks like there are more Se-"

"Don't you even say it!" Paladin shouted.

"I mean, I can do that too," Zenith said under his breath, walking out of the living room.

Paladin turned to Blurr. "I hope you're right about them."

"I can feel their energy, babe. They are with us, and your ties to Menzuo will be revealed soon enough, I'm sure of it."

Tenan was standing against the wall with a smile on his face. Slaycick walked over to him. "What's brightened you up, partner?"

"I can see their energy," Tenan replied.

Slaycick looked at everyone in the room. "Whose energy, ours?"

Tenan shook his head. "No, Menzuo and those Twin Powers by his side, Allucio and Desmurose. They have pure warrior hearts. Menzuo is really something to behold, something unbelievably special. Desmurose and that Allucio kid are very light-hearted, but they are serious warriors. Their bond is strong, and that will keep them safe."

Slaycick looked into Tenan's clouded eyes. "And you can see all of this, how?"

"See it and feel it. It's part of my new gift," Tenan answered. "Honestly, I judged Allucio wrong as well. He's very kind-hearted, but has no game with the ladies."

"I think he's growing on you, Tenan," Slaycick said with a chuckle.

Tenan nodded. "He might be, but I have to keep him on his toes."

Slaycick looked over to Rekluse as he leaned up against the wall right next to Tenan. "Maybe you need to use that energy to feel out your girl's spirit. Before we make a move, you need to have a moment to explain all of this to her."

Tenan sighed heavily as he could sense the heartbreak within Rekluse. He wanted to ease her pain and worries but needed to find the right words to say. He stood silently next to Slaycick as he gathered himself with his newfound ability. Everyone in the room was preparing for their next moves.

***

"Lower your energy levels," Menzuo said as he, Allucio, and Desmurose flew closer to Dr. Bernstein's destroyed laboratory. "The temperature is dropping, so we must be close to the impact area."

"Got it," Allucio replied.

"Got it," Desmurose followed.

They all lowered their energy as they flew closer. Skimming through the sky, the three warriors could see an area to their right, covered in ice. A large gray cloud floated motionless about one hundred feet from the ground. Several Super-Normals with flying abilities circled the sky, just below the cloud. No more than five hundred yards to the right was an area enveloped in a thick, charred substance resembling lava. A thick dark mist bubbled towards the sky, letting the young warriors know that life was not habitable in that region.

"The area looks as if it's been split between fire and ice," Desmurose said, noticing the air from the heat and cold pushing up against each other.

"Menzuo, can you enclose us in that space-gel?" Allucio asked as they flew closer.

Without hesitation, Menzuo waved his hand in a circular motion. In an instant, the three of them were completely surrounded by the gel. "We have to make sure we fly below those clouds in the cold region. We can't let those Super-Normals see us," Menzuo said as they shifted directions. "The way that they are flying up there, it looks like they are possessed by the mist of the Dark Spores. The cold is slowing them down and keeping their energy levels dormant."

"You see that?" Desmurose said, pointing. "In the middle of the split between the heat and cold. That must be where Dr. Bernstein's lab was."

Menzuo eyed the locater Lydia gave him. "There is an entrance about a mile away that can lead us to the lower sub-level bunker."

"Let's get a move on and grab that serum," Allucio said as the Solar Warriors flew towards their destination.

A few moments later, they landed near a hatchway made with steel doors. Menzuo looked at the locater. "This is the way in."

A stiff cold breeze blew past them. Desmurose looked at his suit, observing that it was still covered by the space travel gel. "Looks like this stuff is keeping us safe from the cold temperature."

"Yeah, we're lucky," Allucio added. "I think it's also keeping that mist away from us as well."

Menzuo nodded. "It does seem like it, but remember, there isn't a long time limit to these gel suits, so we have to move it."

"How much time do you think we have?" Desmurose asked.

"Probably another twenty minutes or so," Menzuo answered. He quickly opened the hatchway, and they all made their way down, deep into the tunnel.

Descending deeper into the ground, they could see a bright light at the end of the tunnel, leading to an open area. "I can feel a dark energy down here," Desmurose said, tensing his muscles.

"I can too!" Allucio added as he readied himself for an oncoming attack.

"Wait!" Menzuo hissed. He analyzed at the locater, noticing several red dots on it. "There are about thirty heat signatures down here."

"Why can't we just take them all out?" Desmurose asked.

"Remember what Lydia said," Allucio followed. "This place is unstable and we cannot try to fight whatever is down here. We don't know what condition these people are in or what it may do to this area."

"Allucio is right," Menzuo added. "We have to maintain stealth down here as long as possible."

Desmurose sighed. "So, where do we have to get to?"

"Looks like we're just a few hundred yards from the bunker that Lydia found at The Beacon," Menzuo replied. "The serum should be in there. It's the only place that Dr. Bernstein has left standing here. It's our only hope."

Allucio peeked out to the open area, looking to his left. "I can see them. They're on their hands and knees like they are praying."

Menzuo and Desmurose peeked as well. "I don't think they're praying," Menzuo said as he looked closer. "They look like they're stuck to the ground. I can feel their energy, but this is strange."

"Maybe it has something to do with the Dark Spores' mist. We honestly don't know what it does to people," Desmurose followed.

"Well, let's not find out. We have to get to that room," Menzuo said. "Move carefully. We don't want to aggravate these things."

Allucio and Desmurose nodded and then followed Menzuo's lead towards the bunker doors, slow and steady. Each step was taken lightly. The Solar Warriors studied the people that were to their left. As they got closer, the young warriors ascertained that the people's hands and legs were incased into the cemented floor. A swirling mist moved counter-clockwise around them as if creating a forcefield around them.

"This looks crazy!" Allucio said a little too loud.

The trapped people shook violently to the sound of his voice. "Shhh!" Desmurose insisted. "Do not wake them. We don't want a fight down here."

Allucio patted his chest and whispered. "My bad…my bad." He placed his hand over his mouth.

Just as they reached the door, Menzuo looked back at his friends. "This has to be it, fellas. Let's get in there, grab this serum and bounce."

"We're right with you. It's getting uncomfortable down here," Desmurose said.

"Yeah, it's getting a little cold," Allucio added.

"Damn, the space-gel is wearing off," Menzuo said. "We really have to hurry."

Menzuo slowly turned the knob on the door, holding it tight as it opened, careful not to allow it to make any noise. He motioned for Allucio and Desmurose to follow him in. Just as they entered, he closed the door behind them.

"Alright, where can this stuff be?" Allucio asked.

"You two search those cabinets, and I'll work over here near the lab tables," Menzuo said.

They split up and went on their search. The young Prince walked deeper into the room, turning a corner where the lab tables were. Searching through the drawers, Menzuo continued to come up empty. He moved quickly around the room, hoping to find something that would lead him to the serum. After a few minutes, Allucio and Desmurose joined him. "Nothing, man! We didn't find anything," Desmurose said. "How about you?"

Menzuo shook his head. "I came up empty, too. I just don't get it. It has to be down here."

"It was a shot in the dark, Menzuo," Allucio said. "That Dr. Bernsein probably lost all of his work in that explosion. Whatever he had down here looks like it was just an experiment."

"Wait a minute," Desmurose said as he looked at a blackened window. "What's behind there? I can feel something."

Menzuo and Allucio focused on the energy as well. "Yes, I feel it, but how do we get in there without breaking the glass?"

Allucio walked closer to the glass and noticed a silver button. "Maybe if I push this…"

"Don't!" Menzuo shouted, trying to stop him, but it was too late.

Just as Allucio pushed the button, the blackened glass cleared. They were all able to see inside the hidden room.

"What the hell is that?" Desmurose asked as he walked closer to the window.

Inside, someone was floating in a large container with tubes sticking out of its body. "It looks like a…" Allucio began.

"A Pirate Drone!" Menzuo said. "But how could this thing be down here?"

Allucio noticed a clipboard hanging next to the container. "Guys, the notes on that clipboard reads, 'Experiment 27-14K-457. Unknown alien compound with humanoid extract. Dark mist injection denied. Experimental failure.'"

"Dr. Bernstien captured a Pirate Drone and was experimenting on it? That's impossible," Desmurose said.

"I don't think it's as far fetched as you think," Menzuo added. He noticed an empty canister that possibly held the serum. It was emptied by a tube that stuck into the Drone's body. "Look at the hole on the side of that drone. He had to be injured or near death when he was placed in that container. Dr. Bernstein was probably trying to make some type of Super-Drone without really knowing what he was dealing with."

"Well, I'm glad that experiment failed," Allucio added. "I just wish that we could've found the serum."

Menzuo dropped his head. "Dammit, I was really hoping that stuff was down here. I didn't want this mission to be a failure."

"It's not a failure, brother," Desmurose said, trying his best to lift his friend's spirits. "We had to take the chance to find it. The risk is always heavy when we're trying to save the world."

Menzuo sighed heavily and then spoke. "Let's get back to The Beacon. We have to figure out what to do next."

Just as they started for the door, a large *bang* rang out from just outside of the room. "Oh, crap! I think those people woke up!" Allucio said.

The banging grew louder and the door began to bend off of the hinges. "But we can't fight them with our powers," Desmurose said. "We would risk being stuck down here or even worse."

"The place could explode," Menzuo added. "We have to let them in."

Allucio turned to Menzuo with a confused look on his face. "What, let them in? What's your plan?"

"We let them rush the room, then we use our ability to slow time and move out, locking them in."

"That's when we can make a run for the exit," Desmurose added.

"Smart man, this one!" Allucio said with a smile.

The banging grew more violent as the warriors backed up against the glass. "Here they come!" Menzuo shouted. One last loud bang busted the door wide open. "Wait for it!"

"For what?" Allucio screamed.

"Wait for it!" Menzuo maintained. As the flood of possessed Super-Normals closed in, Menzuo finally barked, "Now!"

"Sensing Densor!" the three warriors shouted, instantly stopping time.

Without hesitation, they flew over the crowd and exited the room. Desmurose shut the door, just as time sped up again.

Menzuo looked down and noticed that the space-gel was fading. "Let's go! Times up!"

The Twin Powers could feel the temperature dropping all around them, and a shrill cold ravaged their bodies. "Oh, this is not good!" Allucio said as his heart riveted in his chest.

Without hesitation, the three warriors sprinted for the exit. Just as they were about to reach the steps, the possessed flying Super-Normals they encountered earlier made their way into the bunker.

"You have seriously got to be kidding me!" Desmurose shouted as he and his friends backed up. "Can we get a break?"

"I don't think so!" one of the possessed Super-Normals shouted as it appeared from the darkness of the hallway. The right side of his face was melted off, revealing layers of shredded muscle and white bone. His clothes were tattered with ice shards hanging from it, from clearly being overexposed to the frozen area. Four others possessed Super-Normals followed right behind him.

"We don't want to fight you!" Menzuo said, quickly raising his energy level. Allucio and Desmurose did the same. "This place is too unstable for a battle."

"We don't care," the possessed one spoke. "We're already dead!" He shouted, charging forward.

The door to the lab burst open and another flood of possessed Super-Normals rushed in from behind.

"This is not going to be good!" Allucio said.

"Get ready to protect yourself! We have no choice, but try your best to not make this place explode!" Menzuo shouted.

As the three protectors took fighting stances, a portal opened up directly above their heads. "Jump!" Tenan yelled.

Menzuo, Allucio and Desmurose looked up. "How?" Allucio asked.

"Don't ask how! Just jump!" Tenan repeated.

Without a second's more hesitation, the three warriors jumped into the portal, just as the crowd of possessed Super-Normals filled the space they once occupied. The portal quickly closed, and Menzuo, Allucio, and Desmurose vanished from sight.

Moments later, Menzuo, Allucio, and Desmurose walked through another portal that led to the Balcony of The Beacon. The Majesties were there. Paladin and Blurr rushed out to the balcony as they felt the energy surge. "How did you guys get here so quickly?" Paladin asked.

Allucio looked over to Tenan, who wore a smirk on his face. "I really have no clue, but I think you need to ask Tenan that question."

Everyone looked to Tenan. "When you guys left, for some reason, I could lock right on to your energy. Being that it was such a pure energy, I could follow you all on this journey. I lost you three a couple of times, maybe because you lowered your levels far enough to be undetected. Albeit, I sensed a spike in energy, it felt like my mind was placed right in that bunker with you. I'm still unsure how I'm able to see things so clearly, as this is all new to me, but I was there."

"Well, I'm glad that you were," Allucio followed. "That place was crazy scary. You really got us out of a pinch."

"We are grateful for your new gift, Tenan," Menzuo added. "It really came in handy."

"You're welcome," Tenan replied.

"I'm really glad that you all are safe, but time isn't really on our side right now," Paladin jumped in. "My team and I are preparing for our deep space travel, and we need everyone to stay alert. It seems that we have more threats coming than we can manage."

"Paladin's correct," Tenan said. "I can feel another dark energy located in the outer realm of this universe. Unfortunately, it is faint, but I can feel it growing. This energy is unknown to me, though."

Menzuo's head snapped around. "Did you say a dark energy from the outer realm?"

Tenan nodded. "Yes I did, why?"

"What do you think it could be?" Blurr asked.

"It has to be Lord Fetid, ruler of planet Excervo," Menzuo replied. "He is the Lord of the Pirate Warriors. A pure evil that wants to rule this universe. He's nothing to take lightly."

"Super-Normals, Oramite giants with the return of Natas Selur and now the Lord of Pirates? What's next, pink rainbows and unicorns shooting gummy bears from the heavens?" Allucio said jokingly.

"No *Se-Crets* here!" Thief joked.

"Seriously?" Paladin asked, staring at Thief.

"This can't be good," Menzuo followed, eying Allucio and Desmurose. "We have to contact the other Solar Warriors."

"How can we do that from here?" Desmurose asked. "Can Tenan portal jump us out there?"

"Unfortunately, it will be too risky for me to do so," Tenan said. "My gift is still new, and I wouldn't want to risk trying to place you there. It took me a long time just to get back here on my own. The portal jump from the bunker, back here was simple, but this…this is something that I have to perfect."

"We understand, Tenan. It was worth asking," Allucio said.

"Don't worry, guys," Menzuo said. "I can connect with them telepathically. It's something I picked up on my personal journey. I've spoken to Solar already, so I should be able to reach the others."

"It's worth a shot," Desmurose said. "What do you need to do to make this happen?"

"Just a quiet space and time to focus."

Lydia stepped forward. "My lab on the second floor is empty. You guys can use that room. I'll bring you there."

"Thank you, Lydia," Menzuo answered. "Lead the way."

Paladin turned to Blurr. "I think now is as good a time for us to go. Aganathin is in recovery, Menzuo and his Twin Powers have to focus on connecting with their team, and we have to figure out how to survive this deep space travel."

"Are you sure that this is what we need to do, babe?" Blurr asked.

"I've already contacted Washington," Paladin said. "Admiral Hankerson will provide what we need. And of course, I'm not one hundred percent certain of any of this, but what choice do we have?"

Menzuo turned to Paladin as he overheard his conversation with Blurr. "Paladin, wherever your mission takes you, we believe in you. Be safe, and make sure that you return in one piece. We have a lot to figure out."

Paladin nodded. "I'm looking forward to our conversation. And Menzuo, I do trust you."

Menzuo nodded, then followed his friends and Lydia to the lab on the second floor.

***

They took the elevator down. As the doors opened, they entered an empty room. "Here it is," Lydia said. "I'm in the middle of renovating this room, so everything had to be removed."

"This is perfect, thank you," Menzuo said.

"Well then, I guess I'll leave you guys to it," Lydia replied as she walked back into the elevator. "I'll be upstairs with everyone else when you're done." The doors closed.

Menzuo walked to the center of the room with his two best friends. "Let's get to it." They all sat on the floor. "Grab hold of my hands and focus on my energy. Once we're connected, I'll reach out to Solar. From there, I'll try my best to connect with the rest of the team."

"Okay, I'm ready," Desmurose replied.

"I'm ready, too," Allucio followed.

They all closed their eyes. Allucio and Desmurose focused in on Menzuo's energy. Within seconds, they were connected. "Whoa, this is cool," Desmurose spoke telepathically.

"I can feel the energy coming from you both," Allucio said telepathically as well. "This is some new level hero stuff."

"I know, right?" Menzuo said telepathically, proud. He quickly calmed his joy and refocused. "Okay, okay, now is the hard part. I have to try and connect all of us with Solar. Here we go."

Menzuo took a deep breath and focused on his brother's energy. Grabbing tighter to Allucio and Desmurose's hands, his focus strengthened. "I can sense Solar's energy now."

"I can feel him too," Desmurose said.

"I can, too. Wow, he's strong!" Allucio added.

A smile fell upon Menzuo's face. "Solar, it's me, Menzuo, and I am with Allucio and Desmurose. We need your help."

CHAPTER 20

INTO THE STREAM

"Everyone all set?" Paladin asked as he, Blurr, Thief, and Zenith stood atop The Beacon. His eyes swept over all of them.

"So, what's the wager here?" Thief asked.

"No need to take your money, I've got plenty of it," Paladin said.

"Keep the cockfighting to a minimum, guys," Blurr said. "We've got work to do."

"You're right, babe," Paladin said in a low voice. Behind his mask, no one could see the devious smile splitting his face. But before he could take a step, Blurr had already streaked into the night sky, scorching the blackness in a stream of baby blue and gold.

"Not fair!" Thief screamed, joining her.

Paladin shook his head. "I knew they'd get the drop on me. Guess it's just me and –" he turned to look for Zenith, but to his dismay, he was gone as well. "Aww, crap. I'm not going to be last." Paladin charged his speed variant and ripped into the air after Thief and Blurr.

The race proceeded for about three minutes, with Blurr finally holding off a strong charge from Thief and Paladin, with Paladin narrowly out leaning Thief as they touched down just outside of Fort McNair. Thief crashed into Paladin, and they both rolled along the ground, trenching up grass and dirt.

Blurr stood before them, gently brushing off her shoulders. "I was wondering when you two get here."

Paladin stood. "No fair, you're like, phasing in and out with crazy powers nowadays."

"Yeah," Thief said, now standing too. "I could barely drain anything from you."

"Cry babies," Blurr said.

Paladin looked around as his helmet retracted. “Where’s Zenith?”

“Meditating,” Zenith said, floating on a tree branch just above them.

“What?” Thief yelled. “Don’t tell me you made it here before us?”

“Teleportation is a fine way to travel,” Zenith said.

“When did you learn to do that?” Blurr asked.

“Se-Crets,” Paladin said in a mocking voice, making air quotes.

Thief shook his head. “It’s just not funny when you do it, man, just not funny.”

Zenith floated down, just as sirens blared and an army of vehicles mobilized around them; complete with a helicopter, APCs, and two tanks. “I guess the welcoming committee is here.”

The group held their hands over their heads. “Relax, gentlemen and beautiful lady,” a friendly voice said as the door of one of the army jeeps opened.

“Admiral Hankerson,” Paladin said.

Hankerson approached them. “The one and only.” He shook Paladin’s hand. “Didn’t I give you strict instructions to use the front gate and ask for me?”

“Well, why spoil an awesome opportunity to make a grand entrance?” Thief said.

“You Capes and your *theatricality*,” Hankerson said, smiling. “Come with me. We’ve got the Overdrive 2 prepped and fueled.”

Blurr and Paladin followed Admiral Hankerson, and Thief hung back, waiting for Zenith to touch down. “Hey, Zenith,” Thief whispered.

Zenith turned. “Yes.”

“Thanks for not busting me back there. You know, about my lingering feelings for Blurr. I mean, I know you must know.”

“Don’t have to be a telepath to see that. People see what they want to and ignore what they don’t,” Zenith said mildly.

“Yeah, I know. But still…thanks.” Zenith nodded, just as he was about to join the others, Thief grabbed him by the arm. “But honestly, why did you hide the truth?”

"Some Se-Crets are best left for a later time," Zenith said and eyed Thief's hand around his forearm. Thief noticed and loosened his grip. Zenith walked off, and Thief followed after.

Inside the hanger bay of Fort McNair, there was the expected amount of traffic. Military troops scurried about tending to various tasks, as security personnel made final checks on vehicles and equipment, not giving too much fanfare to the world heroes; although undoubtedly, everyone knew they were present.

"This way folks," Admiral Hankerson said, waving the team forward as he approached a large spacecraft.

The ship was massive, about the size of four school buses side by side, with sleek lines and an elegant design that would make the most sophisticated foreign luxury car salivate with envy. "It seems bigger than before," Paladin said.

"That's because it is," Hankerson said. "Recall that the USS Overdrive 1 was the prototype, and we used it's Gamma Lasers to punch the first hole in Q-18 when it was larger. This baby is decked with double the firepower and larger warp cores capable of faster deep space travel. So, quite naturally, we need to build it bigger."

"How much bigger?" Thief asked.

"About a fourth, give or take," Hankerson said.

"Admiral, we're humbled by your generosity and very appreciative of the Army's help in this matter," Paladin said.

"Don't be. This is Uncle Sam we're talking about here, Paladin. We don't give without needing something in return. Now you Capes saved the world, and I get that. And we are indebted to you in the highest way. But, we need your word that when you return, you'll bring this back in one piece, and we finish our conversation about the F.R.I.E.N.D.S. Initiative," Hankerson said. "Don't think we forgot about our little conversation."

"Don't worry, Admiral, you have our word," Paladin said.

"Hey Admiral, while we're talking about words and all, how's our boy Slingblade doing in the can?" Thief asked.

Paladin could see the distrust swirling in Thief's eyes. Yes, they all knew the government couldn't be trusted, but this wasn't the time to play sleuth again. "Don't worry the Admiral about that, Thief." Paladin rushed over and grabbed Thief by the arm. "There'll be plenty of time to answer those questions when we return, okay?" He gave Thief's arm a squeeze. "You clear?"

Thief glared at Paladin and then back at Admiral Hankerson. Blurr was in his periphery, narrowing her eyes at him. The moment of silence as everyone awaited Thief's response was suffocating. Finally, Thief broke from Paladin's grip. "Crystal," he said as he walked to the USS Overdrive 2.

Blurr joined Thief as they entered the USS Overdrive via the aft bay door and Paladin had some final words with Admiral Hankerson. "Thanks again Admiral. We'll be in touch."

"See to it that you do. I hope you find what you're looking for. From what you told me on the phone, this is as essential to our survival as it is Blurr's," hankerson said.

"Indeed, Admiral," Paladin said.

"Anything else that you need, feel free to contact us via the sonic radio equipped on board," Hankerson said. "Signal modulates in real-time, so it'll be like chatting on a cell phone," Hankerson said.

"Will do," Paladin said as he shook the Admiral's hand and walked off.

Before he could let go, Admiral Hankerson tightened his grip and pulled him back. "Keep your Cajun friend on a short leash, Paladin. I've seen his file. He's not one to trust completely."

"I trust him just fine." Paladin pulled away. "Good day, Admiral."

Paladin boarded the USS Overdrive 2, and the aft door shut behind. He made his way to the cockpit, which was virtually spotless, sporting four shiny leather chairs – a front and back row of two – and a wide front facing glass canopy, offering a full two hundred and sixty-degree viewing angle. His mouth dropped. "Wow, this one is even sweeter than the first."

"Leave it to Uncle Sam to go even harder to the rim the second time around," Thief said.

Paladin shot him a look and headed towards the front two chairs. "Blurr, you're with me."

"Oh, so now we're going to go all cold, bud?" Thief said.

Paladin sat down, and Blurr joined him. "Don't scare the Normals, remember? You have to play fair, Thief."

Thief plopped down in a chair directly behind Paladin. "I know, but recall that I was a detective. It's kinda hard to just blow off bull-crap when I see it. I gotta call it out, you know?"

"Just don't know why it's so hard for you to ignore your own crap, you know?" Blurr added.

"Ha, ha, ha," Zenith chucked, taking his seat as well.

"Did he just laugh?" Paladin asked.

"Then you know what that means. Hell just froze over, and I'm just waiting for that cow to jump over the moon. We're doomed," Thief said.

Paladin fired the engines and activated the sonic radio. "O2 is ready to go."

"USS Overdrive 2, you have a clear bay and are prepped for launch. Safe travels," a female voice rang out across the intercom.

The USS Overdrive lifted in place, jostling for a second or two, and then cruised out of the hangar bay. Once it cleared the building, the nose tilted skyward, and in a flash, the ship bolted into the atmosphere. After breaking orbit in what seemed like seconds, the ship drifted into space, passing an endless sea of space junk and Earth debris. The ship steadied and righted itself, allowing everyone to safely stand after Blurr activated the artificial gravity.

"Alright Zenith, it's showtime," Thief said.

Zenith stood, and Blurr loosened her seatbelt to join him.

"Thief, take the controls. I want to listen in on this," Paladin said.

"Roger that," Thief said, moving into the front row.

"Alright Zenith, give it to me straight," Blurr said.

"Once outside in the spacesuit," Zenith started, "I will connect with you telepathically, slowly deciphering the coordinates of the Rothandians in the outer time zone. It will be difficult at first to allow me to pass between the natural mental barriers that most humans innately have. Nonetheless, all you need to do is focus, and you'll be fine."

"How does one do that?" Blurr asked.

"Focus on the thing that is most dear to you," Zenith said.

Blurr eyed Paladin. "Like this clown here?" she joked.

"Precisely," Zenith said.

"Really, Z," Paladin said. "I thought we had a moment back there."

"Back where?" Zenith asked.

"On Earth. You know…any moment back on Earth," Paladin said weakly.

"No, I don't recall," Zenith said. He turned back to Blurr. "When you finally relax, just do what comes naturally and begin to run. Running in space is much like doing the same in the ocean. It's not the same as it is on Earth. It's a give and take scenario, but you must always understand that you are not in control. The space around you is. You must both yield and take control at the same time if you are to successfully generate speed. Can you do that?"

"It's not a matter of if I can Zenith, it's a matter of I will," Blurr said.

Zenith's eyes widened. "Now, you are ready. Take a spacesuit and call me when you're finished. But hasten. We are running out of time."

Paladin and Blurr slipped into a side cargo hold and did their best to load Blurr into the spacesuit as quickly as possible. Arms and legs were the first to go on, with the glass helmet being the last piece to don, but before Paladin lowered over her head, he took a moment to speak his peace. "Are you ready for this?"

"Ready as I ever will be."

"Don't do the whole big girl panty thing with me, Karla. Level up. If you're scared, say so. You don't have anything to hide from me. I'm here for you, as transparent as ever. You are my heart and soul. I am intertwined with you for eternity. And nothing can break that…nothing is going to take that away from us. Do you understand?"

Blurr nodded as tears filled her eyes. "I do. Sebastian, you share every portion of my heart, and I am so in love with you. Every fiber, every cell, every part of me burns with a desire to fill you with happiness."

Paladin leaned in and kissed her as passionately as he could, minus the S4 and spacesuit between them.

"Quickly. We must hasten," Zenith said from behind, breaking up their moment.

Paladin rolled his eyes and shook his head. "Alright already." He and Blurr shared a smile as he lowered the space helmet over her head and secured the locks in the sides, front, and back. Paladin gave the glass shield a tap. "You good?"

Blurr smiled back and flashed a thumbs up. "Always."

Zenith took Blurr by the hand and closed his eyes. In seconds, they vanished and reappeared outside the ship. "I got them, Paladin. Heads up," Thief said.

Paladin rushed to the cockpit and took the seat next to Thief. They gazed out the front of the ship and locked on to the image of Zenith fastening a black tether to Blurr's space suit about a hundred yards in front of them.

"So, S4, huh?" Thief asked.

"Yep."

"What's the last variant again?" Thief asked.

"Sensing. Allows me to change variants intuitively on the fly."

"Convenient little perk."

"Let's just say you'll never catch me slipping," Paladin said, eyes glued on Blurr.

"Easy fella, we're on the same side. Remember?"

Paladin made eye contact with Thief. "I do, but sometimes I forget. Or, I just want you to remember."

"Don't worry. I know."

"Sometimes I think you forget. Leaving like you do."

"Hey, I came back, didn't I?"

Paladin nodded. "You did," he said weakly.

"All this space travel and Dark Spore mist mumbo-jumbo is a little much. You scared?" Thief asked Paladin.

"Pissing in my pants," Paladin replied.

"Don't worry, she's a tough cookie. She'll be fine. If anyone can pull this off, it's Karla."

Paladin sat back in his chair and sighed. "Yeah, I know. The problem is, I fear she's taking on too much. I don't like pushing her, not until we know exactly what's going on."

"Yeah, I know what you mean bloke. Can I give you a word of advice?"

Paladin looked at him. "Shoot."

"Karla's like a wild stallion. You can't bridle her, or you'll kill her spirit. She has to flow and be what she wants to be. What she's gonna be. In the end, it's better for everyone that she is."

Paladin nodded. "You're exactly right. But, I have special plans for her and me when this is all over." Paladin slowly looked over to Thief as his eyes widened. The silence pause between then was a dead give away of what Paladin had in mind. He turned away and whispered, "I just hope that whatever she becomes is something the whole world can handle."

Zenith vanished from view and materialized behind Paladin and Thief. "She's ready."

Blurr began her attempt at running in space, churning her arms and legs as fast as she could. It was weird for both Paladin and Thief to finally see her move in what seemed like stop motion photography. It was a far cry from the hummingbird-like flapping of her appendages they were accustomed to.

Zenith closed his eyes and initiated the telepathic connection. Moments later, Blurr became one with her natural speed, and her arms and legs moved like whirling helicopter blades, barely visible to the naked eye. She bolted out in front of the spaceship, and the black tether tightened, whipping the ship behind her in a blazing wake of speed; jolting Paladin and Thief back in their seats. Zenith maintained his composure, floating in place, unaffected by the sudden onset of inertia.

As Blurr continued to pull the ship through space, Zenith deepened his connection, providing subliminal cues to coach her to transition to the next time dimension. Before long, Blurr and the USS Overdrive began to flicker in and out of sight, becoming one with the Speed –Stream.

"She's doing it," Paladin grunted, looking down at his hands as they phased in and out.

"You're right," Thief said, noting his own legs fluxing as well.

Paladin found it difficult to breathe and slowly started to lose consciousness. "Karla…hold on…hold…"

All at once, a sonic boom erupted, and the ship exploded into a bright ball of lightning, taking the entire team with it, into the Speed-Stream.

CHAPTER 21

REUNION

A large, warehouse garage door opened as Natas' titanic hand manually lifted the steel-plated panel, breaking the lock and jam that sealed it from the inside. The behemoth and the two giants behind him looked around cautiously before stepping inside. The large warehouse located on the southside of Hero City was the only place big enough to house the three hulks inconspicuously. Once inside, Natas closed the door behind them.

The three of them walked in between large isles of kitchen appliances, pipes, wood, and other equipment that were neatly stacked on tall shelves minimally taller than the giants in height. The warehouse was dark, and the only light came from a few emergency lights that flickered on after the building's closing hours. They walked to the back of the warehouse and took a seat on the floor as they uncloaked from invisibility mode.

"The deed is done. The young Super-Normals have retrieved the doctors, and they will be here shortly. My young apprentices are becoming quite the formidable tyrants. They went head to head with two members of the Majesties and won. With all of us fighting together, we'll easily demolish the rest of them. The Majesties won't even stand a chance. Then, I will become the ruler of this god-forsaken planet and set up decrees that will finally make this place run the way it should," Natas said with a fiendish grin.

"Father," Gath said. "How did you know your back-up plan worked successfully?"

"I've been around for centuries, son, schemed many wars and strategies to divide country against country, brother against brother, husband against wife. If there is one thing I've learned over these thousands of years, it's to always be a few steps ahead of your enemy," Natas said. "Every step I've taken has been calculated up to this very moment. I've been behind it all; Dr. Bernstein releasing the Dark Spores mist into the atmosphere during the storm, creating Super-Normals, and even Tanwar Terah creating you giants. You name it. It's my telepathic whispers that drive mankind to make aberrant decisions. Those teenagers were rebellious Satanists before they even got their powers; mad at the world and their parents. It was easy to coerce them. They've been waiting in the wings for a while."

"What about the Majesties and Amaruk?" Siph asked. "Did you account for them?"

"The Majesties and Amaruk were what I call 'necessary inevitabilities,'" Natas said. "You can't see them coming, but they are necessary whether you like them or not. In any case, I've learned not to trust anyone who is not a part of your immediate circle and to always be prepared for anything – in loss and in victory…always be prepared."

"And the portal dweller, Father…why is he important to you?" Siph asked.

"Ha!" Natas replied as he cracked his knuckles; forearms resting on his knees. He fisted his hands several times before continuing. "I fought a portal dweller thousands of years ago. Their gift is one to be coveted. The ability to access heaven and hell and everything in between is the closest thing to omnipresence. My objective was to place him under my command and use him as a vessel to get me into the gates of Heaven once again. The gulf between heaven and hell can't be crossed by any angel, demon, or human soul that has died and gone to either place…but that's not so with the portal dweller. That's a gift that God gave to a very select few."

"What is the name of the one you fought with, Father?" Gath asked.

"Titus," Natas said lowly as the memory almost pulled him into a daydream. He rubbed his face with his hands. "In his human form, Titus was one of the toughest men I've ever battled. He was tenacious, feerless and very clever. I defeated him in his mortal body, but he still got the upper hand."

"How so?" Gath asked.

After a few moments of silence, Natas sighed and answered. "He became something else – a rare promotion by the same God who booted me and several others like me out of our heavenly home. I haven't seen Titus in many years, but I can see his fingerprints all over the Majesties. They must be destroyed."

Gath and Siph looked at their master, seeing a somberness in him that they had never witnessed before. Natas took a deep breath and let it out slowly.

"And when we capture this portal dweller, what happens when he opens the heavenly realm for you?" Siph asked.

"Earth has had two world wars," Natas said with an evil smirk. "I was there for both of them. Let's just say that Heaven is due for its second war as well…on Earth as it is in Heaven."

***

A few hours passed as Natas, and the giants rested in their temporary hideout. They awoke at the sound of the garage door opening as several voices echoed throughout the warehouse.

"Come," Natas said. "They have returned."

All three of the giants walked towards the same loading area they entered through. Mystikal stood next to the soldier while Flame, Arctic, and Decibel waded in the background with Dr. Samir as the three enormous figures approached them. Dr. Samir made his way to the front slowly as he gazed at the two giants and Natas in his new body.

"Master Natas, is that you?" Dr. Samir asked as his mouth dropped in awe.

"It is," Natas replied. "Alive and in new flesh."

The two walked towards one another as Dr. Samir looked up at the gigantic Natas Selur as he drew nearer. His face was just below his pelvis as the two stood just inches from each other.

"How is this so?" Dr. Samir asked excitedly as he began to circle Natas in admiration, slowly dragging his fingers across his massive arms and then his back. Natas lifted his arms and hands as Dr. Samir esteemed the new colossal body of his superior. "I thought they murdered you. But here you are now; big as the giants that I helped create. Who was able to pull off such a feat?"

Dr. Samir rubbed the new material of Natas' red suit. He did the same with two giants, Siph and Gath. The Super-Normals waited in silence as Dr. Samir emotionally took in the joy of seeing his family again.

"Much has happened in the last few weeks, Dr. Samir," Natas said. "Nonetheless, fate always has her way. Forces beyond this galaxy were her servants, and they repaired me, made me stronger. I have much to tell, but we must direct our attention to eliminating the Majesties of Canaan and capturing the portal dweller."

"Do we know where they are?" Dr. Samir asked.

"No, but they're somewhere here in Hero City," Natas said. "We'll draw them out. They always run towards the fire, and this time we'll make them burn. Mystikal, thank you for your help. Mirage, you can let go. You're safe."

Suddenly, the soldier wearing brown fatigues phased into a skinny man wearing a tight, black leather suit with a gold belt around his waist. He adjusted a red mask on his face and slowly pulled it off, revealing a semi-wrinkled face with gray hair.

"You can never be too safe," Mirage said. "Nonetheless, you'll be happy to know that everything is in place back in Israel. I even left a few…hmmm…parting gifts at the Prime Minister's House before that ball-headed bastard knocked me out."

"Very good," Natas said. "Your sacrifice will be rewarded, Mirage. I thank you for stepping up."

Natas looked to the three teenagers. "You're up next," he said. "Are you ready?"

"We've been waiting for this moment for a long time," Flame said. "We're going to annihilate the Majesties. They're already down two members."

"I love your resolve, young one," Natas said. "But don't get too cocky. You're very powerful, and the way you maintain that power is by never underestimating your opponent. The Majesties won't make it easy, but your job is only to draw them out. When they show up, my sons and I will blindside them. Then all of us will finish them off together. “

“Decibel and Arctic, let’s light this city on fire,” Flame said.

The three teens walked out of the warehouse with the intent to desolate Hero City and all that were in it.

***

Blessed stood on the balcony, looking out over the city as the cool wind off the lake brushed across his face. Slaycik walked out and came and stood next to Blessed, giving him a light tap on the shoulder.

“What’s on your mind, Boss?” Slaycick asked.

“Man, what isn’t on my mind is the question,” Blessed chuckled.

“Ha-ha! Yeah, I understand.”

“I put a call into D’mitri. He’s on his way.”

“D’mitri as in Paraflyte?”

“Yes. I think I have a way to help Aganathin. I’m not sure it’s going to work, but it’s worth a try.”

“I’m looking for a super-strong, bald Jewish guy and a fast British-Jamaican with dreads,” a voice said from above them.

Blessed and Slaycick looked up to catch Paraflyte floating above them. The handsome Russian man lowered himself to the balcony and embraced his new friends.

“I’m sorry about Aganathin,” said Paraflyte. “I came as soon as you called me. Your coordinates were easy to find.”

“Thank you,” Blessed said. “Unfortunately, troubling times are upon us. A major war is brewing, and it’s much bigger than the fight in Syria. I’m also sorry to inform you that Natas may be behind it all.”

“What do you mean, Natas?” Paraflyte asked in shock. “I tossed him into Tenan’s portal half-dead and with his arms missing. How the hell is he back?”

“Something or *someone* revitalized him. And from what we’re being told, he’s bigger and much more powerful,” Slaycick said.

"Unbelievable!" Paraflyte exclaimed. "Whatever the Majesties need from me, I'm here to give it."

"We appreciate it," Blessed said as he made his way inside The Beacon. "Let me take you inside where Aganathin is resting. The man who owns this place, Paladin, just went on a mission along with several other Super-Normals. In addition, we've met some other gifted beings who are not from this planet. They've been helping us fight. None of this stuff is by coincidence. You can see the signs. The clouds are closing in from a distance."

"Indeed," Paraflyte replied.

The three of them walked into the room where Rekluse, Kasitia, and K'nia sat across from Aganathin on a couch while he slept in Paladin's bed. Tenan stood against the wall behind the bedroom door deep in his own thoughts. They were all surprised to see Paraflyte.

"D'mitri…we meet again," Tenan said with his head down.

"Tenan," Paraflyte replied, feeling somewhat awkward. "How are you?"

Tenan looked up, showing Paraflyte the whites of his eyes with no pupils. "I'm okay, but life has had its sacrifices."

Doing the best to hide his astonishment, Paraflyte nodded gracelessly and looked away. The others were unaware of Blessed's unilateral call to bring Paraflyte into the mission, so they waited silently for his explanation.

"I'm going to try something," Blessed said, getting right to the point. "Rekluse, I remember you explaining to me how Paraflyte used his body as the source to create Oramite suits and weapons before he came into the truth. I know this is a painful process for Paraflyte, but he promised us after the fight in Syria that he would help us when we need him. I called him tonight to see if we could help do something about Aganathin's arm. I have a plan, but I don't know if it's going to work."

The mood in the room was grim until K'nia spoke up. "Thank you for coming to help out, D'mitri. I know you helped us out in Syria after a drastic change of heart and I would say it's kind of soon to see you, considering that you were trying to kill us all not too long ago.

Nonetheless, Aganathin was the first one to extend an offer of forgiveness to you without ever really talking it over with any of us. You shot out of Syria before anyone of us had a chance to really talk to you and tell you how we feel. Yet, if you're here to help Aganathin, then I'm ok with it. I'm not speaking for everyone though."

"Listen," D'mitri replied. "I understand that I held hatred in my heart for many years towards Israel because of an atrocious act that I believed they were responsible for. That hatred caused me to hurt many people, and I'm sorry. I can't go back and change my acts. If I could, I would. Nonetheless, moving forward, I can show you all that I'm here as an ally to the Majesties of Canaan for the rest of my life. It's the reason I came as soon as Blessed called me."

The room remained silent for a while before Tenan offered an extension of forgiveness. "I forgive you, D'mitri. You hurt the lady in my life that I love unconditionally and you tried to murder me, but I sincerely forgive you. I'm able to do it because of men like Aganathin and because of the things God has been showing me lately."

"Thank you, Tenan," D'mitri replied.

"Alright. I hate to break up this emotional moment as needed as it is, but time is of the essence," Blessed said.

"It is," D'mitri agreed.

Paraflyte reached down and pulled up his pants leg, revealing the calf portion of his leg. He grabbed his left calf muscle with his left hand and began to squeeze, gradually tightening his grip. Suddenly, his leg became black and altered into what seemed like pudding. He pulled the black substance from his leg as it snapped away like a potter preparing a piece of clay. Paraflyte grunted doing his best to muffle a scream into a grunt by biting firmly on his bottom lip. The pain was agonizing. It took a few seconds for his calf muscle to form back whole again.

The black pudding-like substance Paraflyte pulled from his leg began to glow with a dark purple luminosity around it. "Fresh Oramite," Paraflyte murmured and gave the gooey substance to

Blessed as he remained crouched over, waiting for the pain in his leg to subside.

Blessed pulled the covers back from Aganathin, who was knocked out. He held the Oramite substance against Aganathin's arm with his left hand and touched the top of his shoulder with the other. Blessed closed his eyes as his hands burned red. As he held the Oramite in place, it began to melt and fuse into Aganathin's shoulder, where his arm used to be. The Oramite seeped into the pores of Aganathin's skin; attaching itself to the nerve endings. As Blessed let go, the Oramite formed into a new arm.

Aganathin remained asleep throughout the entire process, and, in a matter of seconds, he had a brand new attached arm. The rest of the team watched on in amazement as they admired the gift of their fearless leader. Blessed's decision became unanimously accepted and praised by the team. The Oramite took on the color of Aganathin's chocolate-colored skin. He stirred a few times as he struggled to attain comfort.

The team watched him a bit until Blessed ordered everyone out of the room so Aganathin could rest. As everyone filed out to the living room, Tenan tapped Paraflyte on the shoulder and thanked him before walking out on to the balcony. The other Majesties thanked Paraflyte as well for his commitment and expressed their gratefulness to Blessed with hugs. Rekluse saw Tenan head out to the balcony and followed after him.

"That's mighty big of you," she said as Tenan turned around. "You forgave the guy who tried to kill you and me. I owe you an apology, and I hope that you can forgive me like you forgave him."

Tenan stepped toward Rekluse and gently grabbed her hand. "It's me that owes you an apology," Tenan said. "I have to do a better job of communicating with you. I never should have portal jumped out of here like that. It was rude and I left you in a position of worry and concern."

"Look, Tenan," Rekluse said. "I know that relationships have sporadic up and down ebbs and flows that come with challenges. Nonetheless, I just need you to know I'm here for you. Seeing you come back without your sight just set me off, but then I see you fight through your emotions to forgive D'mitri. I mean Paraflyte, or whatever his name is. It just reminded me how selfish I was being."

"We have a lot to talk about, I suppose."

"We do, but let's do it after we get through this. I don't want us getting caught off guard by being all soft and sentimental."

"Agreed," Tenan laughed.

Abruptly, several loud explosions rang out several blocks away that startled the couple. The rest of the Majesties spilled out to the balcony to join them, intent on finding out the location of the explosions. Large fireballs could be seen slamming into several buildings off in the distance.

"More Super-Normals!" said K'nia.

"Yeah," Blessed said. "If I had to guess, that's the kid we saw from yesterday at the Prime Minister's House, which means his friends are with him. Majesties, let's put this fire out. Be careful and watch each other's backs. Tenan, let's open a portal. It's time to put these kids to bed."

CHAPTER 22

CHOICES

As Menzuo, Allucio, and Desmurose continued to meditate in the lab, they were able to fully connect with the rest of the Solar Warriors team. The team consisted of Princess Amiata and Nuncio from planet Bralose, Scoop and Wyler from planet Walonoke, Solar, and Master Renzfly on their home planet of Yardania. Everyone focused on Menzuo's energy and their minds were led to a dormant land surrounded by mountains and valleys of green grass.

"Wow, where are we?" Princess Amiata asked as she walked with Nuncio by her side. "This doesn't seem to be a place that I've ever heard of."

"You haven't," Menzuo said as he stepped forward. "We are in my training realm. This is where Master Renzfly brings me in my sleep so I could train under his guidance."

"I remember this place well," Wyler said as he and Scoop came to view. "Training here with you, Menzuo, was an experience."

"How did you get us all here?" Scoop asked.

"This place can only be unlocked by a Master Yardanian Warrior and his students," Master Renzfly replied as he and Solar walked towards the team. "Not many warriors have trained here, but I'm glad to have you all here."

"Brother, why are we here?" Solar asked, getting to the point as he could tell the urgency of Menzuo's energy.

"I have come to find out that there is a growing evil coming from planet Excervo. I believe that Lord Fetid has fully returned," Menzuo said.

Master Renzfly's eyes widened. "Your knowledge of Exervo is impressive. Solar and I have been watching the change on the planet. We can see something taking place, but cannot feel. Have you felt the energy growing?"

Menzuo shook his head. “No, I didn’t feel it. Allucio, Desmurose and I have met up with some other heroes on Earth; The Majesties of Canaan and a man named Paladin, who leads a team of two other Super-Normals. We had to come together in Hero City to prepare for an inevitable battle against several evil forces that have made their way to Earth. These forces are too big to fight alone. What we are looking to face may cause a true extinction-level event on our planet.”

“Do you need us to come and help?” Nuncio asked.

“No, we can’t risk it,” Menzuo answered. “Something is off with…I can feel it, but I don’t know what it is about this. Maybe it’s the visions that Lord Fetid placed in my mind after I killed his Queen. I’m not sure, but I know we have to be prepared for whatever is going to be released.”

“Menzuo,” Scoop said as he stepped forward. “We will protect our planets with our lives. We need you to protect Earth and make sure that whatever evil is coming, you all will eliminate it.”

“We have your backs,” Solar said with confidence. “Protect Earth and the Energy of All Good and Evil. I know that with the team you all have there, you’ll be victorious.”

“Thank you guys,” Allucio said. “We know that you all will be victorious in any battle as well.”

“That’s right,” Desmurose added. “We’re the Solar Warriors, and we live for this.”

“Just know that we will be ready,” Princess Amiata said.

Just as she spoke, a huge surge of energy flowed through the Solar Warriors’ bodies. “Did you feel that?” Master Renzfly asked.

Everyone looked to the sky of the training realm. “What was that?” Allucio asked.

“Was it Lord Fetid?” Desmurose asked. “That energy was pure evil and very powerful.”

Master Renzfly shook his head. He closed his eyes. “No, it was not the Lord. He just released an extremely powerful Pirate into our universe.” He focused on the energy, making his muscles tense. His eyes shot open. "Havoc! His name is Havoc, and he's heading to Earth."

Menzuo's rage exploded. "We'll meet him before he gets here. He won't even make it to Earth."

Desmurose turned to Menzuo. "Are you thinking what I'm thinking?"

Menzuo nodded. "Zero-G fighting on the moon!"

"Oh, I'm with that!" Desmurose added.

"I believe it's time we all prepare for the worst," Solar said.

"Everyone," Master Renzfly instructed. "Get your armies ready. Princess Amiata and Nuncio, inform the King that there is a threat coming."

"We're on it," Nuncio answered.

"Scoop and Wyler, prepare the Walonokians and Whistlers for the oncoming threat," Master Renzfly continued.

"We are ready," Scoop replied.

Master Renzfly turned to the group. "It's time. Whatever Lord Fetid is preparing to do, he isn't wasting any time."

"This is it," Menzuo said. He looked to his brother Solar. "Be careful. This will be our true first battle fighting individually."

Solar smiled. "Don't worry about me. Master Renzfly has worked me hard since our return home. I am more than ready. You protect yourself as well, little brother, and we will link up soon."

Everyone shook hands then walked off in opposite directions. "Stay focused, guys," Menzuo said to Allucio and Desmurose. "This will not be an easy battle."

"Trust me, bro," Desmurose said. "We are more than prepared for this."

"Time to wake up," Menzuo said.

In an instant, they all faded out of the training realm and were back in the lab located in The Beacon.

The young Warriors opened their eyes, allowing their focus to return. "That was freaking amazing!" Allucio said. "You train there with Master Renzfly? I want in, dude."

"Yeah, me too," Desmurose chimed in. "You've been holding out on us, bro."

"In due time," Menzuo answered. "But first, we have to hurry and get to the moon. We have to cut off Havoc before he arrives."

As everyone stood, a loud explosion shook the building. "What in the world was that?" Desmurose shouted.

"I don't know, but that energy doesn't feel good!" Menzuo said. "Let's get to the balcony."

They bypassed the elevator and shot up the stairs to the top floor. Within seconds, they were out on the balcony and noticed a huge mushroom cloud of fire off in the distance. "This isn't good!" Allucio shouted.

Desmurose looked around, noting that both the balcony and the room was empty. "Where is everyone?"

"I guarantee that the Majesties have made their way to that danger zone," Menzuo answered. "But we can't help them. We need to go!"

"We're ready!" Allucio said.

"Wait!" Lydia shouted as she ran out to the balcony to meet the young fighters. "Everyone has left, and we need to remain connected. With Paladin and our team gone on their own mission, the Majesties heading to their battle and now you boys leaving to wherever the heck you're flying off too, we need to make sure we stay in communication." She handed Menzuo, Allucio, and Desmurose earpieces. "Take these."

"What are they?" Allucio asked.

"These are my IEPCS's – Inner Ear Piece Communication Systems. Put these in your ears, and you all will be able to communicate with me and B.R.A.I.N. here at The Beacon. From there, I can keep everyone connected."

The Solar Warriors placed the devices in their ears, and their IEPCS adjusted perfectly. Menzuo heard three faint chimes followed by a low buzz. "All set," Menzuo answered.

"Good luck wherever you're going, and be safe," Lydia said.

"See you soon," Menzuo said. He moved his hand counter-clockwise, making the space-gel reappear around him and his friends. "Let's go!"

In a flash, the three warriors shot high into the sky like lightning and disappeared out of the atmosphere.

"Well, damn. And I thought I'd seen it all," Lydia joked and then headed back to her work station.

***

Within no time, Menzuo and his best friends made it to the moon. They dispersed their energy throughout their bodies, which created a gravity field around them. "We're in Zero-G," Menzuo said. He looked off in the distance, noticing a spec of fire growing in size as it closed in. He pointed to the light. "Havoc is almost here. Raise your power!"

Without hesitation, Allucio and Desmurose powered up.

***

The energy boost grabbed Havoc's attention as he flew closer. "Aaah, these young fighters are powerful and smart. Taking the battle to Zero-G on Earth's moon. It won't help them one bit." He directed the ship towards them.

***

Menzuo noticed the image gained in speed, recognizing that it was indeed a spaceship. "He's moving faster. Looks like we got his attention," Menzuo said. "Here he comes!"

"Do you feel that?" Desmurose shouted.

"I sure do!" Allucio answered. "He brought backup!"

"A ship full of Pirate Drones!" Menzuo said.

"Oh it's party time! Time to have a *par-tay*!" Allucio replied.

The ship circled the warriors once and then landed less than fifty feet from them, stirring up dust from the Moon's surface. The hatch opened and out stepped a large Pirate Warrior – Havoc. He was wearing a special suit that protected him for the lack of atmosphere on Earth's moon. It was a solid dark green color that had a slight glow to it. A black breathing mask covered his mouth, only exposing his eyes.

"You must be Havoc," Menzuo said. "I suggest you turn around and go back to Excervo. You don't want to face us."

Havoc sauntered towards the three warriors. "I'm glad that you know who I am," he said, stopping about twenty feet from his enemies, "but what you don't know is that I do not retreat from any battle. As a matter of fact, when has any Pirate retreated?"

"From my knowledge, never, but now would be a good time for a first time," Menzuo replied.

Havoc looked at Allucio and Desmurose. "It's good that you brought back up. You're going to need it."

"Back up?" Allucio said. "Menzuo doesn't need back up, but it does help to have friends that will handle his light work."

Havoc cracked a smile. "Light work. If you only knew what light work is in motion for you Solar Warriors."

Menzuo looked confused. "If you have something to say, either say it, leave…or die. It's your choice."

"Well, I choose…die!" Havoc shouted. He spread his arms as wide as he could, instructing the Pirate Drones to exit his spaceship. Within seconds, a flood of Drones flew out and circled above Havoc's head. "I have a choice, and so do you, Prince Menzuo. Life and death choices have to be made. All I want to know is if you're ready to make yours!"

Menzuo, Allucio, and Desmurose fully powered up, readying themselves for the battle. "I've made my choice!" Menzuo shouted. "I choose to protect my planet!"

Havoc chuckled. "Then you shall soon learn how wrong of a choice that is, right before I kill you. Attack!" he commanded his Drones.

The Pirate Drones charged forward. "We got this!" Desmurose shouted. "Super Disc!" A huge green disc flew from his hands and blasted several Drones out of the sky.

"You take that monster out!" Allucio shouted. "Sonic Blade!" A large blue flaming blade flew out of his hands and destroyed a bunch of Drones.

Allucio and Desmurose flew directly into the swarm of Drones, taking them out with every punch and kick they released.

As his friends fought off the threat above his head, Menzuo locked eyes onto Havoc and approached him cautiously. Not once looking up at what his friends were doing in battle. He was confident they had their fight under control. "You have chosen wrong. I gave you a chance to leave."

Havoc walked forward as well. "Choices, choices, choices…young Warrior, how wrong you are. Take this! Tornado Rush!" He clapped his hands together, instantly creating a horizontal tornado that flew towards the Universal Protector.

"Not today!" Menzuo shouted. His eyes began to glow. He dug his feet deep into the ground of the Moon. "Mega Body Attack!" Three huge flames flew from his hands, right into the mouth of Havoc's attack.

Menzuo's attack was so intense that the pressure from the flames diminished the tornado. "What?" Havoc shouted.

It was too late for him to move. The three firebombs exploded right onto his chest, sending him back into the foot of his spaceship.

Menzuo took a second to look up, noticing that Allucio and Desmurose were floating back to back, fighting off every Pirate Drone that tried to attack them. Throwing their massive attacks, the Drones didn't stand a chance against the young warriors.

"That was pure luck!" Havoc shouted.

"It's never luck, just pure skill!" Menzuo replied. "Sensing Densor!" he shouted, instantly disappearing.

As time slowed, Menzuo charged in like a bolt of lightning. He was now inches from Havoc. He raised his hands above his head as if he held a sledgehammer. Time sped up and Menzuo lowered a furious two-handed punch on the top of Havoc's head. The impact sent havoc several feet deep into the Moon's surface, creating a massive crater where he once was.

Without hesitation, Menzuo flew deep into the hole, picked Havoc up by the neck, and floated back to the surface. Looking deep into his eyes, Menzuo smiled. "Like I said, my choice is to destroy you!"

Havoc smiled. "My sacrifice is worth it. I live to serve Lord Fetid, and you don't even know that you have already lost."

Menzuo paused as he landed back on the ground. "What are you talking about?"

Havoc tried to laugh as Menzuo's grip around his neck tightened. "How can I explain…without the ability…to breathe?"

Menzuo loosened his grip, but kept his defenses raised, ready to take him out if he tried anything funny. "Speak!"

Havoc took a deep breath. "How about another choice, Prince? Either save Earth with your new friends or save Yardania with your old ones. As you can see, you can't be in two places at once, so you will lose."

The rage within Menzuo started to rise. He wanted to desperately kill Havoc, but he wavered between the set of choices before him. "I cannot lose. The Solar Warriors are prepared to protect the outer realm at all costs and Earth…whatever threat is coming to Earth, my new team of friends can handle it." He glared at Havoc. "Just know that you have lost."

"Young Prince, I am just a decoy…collateral damage. A stop-gap for Lord Fetid's ultimate plan."

"He has no plan!" Menzuo shouted. "He is not strong enough to execute a plan. That's why he sent you. Another weak Pirate for me to practice on."

"I'm not weak, Prince Menzuo. I *am* the sacrifice. You can kill me if you like, but the distraction has worked," Havoc said. "Earth is at its weakest with your friends separated and the outer realm…well, that beautiful plan will be completed soon enough. I have spoken too much already. Just know that you have underestimated my Lord, and you will pay dearly. Like I said…choices!"

Still confused by everything, Menzuo refocused on his fight. He raised his left hand, as it was engulfed in a red flame. "My new choice is to make you speak. Your life will not be spared, but I will make sure that I'm well equipped with all the information I need to protect this universe. Mega Body Attack!"

Menzuo released a dazzling attack upon Havoc, complete with precision hits on Havoc that rattled his evil opponent. Menzuo strategically took him down, lowering his energy level to make him speak.

Just above, The Twin Powers moved as one, demonstrating the full array of their skills as proven warriors, not allowing a single Pirate Drone to land an attack. Their ability to hold them off and take them out, one by one, truly showed how powerful this Solar Warriors team could be. Victory was on the horizon as the three warriors obliterated their foes.

CHAPTER 23

REMATCH

Tenan's portal opened, and the Majesties stepped out to total chaos in the downtown area of Hero City. The region was a mess, filled with screams of despair and calamity as people scurried for safety, avoiding towering blazes of fire and countless debris of falling buildings. The menacing cries for help could be heard for blocks. Several corporate buildings and skyrise apartments were already on fire as families poured into the streets, fleeing to their cars in an attempt to escape the supposed terrorist attack.

But the Majesties knew it was not the work of terrorists, but of evil Super-Normals. Rekluse noticed a few people frozen amongst the frenzy as if they were paralyzed. A storm of fireballs dispersed from the sky, raining in different directions and striking multiple targets. Police sirens could be heard in the distance closing in on the commotion.

Multiple E.I.E.s filled the sky to take in the festivities. "We've got company," Kasitia said, pointing at the high flying drones.

"That's not all," K'nia said, pointing off in another direction. Suddenly, a teenager riding a hoverboard zoomed by just above the Majesties' heads. He recklessly lobbed fireballs from his hands, striking cars, shops, and innocent bystanders – casualties of Flame's sinister acts.

Arctic trailed Flame on a hoverboard of her own, dispelling rays of white mist from her palms. Anyone or anything hit by the young Latina's rays were frozen immediately. Both Super-Normals were so hellbent on terrorizing the city in their frenzy that they failed to notice the seven super soldiers below them, draped in their black army fatigues.

A third teenager, Decibel, could be seen traveling in the opposite direction coming to meet up with his comrades, also straddling a hoverboard. He yelled, releasing a scream so loud and excruciating that it caused everyone in an earshot to drop to their knees, hands covering their ears. All of the Majesties, including Paraflyte, fell to the ground writhing in pain as the sound equal to that of a thousand fire truck sirens amplified to intolerable levels.

The teens partied up, hovering above the crowd of people, marveling at their work. Their boards rose higher into the sky as Decibel smiled, elated by his handiwork. Flame and Arctic gazed down on the thousands of Chicagoans below them, sharing smirks.

"Go ahead, Decibel," Flame said. "You can make them hear you better than I can."

Decibel, able to project his voice at any level, spoke into an oversized megaphone, carrying his voice for several city blocks. "Behold!" yelled Decibel. "The time of the Antichrist is upon us. You people will have a choice. Join us and live or resist and die. Look around you. You see the evidence of our power. We left you examples of what happens when you resist. If you are willing to serve Natas Selur, remain kneeling. If you oppose, then stand. We'll give you a quick and painless death."

One by one, several brave people scattered among the crowd began to stand up. The teens, surprised by those showing a lack of fear, looked around frantically as they tried to determine who to punish first.

"This has to end now," Blessed said to his team. "We have to take the fight them and redirect their attention on us before they continue to kill more innocent people. K'nia, you have the truest aim of all of us. Can you cut the chord to the microphone?"

"Of course," she said. "He talks too much anyway."

K'nia instantly stood, rolling a few Oramite stars in her hands. Just as the three teens spotted her, she launched a few in Decibel's direction. The stars, moving with the speed of a bullet, pierced his neck; severing his vocal chords. He lost his balance and fell off the board; falling a few hundred feet to his death. Flame and Arctic watched in amazement. Fear filled their hearts and their expressions revealed it.

"Everybody get to safety!" Blessed yelled, prompting the crowd to disperse again. People began to scatter and run out of harm's way.

Arctic and Flame directed their attention towards the Majesties, who were now standing together in unison, bracing for retaliation.

"You bitch!" Arctic screamed. "You'll die for that!"

"Come and get it, pussy cat," K'nia said.

Arctic aimed her hoverboard at the group and darted for them at full speed, launching sharp-pointed ice sickles from her palms. Tenan opened up a portal in front of his team that swallowed the sickles whole.

Arctic flew by, just missing their heads and circled back around, launching more ice sickles. "I can do this for days," she lashed.

At the same moment, Flame charged at the Majesties too and tossed several fireballs their way. The Majesties hastily avoided their attack, ducking and moving out of the way as they dodged the fire and ice projectiles.

As Tenan cleared the assault, he sensed the presence of greater danger as three large shadowy figures emerged from behind a building. Although they were cloaked, they couldn't hide the shadowy silhouette of their souls, which was visible to Tenan. "The giants are here!" he shouted, alerting the team.

"Where?" Kasitia asked, ducking behind a nearby car. "I don't see them."

"Neither do I," Slaycick said, scurrying about.

"They're cloaked in invisibility," Tenan shouted. "Handle the teens. I'll take care of Natas and the giants. He wants me alive, and he doesn't know I can see him."

"Wait, Tenan," Blessed said. "How do you know he wants you alive?"

"I can see his spirit and his intentions," Tenan said. "As crooked as they are, he wants to use me for something. I believe it can work it to my advantage."

"I'm coming with you," Blessed said. "Perhaps we can make them show themselves. Slaycick and Paraflyte, can you and the girls deal with those two?"

"We got this," Paraflyte said. "As a matter of fact, we need to make this fight fair."

Paraflyte touched his collar and a black and grey, army fatigue-mask formed around his face. He bolted into the sky, flying after Flame. Flame turned and launched a fireball, which Paraflyte dodged effortlessly. He pulled his guns from hips and began firing. One of the bullets managed to hit the hoverboard's motor making the villain fall from the sky. As Flame fell from his board, he casted a stream of fire that served as propulsion to slow his fall. The board landed next to him and exploded. "You broke my board, old man," Flame said, pointing at Paraflyte.

Paraflyte shot by as he avoided a pair of fireballs from Flame, who turned his attention back on the Majesties. He launched a few more in Slaycick, Rekluse, K'nia and Kasitia's direction, who barely managed to avoid his attack as well.

Slaycick shifted into hyperspeed and ducked behind Flame who was still holding a throwing motion. Once he got behind him, Slaycick leaned in and rammed his shoulder into Flame's back. The force sent him flying several feet forward and causing him to scrape his face on the pavement. Flame rolled to a halt and stood, gathering himself.

Meanwhile, Arctic focused her attention on Paraflyte and flew in his direction as they converged in a dangerous flying dance. "Try this," she said, casting thirty plus dagger-like sickles at Paraflyte. Paraflyte closed the distance between them, dodging the icy projectiles of the wintery diva, weaving side to side and up and down in a figure-eight motion with a full head of steam. Only one ice shard landed, hitting Paraflyte's shoulder and busting into tiny pieces.

Paraflyte, who was wearing an Oramite laced suit, shrugged it off and kept flying, unfazed initially but soon realized that something was wrong. A block of ice had formed around his shoulder and was increasing in size at an astronomical rate. The weight of the ice dropped him from the sky and sent him crashing to the ground. He tumbled along the street and slammed into a parked car, as the ice shattered around his body.

"D'mitri!" K'nia yelled.

Paraflyte rolled to his knees. "I'm fine," he said, taking a gasp. "Be careful with this one. Don't let her sickles or any part of her touch you. The ice from her hands has nasty effects. We have to be strategic."

"Yeah, she's the one who hurt Aganathin," K'nia said. "But first thing's first. Let's get her off that board. We can fight her better on the ground."

Slaycick stood in front of Flame as he continued to brush himself off. "I'm not one to sucker-punch people, but you threw a fireball at my friends and me. That's a no-no," Slaycick said, waving his finger at him. "Now, we're face to face. So, I'll give you a chance to stand down. We really don't like hurting kids."

"That's kind of you, but I'm not a kid," said Flame, quickly opening his hands. He formed two fireballs and threw them at Slaycick, who side-stepped the balls and charged the teenager, punching him in the face before he could figure out what happened. The teen hit the ground, woozy and seeing double.

"Listen, Kid," Slaycick said. "You can throw those fireballs at me 200 times, and I promise you that you'll miss all 200. For the last time, Stand down."

Flame grabbed his chin and stood, full of rage. "Never! I'm gonna burn this whole city down with you in it. Be still so I can set those ugly dreadlocks on fire."

Slaycick sighed, reached over his shoulder, and pulled his swords from their sheaths. He twirled them in his hands. "Kid, please don't make me do this. I'm giving you a chance to surrender and to let us help you. Your mind has been warped by a lie."

"I'll never surrender!" Flame yelled as he tried to catch Slaycick off guard by firing seven fireballs at top speed in his direction. Slaycick – quick to react – moved to the side and sprinted in hyper-speed towards Flame. Flame's fireballs hadn't even reached

Slaycick's previous position before the Majesties' fastest man was upon Flame. He swung his swords at Flame's extended arms and sliced his hands off at the wrist.

It took Flame a few seconds to register what had just happened. Confused, his eyes darted back and forth between Slaycick and his bloody wrists, trying his best to make sense of what he was seeing. After a few times, it finally registered. "What did you do to me?" Flame yelled.

"I warned you, kid," Slaycick said calmly. "You chose not to listen."

Instantly, Slaycick connected a roundhouse kick to Flame's face that dropped him immediately. Slaycick resheathed his swords on his back as the teen continued to bleed out from his wrists.

Arctic charged towards the three women and Paraflyte, discharging a blizzard-like flurry of ice and snow from her hands. Rekluse flipped out of the way and rolled behind a van as Kasitia transformed into shadow mode and moved inconspicuously along the street. K'nia and Paraflyte weren't as fortunate as flurries from Arctic's discharge hit their mark. Several flakes contacted K'nia's skin, causing her to freeze in place. The flurries that hit Paraflyte formed an icy cast around his entire body, rendering him motionless. Arctic circled back around on her board for another pass and noticed Flame's motionless body lying along the sidewalk in a pool of blood. Her eyes fell on Slaycick, who had pulled his swords from his sheath again.

"I'm gonna kill you for that!" she yelled.

"Come on," Slayick said. "Let's see if I can outrun your snowflakes."

"Alright, I'm through playing with this skank," Rekluse mumbled as she pulled three metallic balls out of her belt pouch.

Instantly, Hero City transformed into a flat, dry desert right before Arctic's eyes. Slaycick disappeared and she was all alone by herself.

"What the hell is this?" Arctic asked to herself aloud. "Mirage is this you?"

"No, bitch. It's me," Rekluse said, as she stood before Arctic, flanked by two cactus plants.

Arctic's hands fisted at her side, covered in snow. "You can make me try to see whatever you want, slut. My abilities work just fine in and out of reality."

"Let's see it," Rekluse said.

Arctic charged her with the hoverboard, unleashing a fury of flurries and ice sickles, which passed through a hologram image of Rekluse. Arctc's eyes widened. "What!" A beeping noise under her feet caught her attention. She looked down and noticed three metallic balls magnetically fastened to the bottom of the board. They exploded, tossing Arctic from her board and sending her soaring in the air. She landed in the middle of the street, knocking her self incoherent. When she finally came to, Rekluse was standing over her.

"Look at me," Rekluse said as she locked eyes with Arctic, making her pupils turn white. "You're going to do everything I say, starting with unfreezing my friends."

"Yes," Arctic said begrudgingly under a trance. "I will do what you say…and unfreeze…your friends."

***

"I can see you," said Tenan as he and Blessed approached the invisible giants. "Your cloak foolery doesn't work on me."

"Portal Dweller. You speak with such boldness," Natas said as he and the giants materialized before them. "So much for the element of surprise. Your abilities go much deeper than I thought. It doesn't matter. My reign over planet Earth is inevitable." Natas smiled wryly. "And your gift will come in useful for me, Portal Dweller."

"Wrong," Blessed replied as he stepped in front of Tenan. "The only thing inevitable about today is your defeat."

"Blessed, the mighty one. You survived the fireball, I see," Natas said as the two sides drew closer to each other. "I remember how well you fought in Syria. You gave my sons quite the battle. Today will not be so. Today, you die. But before I kill you, where's the rest of your team?" Natas asked, looking around. "I heard you're short a man, or should I say…an *arm*."

"Aganathin is fine. And his new arm is much stronger than his former," Blessed replied.

"Interesting," Natas replied, somewhat surprised. "And the speedsters? I was hoping to see them personally for what they did to me in Jableh. I want to hear the sounds of their skulls crack when I crush them with these hands."

"Awwww. Did you miss me, pudding?" Slaycick said as he appeared out of nowhere standing next to Tenan. "I'm right here. This time I'll make sure I chop off your head instead of your arms."

Blessed stepped forward, standing only inches away from Natas, who dwarfed him like a great Oak Tree. Unfazed by Natas' new size, Blessed sized him up. "We beat you before Natas," he said. "And we'll beat you again."

Natas quickly scooped Blessed up, wrapping his fingers around the top of Blessed's six foot eight-inch frame like a young boy picks up an action figure. He tightened his grip as he brought Blessed face to face with him. "I will crush you," Natas said as he continued to squeeze. But his grip quickly loosened as his fingers slowly began to open. Natas gazed at Blessed with wide eyes.

"Rrrrrrraaaaaaaaaah," Blessed yelled as he pried the giant's hand open with his pure brute strength. Natas looked on with amazement as Blessed kicked out of Natas' grasp, backflipping to the floor and landing on his feet. He didn't hesitate to counter with an attack of his own. He cocked back his arm and swung, delivering a powerful blow to Natas' midsection. The punch sent him sliding back a few feet, doubling over in pain. He looked over at his two Giant comrades. "Crush hiiiiiim!" Natas yelled.

Siph, hearing his father's request, lifted his foot at Blessed. As he slammed it down in Blessed's direction, Blessed caught the behemoth's foot with both of his hands and flipped him backward. Siph landed on his head and rolled to a prone position. Gath charged at Blessed in a rage yelling, "Brother!" he threw a wicked haymaker that Blessed tried to block with both forearms. Still, as the beast made contact, Blessed was quickly overwhelmed by Gath's brute strength and rocketed backward some twenty feet in the air.

Tenan grabbed two metallic ball bombs from his back pouch and tossed them at Gath's chest, exploding on contact. "Bingo!" Tenan said. Gath staggered, but remained standing. Rekluse approached next as K'nia and Kasitia lagged behind joining in on the fray. But Siph was back on his feet and quickly dispersed each of the females with complimentary backhands that sent them reeling.

Paraflyte screeched in from above and hovered just above the Majesties and the giants. Siph noticed and took aim, blasting Paraflyte out of the air with lasers that discharged from his fingertips, sending him slamming into a lightpost.

Slaycick dashed in and hacked at one of Siph's arms with his blade, but the weapon bounced off with a clang, only effectively creating a spark that momentarily blinded him. Siph laughed as he mocked Slaycick's futile attempt. "Haha! Puny man, I've been upgraded."

As Slaycick tried to swing again, Siph countered with another dose of lasers. Slaycick avoided the volley, darting out the way. K'nia hit Siph with a barrage of stars shooting from her hand which bounced off of him like bugs on a windshield. Only trace scratches remained along the Giant's armor. As K'nia attempted another attack, Siph opened his hand and zapped her with a pulse blast that sent her flipping into an overturned car.

Rekluse and Kasitia charged once more at Gath, peppering him Oramite bullets from the barrel of their guns. Rekluse conjured an illusion of fighter jets and army tanks that launched an onslaught of missiles and ammunition in hopes of distracting him. But it was useless as the beast merely smirked and tilted his head at her. "Silly games from a silly girl," he slurred.

Natas stood and waved his hand, quickly dispersing away the false images. "Sorry, sweetheart. I've seen that trick before, and it doesn't work on me anymore," Natas said. "But I have a trick for you." Natas extended his arm toward the charging women and easily lifted them into the air like a hurricane. Natas rolled his arms in small circles as he began controlling the women in midair. With his psychokinetic influence, he removed the guns and then finally tossed them aside like ragdolls. Kasitia and Rekluse slammed into an adjacent building, breaking through the walls as the roof caved in on them.

"Rekluse!" Tenan shouted as he sprinted in her direction.

"Aaah," Natas said as if he had an epiphany. "The Portal Dweller has a love interest."

Slayick ran at hyperspeed and rescued the women from the debris. Both Kasitia and Rekluse were disoriented as they groaned in pain. Blessed recovered and charged Gath, leaping in the air with his fist pulled back, ready to strike. Gath quickly turned just in time to catch Blessed in midair and slam him into the pavement. The force was so strong that Blessed's body shattered the concrete, creating an indentation in the street. Gath, showing no mercy, proceeded to stomp the metal-armed soldier repeatedly with his colossal boot until Blessed broke through the surface and splashed into the sewer below, unconscious.

Natas reached down through the hole and took Blessed by the head, pulling him from the sewer and lifting him overhead. He held his body up in the light, analyzing him. "So delicate are you" Natas joked. "But it is admirable that you still think you can best a powerful being like me." He looked over at Siph and Gath. "Like us!"

The other two Giant's shared a smile. "No!" K'nia gasped and quickly charged all three giants in a blood rage. "Let him go," she screamed as she fired stars from her hand.

Siph stepped forward. "This one's mine," he said, before slapping K'nia with a backhand that catapulted her into a nearby store window. Several police cars entered the scene, weaving through the street as they sped toward the conflict.

Gath moved in. "Allow me, brother." He fired a stream of lasers from his hand at the police cars, which exploded on contact.

The downtown area of Hero City was a scene of carnage as buildings blazed with fire and a number of cars remained flipped over in the streets. Countless bodies of innocent casualities were strewn for blocks.

"This ends now," Paraflyte said as he launched into the sky and dash towards all three giants. Natas, Gath, and Siph aimed at Paraflyte with open palms and scorched Paraflyte with powerful blasts. The blasts were powerful enough to drop Paraflyte out of the air for good. His muscle frame plummeted to the ground, creating a large fissure in the middle of the street.

"Majesties!" Natas yelled angrily. "It's over! Come say good-bye to your fearless leader and watch as I crush his head like a grape."

Slayick kneeled over Kasitia and Rekluse as both women stirred, trying their best to regain their composure. Tenan came to Rekluse's side and gently propped her up in his arms as he knelt behind her. "I'm fine, baby," she said faintly. "You and Slaycick go finish them off. I'll make sure Kasitia's okay."

"No. I won't leave you again my love," Tenan said.

Rekluse turned around and used his shoulders to push herself up. "Besides," she said weakly. "I have a plan. I need you and Slaycick to distract them."

Tenan considered his girl's words as she winked at him and offered a slight smile through the pain. It was enough to convince him to follow through. "Okay," Tenan said, smiling back. "I think I might have a little something up my sleeve as well."

Slaycick rubbed Kasitia's back. "Come on girl, get up."

Kasitia shook her head and slowly turned over. "Thank you, Slaycick," Kasitia said breathing heavily. "But Rekluse is right. We have to find a way to beat these bastards. We can't let them win."

Natas approached Slaycick and Tenan, holding Blessed in his hand. He pointed at them with his free one. "Playtime is over. Your leader is about to die at my hand. Who's next?" He directed his sights on Tenan. "I told you I was coming back, Portal Dweller and that I was bringing death and destruction with me. It was necessary. The people, gifted and normal alike, had to know that I am the true definition of power and governance. The new world order will happen under my reign. It is preordained."

The image of Blessed hangin from Natas' hand like a limp noodle sent a flood of rage through Slaycick. He charged at Natas like a bullet fired from a canon. Although Slaycick was invisible to the naked eye, Natas' was able to easily track him as if he was moving in slow motion. "I see you!" Natas yelled as the speedster charged down the street at him. Slaycick went airborn and drew his sword, aiming for Natas' head, but he wasn't fast enough as Natas snatched Slaycick out of the air with his free hand. He squeezed Slaycick until he released his weapon, yelling from the pain. "Finally! The speedster," Natas said as Slaycick squirmed in his grip. "Things are a little different now. Especially when you can't catch a person by surprise. I remember what you and the little fast girl did to me. Where is she by the way?" Gath and Siph chuckled at the sight of their master holding both Slaycick and Blessed, who were too powerless to resist.

"Awww, he looks like a little hamster," Gath laughed. "Crush his head, Father. You have the last laugh."

"Yes," agreed Siph. "Send a message to all who oppose you – to all with abilities and without. You are the supreme ruler of Earth."

Slaycick was able to pull a small knife from his pants leg and attempted to stab Natas' hands, but the blade snapped in half on contact. "Please stop, litte man," Natas said. "Take your defeat like a true soldier."

Without another word, Natas slammed Slaycick head first in the pavement, breaking several bones in his face. He stomped the speedster in his back, pounding him into the concrete.

"You will suffer the same fate you gave me," Natas said as he lifted Slaycick's own sword high into the air over his body.

"Stop!" Tenan screamed in the distance. Natas paused and turned in his direction. "You've won, Natas," Tenan said. He removed his belt with his guns attached to it and dropped it, then raised both hands in the air. "I'll surrender if you spare my friends. But, if you kill him, I'll disappear into a portal and you'll never see me again."

Natas looked down at the injured speedster and plunged the sword into the concrete next to him. "It's a deal," Natas said smiling.

"Let him go too," Tenan demanded, eyeing Blessed.

"That's a negative, Portal Dweller. You're clever. If I let him go, what's to stop you from trying to send me back into space? This guy right here," Natas said as he lifted Blessed's body above his head with the one hand. "This guy is insurance. That way, if you try one of your tricks, he's coming with me."

Tenan slowly approached Natas, and the Giants with his hands raised up. "What is it that you want from me anyway?" Tenan asked.

"Your gift is the gateway to heaven and hell, Portal Dweller," Natas said. "You're going to help me to bring hell on Earth and to wage a new war in Heaven."

"How is that even possible?" Tenan asked.

"Oh, it's very possible," Natas replied, smirking devilishly. "I've been searching for you Portal Dwellers for centuries. The last one I nearly had in my grasp, but I had to kill him, and he became something else. Something else that has been helping you."

Tenan looked up at Natas in a confused state as they were now standing just a few steps away from each other. He pondered his words for a moment, and then the revelation hit him. "Titus," Tenan said as if he had solved a piece to a puzzle.

"I can tell from the look on your face that he never told you, did he?" Natas asked. Tenan remained silent. "He and I fought during the Persian war in the days of Daniel the prophet. I allowed my temper to get the best of me. I murdered the one person who I needed the most to bring about my plan. Now, here we are, thousands of years later, and I will not make the same mistake. Why? Because the lives of your friends depend on it."

Suddenly, a vision crossed Tenan's mind. A lake of fire and brimstone, along with countless armies of demons, filled his gaze. In the darkness of his natural eyes, he considered a plan: opening up two portals under the giants as he did back in Syria, but it was risky. He knew that Natas would definitely kill Blessed if he did. Natas' remarks about opening portals to both heaven and hell rang true in his mind's eye. *It could work*, Tenan thought to himself.

At that moment, he knew what had to be done. His previous trials with portal jumping and losing his sight had prepared him for this very moment. And he was ready. He had already accessed the heavenly realm, but he hadn't ever considered opening a portal to the depths of hell. As the vision played out in his mind, it finally faded and smile bloomed across his face.

"So be it," Tenan said confidently. "But please, allow me but one moment before I surrender. You will have what you wish for."

Tenan looked over to his right and opened a portal. He could see Menzuo was holding a weakened Havoc by the neck.

"Speak!" Menzuo yelled at the Pirate Warrior. "What is going on in the outer realm?!"

"Death," Havoc replied.

At that moment, Menzuo looked up and saw Tenan through the open portal. "Blessed!" he gasped.

"A little help, please," Tenan said as he smiled faintly. "Like, now."

Before the Giants could react, Menzuo released Havoc and flew speedily through the portal followed by Desmurose and Allucio, screaming, "Sensing Densor!"

The Giants froze abruptly, unable to move as the attack rendered them immobile. Tenan closed the portal behind the Twin Powers.

"Quick, Allucio, grab Blessed," Tenan said as he pointed at Natas.

Allucio swiftly flew over and pried Blessed from Natas' hand and flew him away to a safe location. A frozen mist enveloped all three giants, as Arctic – still under Rekluse's mind control – turned them all into blocks of ice. When she was finished, Rekluse chopped her in the back of the neck, knocking her unconscious.

Allucio flew by her side. "Out cold!" he laughed. "Pardon the pun." Rekluse glared at him and then rolled her eyes.

The two of them joined Tenan as he approached the three ice blocks. Rekluse, Kasitia, Menzuo, and Desmurose lagged behind them.

"Thank you," Kasitia said as she gently touched Allucio's shoulder. "You three have helped us save this city."

"For the time being," said Allucio. "Unfortunately, there's more coming."

"And when they come, we'll send them right to the hell that they belong in," Tenan said. He closed his eyes and after a few seconds, three portals opened up underneath the three giant blocks of ice. A gruesome and chilling noise of souls wailing in agony could be heard screaming and yelling from depth of the portals. The three giants plunged through the portals as billows of steam and smoke escaped. The portal closed and the cries silenced.

Everyone stood in silence until Allucio broke the ice with a question. "Wait a minute, everyone thinking what I'm thinking? Did you just, send them to –"

"Yes," Tenan replied cutting him off. "And there's no coming back from that. Come, we must check on the others."

"Wow!" Allucio continued. "And you sent them there in a block of ice. That's some irony for your ass. Remind me to stay on your good side, Tenan. Sheeeesh!"

Kasitia looked over at Arctic. "What is your plan with her?" Kasitia asked Rekluse.

"I'm not sure yet," Rekluse replied, looking at the young teen, laying unconscious on the street. "I wiped her memory of tonight's events. She's still a child, and we already put down two of her friends. I'm thinking of showing this one some mercy. Some mentoring might be in order."

"Sounds like a plan to me," Kasitia said.

Menzuo walked over to Slaycick and picked him up slowly.

"Careful with him" Tenan said. "His spine is fractured. When Blessed comes to, he can help heal him."

Menzuo nodded and gently lifted Slaycick in his arms, while Desmurose flew over to Paraflyte. "Is he one of ours?" Desmurose asked.

"Yes," Tenan said as he opened another portal.

Desmurose draped Paraflyte over his shoulder and helped him up from the street. A few seconds later, K'nia emerged from the store's broken window, clearing glass from her body and hair.

"K'nia!" yelled Kasitia as she ran over to hug her sister. "Are you okay?"

"Yeah, sis. Are you?" K'nia asked.

"Yeah, a little banged up, but I'm fine," Kasitia replied.

"Everyone's accounted for," Tenan said as he opened a portal.

Several E.I.E.s zoomed in to get a closer look at the heroes. "That's going to make for one hell of an episode," Lydia said, joining them on the street.

"Popcorn ready?" Allucio joked.

Several more cop cars arrived on the scene and approached The Majesties. Tenan stepped forward.

"I recognize you," one of the officers said as he quickly scanned the group and gazed in awe at Tenan. "Are you alright?"

"I am, but several members of my team are hurt really bad. I need to get them back to headquarters," Tenan said.

"Headquarters?" the cop asked. "Don't you mean a hospital?"

"We got it covered," Tenan said as he patted the cop on the shoulder. "What's your name?"

"Will. Officer Will Haggert," the cop replied.

"Nice to meet you, Officer Haggert. I'm Tenan. Tell your commanding officer I'll be down to the station to give a statement soon as we get situated. We'll be back to help with the city clean up."

"No need, sir. You're heroes. This city owes you a debt of gratitude," Haggert said.

"Thanks. The threat that terrorized your beloved Hero City has been eliminated, but there will be more on the way," Tenan said.

Before the officer could respond, Tenan and the heroes, along with Lydia, stepped into the portal and vanished as it closed behind them.

CHAPTER 24

BLITZ

"I'm not laughing!" Thief screamed as Paladin continually mocked him, pointing at his face.

"Come on, big baby, it's just a little motion sickness," Paladin said, helmet retracted, wearing a wide smile across his face, as the USS Overdrive broke from the Speed-Stream and cruised at a respectable pace.

Stars finally became more visible in real-time as they streaked through space, a far departure from the continual of white bands of light contrasting against deep darkness of space. The entire trip lasted for roughly about five minutes or so – at least that's what Zenith said – but felt like only seconds to Thief and Paladin as Blurr dragged their vessel behind her, leaving only space and time in her wake.

"How's she doing anyway?" Thief asked Paladin.

Paladin leaned forward in his chair and analyzed the large overhead monitor. Numbers burned in the top right corner as multiple lines with jagged bumps and dips danced across the center. "Vitals are holding steady," he said finally.

"Great," Thief said. "How long until we arrive?"

Paladin shrugged, and then his eyes beat over to the empty voice before them. "Not sure, but I'd wager that we're getting close."

A single red spec materialized before them, growing larger as they continued to advance. "We're here," Zenith said, before vanishing.

He reappeared out front, next to Blurr, and motioned with his hands towards the ship. In a flash, both he and Blurr were transported back inside. Paladin jumped from his chair and ran over to her. He helped her remove her space helmet and gave her a hug. He pulled back and planted a soft kiss upon her lips. "You're freezing," he said as he pulled back.

Blurr seemed unfazed by the decrease in temperature. “Oh really? I hadn’t noticed. Wait a minute.” Blurr stepped back and began to shiver, her entire body a mere shadow of itself. When she finished, she reached out for Paladin’s hand again. “Better?”

Paladin pulled back and rubbed his hands together. “Man, you’re burning up. I can feel the heat even through our gloves.”

“Sorry, babe,” she said.

“You made it,” Thief said, over Paladin’s shoulder. “Good to see you in one piece.”

“Good to see you, too,” Blurr said.

Paladin nodded her over to the cockpit. “Come check out your handywork. It’s kinda beautiful.”

“What, you didn’t think I had a good enough view from out there?” she joked.

“Point taken,” Paladin said, as the red planet continued to zoom into view. “It’s just…I think it’s really cool, you know?”

Paladin sat in the command chair and Thief took the seat next to him. Blurr remained standing, gazing out at the planet in a daze. Paladin made a few final checks on the forward console and prepped for landing. “I’m picking up initial space log reading scans from the Overdrive. Ambient temperature…oxygen, nitrogen, argon and carbon dioxide. This is crazy.”

“What?” Thief asked.

“The atmosphere has the same molecular makeup of the gases back on Earth,” Paladin said. “Honey, check this out.” Blurr remained silent, preoccupied by the planet. “Honey, you okay?”

Finally, she turned to look at him. “Yeah, I’m just…enjoying the view.” Paladin nodded.

“Final preparations on tap. A couple of wind storms are in the atmosphere. We’ll have a little chop on our way down,” Thief announced. “All personnel, get ready for some turbulence.” He looked over to Zenith, who stood motionless, unaffected by his words. “Well, all except you.”

The USS Overdrive dropped out of space and pierced the planet's atmosphere. Lightning storms lit the sky as thunder clapped. The ship shook vigorously but held together. "I'm scanning for a flat area to bring her down. Hold on," Paladin said as he gripped the cyclic in his hand. Moments later, the ship was skimming the surface on a vector for a wide patch of flat grassland just a few hundred yards away.

"She's a beauty," Thief said, observing the lush vegetation of the alien world.

As the Overdrive decreased speed, Paladin dropped the landing gear, and the ship hovered momentarily and then finally touched down, safe. "Debark," he said.

Thief exited first, followed by Paladin, while Blurr lagged behind walking slowly. "You feel it too, don't you?" Zenith asked her.

Blurr shook her head and left Zenith inside to join the others. Paladin held out a small device and waved it from side to side, still taking a final analysis of the planet. "It's red. Everything's red," Blurr said as she knelt down to touch the ground. "Trees, grass, and even the ocean we fly over. All red."

"Yeah, there's a ton of iron deposits all around us, deep in the soil," Paladin said.

"No wonder the vegetation is taking on such a red hue. Probably a ton of it in the water as well," Thief added. He looked back at the Overdrive. "What's up with old blue? Not going to join us?"

Paladin turned in Zeniths's direction. "Zenith. This is the place, right?"

"I led the Conduit here, didn't I?" Zenith asked, sounding somewhat annoyed.

"So where's the welcoming committee?" Thief asked.

"Come on down and join us," Paladin yelled at Zenith.

"I cannot do anything else. You have what you need. Time will fulfill itself soon enough," Zenith said. The hatch to the Overdrive slammed shut, erasing Zenith from the group's view.

"Well, can't say I wasn't waiting for it," Thief said.

Paladin folded the small device in half and slid it into a small compartment on his utility belt. "For sure." He looked over to Blurr, who seemed distant, staring into the horizon. "Babe, you okay?"

"This way," Blurr said, pointing off in the opposite direction. "It's this way."

"What is?" Paladin asked. Blurr assumed a running position and in a flash, sped off out of sight. "Wait!" Paladin changed to his speed variant, and he Thief zoomed after her as the red horizon churned up clouds of crimson-colored dust in Blurr's wake. If not for the S4's infrared HUD and navigational display, Paladin could have easily been lost, missing any chance to keep up with Blurr. As the group rounded a large mountainside, Blurr banked left and proceeded to climb the tall mountain as the others followed. When she finally reached the top, the hilly terrain finally leveled off, revealing a flat plain with a large crater in the center. Heat could be felt emanating from the center.

Paladin pulled up short of falling in as he hit the brakes. "A volcano?"

Thief floated in next to him. "Looks like it." He whipped his head in Blurr's direction. "What gives, little lady?"

Blurr turned to the both of them, her eyes were stark white. "Karla?" Paladin said.

Before she could answer, a loud rumbling interrupted her as an explosion of lava launched into the sky from the crater. Paladin dove sideways and cradled Blurr, activating his strength variant, just as the lava dropped groundward and splashed against his suit. He stood over her and protected her body from the remaining lava trails. When the shower of red fluid finally stopped, he helped her to her feet. "What's going on with you, babe?"

Blurr pointed behind him. "There!"

Standing before them was an angelic-looking being, hovering above the crater. A shirtless male – from what they could make of it – was about three times their height, with muscles that rippled along his chest, shoulders and arms. A black skirt was swagged around his waist, and a crown of red tassels and leaves adorned his head. Thief took a defensive position in front of Paladin and Blurr. "There's your committee," he said.

"Who are you, who invades our planet?" the being asked. His voice bellowed like the sound of heavy thunder.

Paladin spoke up. "We don't mean you any harm. We're here for something. An object of great power, artifact."

"And what would you be in need of such an artifact for?" the being asked.

"It is to control a wicked substance that threatens to destroy our world. A Dark Spore mist," Paladin replied.

"Ah, the mist has arrived at your planet. What universe?" the being asked.

"Um, it's, um," Thief tried to speak, but suddenly experienced a brain fart. "Anyone know what universe we are from?"

Blurr stepped forward. "Who are you?"

"My name is Terez," he said. His eyes narrowed at her. "Your eyes. You have the sight. Are you not from the same world?"

"I am. These are my friends. We are in need of that artifact. Please help us," Blurr said.

"You come to my planet, asking for items you shalt not understand. And what do you have to offer in return?" Terez asked.

"The mist. You know what it is?" Paladin asked.

"Everyone knows what the mist is, but the real question is, what is it used for?" Terez asked.

Thief shook his head. "Too many questions, and honestly, I'm getting bored. We don't have time for the back and forth, chit-chat buddy," Thief said. "So either you know where the artifact is and can give it to us, or you don't."

"Thief!" Paladin yelled.

"Naw, forget that," Thief said as he approached Terez. He pointed at him. "Now look, I don't care what the Dark Spore mist is for, or quite frankly who you are. The Traveler's left something behind for us, and we need to get collecting. So you gonna to help us or what?"

Terez shook his head and folded his arms across his chest. “So disrespectful.” He held out his hand and instantly, an image of the same knife that Titan wielded back in Hero City materialized.

“It’s the knife!” Blurr said. “Are there two?”

“No, there is only one,” Terez said. “One for each plane of time. And if you want this one, you must deem yourself worthy of it. You’ll have to fight me! But that would be a big mistake as none of you are strong enough to match me.”

Thief cracked his knuckles and rolled his neck. “Funny you should say that.”

“Alice!” Paladin shouted, but before he could stop him, Thief took off headed towards the giant. He landed a punch to Terez’s face that knocked him back one step, but he maintained his position, still floating.

“Now, give me the damn knife!” Thief demanded.

Terez smiled and winked at him. “My turn.” Terez bolted towards Thief and landed a punch square in his chest. Thief flew backward so fast that Paladin couldn’t even track him. All he could do was follow the sound of trees ripping apart to know his relative position, some three hundred yards away. Terez straightened and tossed the knife up and down in his hand. “Next.”

Paladin’s blood boiled. “If you insist.” Paladin activated the strength variant, and the S4 ballooned into the size of Terez in a snap. He leaped at Terez and grabbed him by the shoulders, landing back on the ground. Paladin spun around on one foot three or four times before slamming Terez into the ground. He stood over him and raised his foot, intent on stomping him. Before he could, Terez sprung back to life and kicked Paladin in the chest, launching him up into the sky about a hundred feet.

Paladin switched to speed mode and zipped back towards Terez before he could stand and slipped into stealth mode. Terez’s gaze fixed on no place in particular, but just as Paladin closed in to attack, Terez popped up and delivered a roundhouse kick that hit its mark on Paladin’s armor. If not for the intuitive sensing upgrade of the S4, changing him back into strength mode, he would have never survived such a blow. As it was, Paladin stood his ground, catching Terez by the leg and delivering an elbow to the Terez's knee.

Terez released a blood-curdling scream that made Paladin release his grip in an attempt to cover his ears. Terez spun around on one hand and foot, before kicking once more and landing another kick on Paladin. This time, he couldn't block it. Paladin launched into the giant crater as an explosion of hot lava filled the sky.

"No!" Blurr yelled.

Thief collided with Terez and quickly raced into the sky. The two exchange a flurry of blows and kicks, with occasional blocks and counter punches that made loud noises similar to those in the thunderous skies. As they continued to climb into the atmosphere, power surged through Thief's body, but it wasn't coming from Terez. *Where is this coming from?* Thief thought as his punches seemed to only get stronger as the fight waned on.

Blurr ran to the edge of the crater and peered inside, looking for Paladin. "Sebastian, where are you?" she screamed, frantic. The ground burst open behind her and Paladin emerged.

His body was flaming red and on fire. "I'm fine, baby," he said. As Blurr instinctively leaned in to touch him, he stepped back. "No, it's dangerous. Stand back." Blurr took his cue and held her ground. Paladin looked up in the direction of Thief and Terez, noting that they were still engaged in fisticuffs. "I'll be back!"

Paladin engaged the speed variant and peeled into the sky. In seconds he had joined the fray, switching back and forth from speed to strength, assisting Thief in delivering blows to Terez that jarred him, keeping him on the defensive and quelled his ability to attack.

Finally, Thief slipped behind Terez and weaved his arms through Terez's, holding him in place while Paladin delivered punches to Terez's face, chest and stomach at lightning speed, even though he was mainly using his strength variant. "Yield!" Thief screamed. "Yield I say, yield!"

Finally, Terez managed to answer; a loud cackle that sent a wave of chills down Paladin's spine. "What's…so…funny?" Paladin asked in between blows.

"You really think you've won," Terez said.

In a blink of an eye, Terez slipped from Thief's grasp and floated just above the two of them. He extended his arms – fingers splayed to his side – and slammed his hands together. The final sound of thunder shattered the sky, drowning out any and everything around it. A large sound wave enveloped Thief and Paladin, sending them hurling back toward the mountain. They both crashed into the ground, forging personal craters of their own. Blurr came to Paladin's side. "Sebas? Sebas, are you there?"

Terez appeared behind her, still laughing. "Leave him, Conduit. He's pathetic and frail. Him and his friend. I knew the blue one was trying to drain my powers, and I gave him all he could handle. It was a cute fight, but nothing I couldn't handle. But they are still human. Not immortal…not like me…not like you."

Blurr stood. "What?" she groaned. Tears trailed from her eyes.

"You know your purpose, your…destiny. It is not with him or those feeble humans you call family. It is with me. With us. The Traveler's knew it, and that's why they sent you here." He offered her a hand. "Now, join me."

Blurr's hands fisted at her sides. The tears that stained her cheeks quickly evaporated. Her hair swirled wildly as hurricane-force winds swirled around her, and her eyes filled with lightning. "Leave…my…man…alone!"

Before Terez could react, Blurr attacked, pummeling Terez with a series of kicks that knocked the wind out of the giant. With each successive blow, Terez tried to counter, blocking only those aimed for his face. But Blurr was getting faster, connecting with his body as she landed dangerously closer to Terez's face.

"You mustn't," Terez gasped.

"No! Indeed I shall!" Blurr said. She moved so fast that she began to phase in and out of sight, making it impossible for Terez to hit her. With two final attacks, Blurr slammed her heel into Terez's stomach and then uppercut him underneath his jaw.

Terez spiraled out of control and whirled to the ground on all fours. He held up a hand to her. "I yield!"

Blurr stood over him. “Oh no…it’s too late for that.” She lifted Terez overhead with one hand, holding him by the neck. Blood dripped from the corner of his mouth. “And now I…will…finish you!”

Blurr cocked back with her free hand, but before she could swing, everything went black.

CHAPTER 25

A TIME TO HEAL

"The giants have suffered a most unredeemable defeat," General Swadin said as he walked next to Judge Amaruk. The two extraterrestrials strolled invisibly among the carnage of Hero City as firemen, police officers, and paramedics scurried to fulfill their duties in the wake of disaster.

"They have, and it was the very reason we allowed them to wage war on those with abilities first," Judge Amaruk said. "It is important that we first know the enemy before we engage. The Giants' overzealous assumptions that they would overpower their enemies served as our opportunity to gauge our potential opposition. Now we know what we're up against."

"And we should strike now, sir!" General Swadin exclaimed excitedly. "They are injured. Yes, the Giants lost but not before severely weakening the champions of Earth. We can take them."

"In due time, General Swadin. We can, but now is not the appropriate time. We are going to train up our army, build our numbers, and teach them all the secrets to the sorcery, alchemy, science, and magic that the Necromenian culture was built upon. Stratus and the World Harvesters may have destroyed our planet, but we will be rulers of the galaxy. As my top general, I will also teach you things that I have learned. You will increase in power too."

"I'm humbled, sir. Forgive me of my impulsive nature. You are correct in your approach."

"No need to apologize, General Swadin. Your passion is appreciated and needed. We still have much to learn about our potential opponents on Earth. They have allied themselves with powerful warriors from within this universe who are not to be taken lightly. These heroes have something much more powerful than Oramite or Sinathyst. They possess a strong will, and that will is what defeated the Giants. Not weapons! It's not to be underestimated. Perhaps coming against them right away as an enemy is not the solution."

"What do you mean?"

Judge Armaruk folded his arms behind his back and sighed heavily. "I mean there are other ways to bring the champions of this planet under our agenda. War it seems is most likely imminent, but we don't have to blitz them just yet. Some of them possess unique gifts that we can use to our advantage. They just need a little coaxing. Then we'll wind them up and point them in the right direction," Judge Amaruk said, smiling. "In the meantime, let's get back to the ship. I want to begin training our army. I have numerous ideas I want to put into action."

Judge Amaruk extended a hand to General Swadin. He took it and Judge Amaruk lifted into the sky, bringing Swadin with him as they sailed effortlessly to their vessel that hovered thousands of feet above, quiet, inconspicuous, and out of sight.

***

The Majesties stepped out of the portal and right into the living room quarters of The Beacon. Allucio slowly lowered Blessed's large frame onto the sofa. Desmurose and Menzuo placed Paraflyte and Slaycick on the floor next to him. Rekluse, who had been carrying Arctic, placed her on the floor close by and took a seat. Battered and badly bruised, the heroes each found a place to sit and gathered themselves. As they rested, Aganathin walked in.

"Aganathin!" Kasitia shouted as she raised to her feet while the others stood with her. "How are you feeling?"

"Renewed," Aganathin said with a look of apprehension sprayed across his face. He studied his left arm for a few seconds. "How was this possible?"

The room remained quiet for a few awkward moments before Tenan spoke up. "Blessed summoned a familiar acquaintance," Tenan said, pointing to Paraflyte, who was still lying motionless on the ground. "He removed Oramite from his body in the same fashion that he used to produce Oramite weapons. Instead, this time he used it for a greater good." Tenan pointed at Aganathin's new arm.

"Blessed was able to fuse the Oramite to your shoulder," K'nia said. "It was really weird and cool at the same time. The Oramite formed into your new arm, as if it knew what to do."

Aganathin's eyes bounced slowly across each of his team member's faces and then back to his arm. He waved it back and forth a few times, winding it forward and back.

"How does it feel?" Tenan asked.

"Surprisingly good. Like it's always been a part of me," Aganathin answered. "But I feel like there's something else to it."

"Hmmm. Maybe it's just a matter of your nerve endings getting used to the Oramite as an attachment," Tenan replied.

"Perhaps," Aganathin replied. "But it feels like it's more than that. It's like it's formed a unique with my body."

At that moment, Blessed began to stir on the sofa. He mumbled a few words that nobody could understand as he was coming out of his unconscious state.

"Easy, big fella," Allucio said as Blessed tried to sit up. "We got you."

Blessed wiped his eyes as Allucio put his hand behind his back to hold him steady. Blessed looked around the room as his eyesight came into focus. His eyes brightened as he was met by a smiling Aganathin standing before him.

"Aganathin, how are you, friend?" Blessed asked faintly.

"I'm good," Aganathin replied. "I'm a little upset that my team went into battle without me, but outside of that, I'll be okay."

Blessed nodded and scanned the room a few more times. He noticed Paraflyte and Slaycick lying on the floor. A look of concern splashed across his face as he eyed Arctic; the wintry villain lying on the floor a few feet away.

"What happened to the Giants?" Blessed asked as he rubbed his hand across his bald head and then his face.

"They're gone for good, Blessed," Tenan replied.

"Are we sure?" Blessed asked skeptically.

"Unless there's a way out of hell, I'm pretty sure they're gone," Allucio said.

Tenan smirked slightly. "Trust me, boss. They're gone for good, but I'm afraid Natas and the Giants were just the first wave of attacks. Whoever or whatever repaired him is still out there. And they're coming."

"Are you able to see who it is, baby?" Rekluse asked.

"Hardly," Tenan said. "There is some kind of magic or spell that's keeping me from seeing them completely, but I know they're here."

"And we don't stand a chance against them if we don't have our full compliment of soldiers," Blessed said as he stood up from the couch, stumbling a bit. He straightened and walked over to Slaycick, who was lying face down on the floor. Blessed moved his hand slowly behind Slaycick's head, then down his neck until he reached his back. When his hand stopped, Blessed closed his eyes.

The broken bones in Slaycick's back instantly realigned and fused back together. Blessed turned him over and put his hand over Slaycick's face. Slaycick's swollen face began to shrink as the broken bones in his jaw, and nasal cavity repaired instantly. After a few seconds, Slaycick gasped and sat straight up, breathing heavily.

"It's okay! It's okay! It's okay, Slaycick!" Blessed said, trying to calm his friend down. "It's me, Blessed. You're safe."

Slaycick looked around the room, slowly taking in his team standing around him. In a sigh of relief, he sunk back to the floor, sliding his hands over his face. "Oh my God," Slaycick said. "What the hell? Did we win? Somebody, please tell me we won."

"We're okay for now, friend," Blessed said as he made his way over to Paraflyte. He touched Paraflyte's collar and his masked dissolved, exposing his head. Blessed placed his hand on Paraflyte's head, and after a few moments, the flying Russian was coherent. He woke up groggily.

"Move slowly," Blessed said. "We've been through a lot tonight. Let your bodies recover."

Blessed looked at the young Latina teenager lying on the ground. He studied her for a while.

"What's she doing here?" Blessed asked. "This is the one who severly injured Aganathin, and she lies here? Alive? Why?"

"I made the call," Rekluse said. "Trust me, I'm hardly one to show mercy to my enemies, but…this one…this one reminds me of myself when I was her age; rebellious, reckless, and out to hurt anyone who got in my way. But through the counsel of a mentor who became a big sister to me, I was restored and rehabilitated emotionally, mentally, and spiritually. I figure I can do the same with this one."

Blessed sighed as he considered Rekluse's words. He looked at Aganathin who simply raised his eyebrows and shrugged; deferring that the decision was Blessed's decision to make.

"I think that is something you and Aganathin should discuss, Rekluse," Blessed said. "I know I made a decision earlier without consulting the team and regardless of how things worked out, that was wrong of me. I don't want that to become a norm amongst the team. I apologize to you all for making a unilateral decision. As your leader, I will make a point to not let that be a habit."

"Brother, it's not easy to lead," Aganathin said as he placed his hand on Blessed's shoulder. "Especially in a time like this. Sometimes when you're in charge, unilateral decisions have to be made. You made the tough call and because of it, I have a new arm. We love you and your leadership, boss. If it's alright with you, then it's alright with me."

"Thank you, brother," Blessed said to Aganathin and then focused his attention back to Rekluse. "Okay. Keep a close eye on her. I would bind her up if I were you. When she comes to, you need to have a heart to heart with her. If she's cooperative and willing to submit herself under our leadership, then we'll take it on a day-by-day basis. But, if she gets out of line Rekluse, I won't hesitate to put her down. She's your responsibility."

"Understood," Rekluse replied.

"Blessed, if I can say something," Tenan interjected. "Before we get on with our night, I wanted to acknowledge that we could not have defeated Natas and the Giants tonight without these three young men. Menzuo, Allucio, and Desmurose, thank you for responding to our call for help. Natas and the Giants had the drop on us until you showed up."

"It was our pleasure," Menzuo said. "But I've been meaning to ask you. How did you know where to find us?"

Tenan smiled and said, "The best way for me to describe it is like an internal tracking device. If I've made contact with you, been in the room with you before, or been near you, then I can find you. It's like an animal with a keen sense of smell tracking his master or herd; except I'm using a different sense. One not associated with sight, smell, touch or taste. It's something within the spirit that I've tapped into. Once I've locked in on my target or destination, that sense allows me to open portals wherever my targets are. That's how I was able to find you on the moon. My portals override time and distance, allowing me to go anywhere I want at any time."

"That's a freakish gift," Desmurose said. "I'm jealous."

"Tonight, you sent those Giants to the depths of hell…literally," Allucio said. "I'm just curious. Are you able to open portals to heaven?"

Tenan looked up at Allucio, showing his all white pupils. "At a cost," he said.

Allucio nodded and smiled.

"Thank you to all three of you," Blessed said. "We are in debted to you, Menzuo, Allucio, and Desmurose. We may have underestimated you because of your youth. That will never be the case moving forward as we fight together to save this world. God has placed us in this fate together for a reason."

"He's right," said Kasitia. "Our coming together is imperative and for the purpose of defeating any evil that's upon us."

"Thank you mighty warriors," Aganathin said.

"We appreciate you," Slaycick chimed in beating his chest with his fist. "Much respect."

"We haven't met," Paraflyte said. "But I'm sure we'll get acquainted. Thank you for aiding us."

The three nodded and accepted the Majesties' gratitude.

"Listen you all," Blessed said. "Tonight has taken a lot out of us; nearly to the point of death. Let's rest while we can. For tomorrow brings a new reckoning. Lydia, please let me know when you hear from Paladin and the rest of the team."

"Will do, Blessed," she said.

The heroes dispersed to different parts of The Beacon; finding a spot to stretch out so they could shut their eyes for a short time. Lydia spotted Tenan and Rekluse heading out to the patio and followed them out.

"What about Thief, Paladin, and Blurr?" Lydia asked as she closed the patio's balcony door behind her. Tenan and Rekluse turned around. "Can you locate them?"

Tenan looked at Rekluse and rubbed his chin. She nodded and smiled.

"I can try," he said.

He closed his eyes and began to travel throughout his mind, locating millions of galaxies and planets. He saw life forms of many kinds as he tried to trace the whereabouts of the three heroes. Moments later, he opened them.

"You have something?" Lydia asked.

He turned in Lydia's direction. "I found them. They're in great danger…and something has happened."

CHAPTER 26

FATE OF THE UNIVERSAL PROTECTOR

As the Majesties found places to rest within The Beacon, Menzuo, Allucio and Desmurose made their way back to the second floor, to Lydia's empty laboratory. They needed time to discuss their mission on Earth's moon and also the calling back to Earth to help the Majesties defeat their opponents in battle.

"Man, I'm glad we got back in time to help the Majesties defeat those Giants," Desmurose said.

"Did you see how freaking huge they were?" Allucio added. "And that one that had Blessed by the head. He was holding him like he was about to squish it like a grape."

"That was insane!" Desmurose said.

"But Tenan…he sent them straight to H-E-double hockey sticks. Hell, man…hell! He has access to Hades!"

"That's creepy as hell, no pun intended. We're lucky he's on our side," Desmurose added.

"Trust me, I know first hand how it feels to travel through one of those portals unexpectedly," Allucio said. "At least he just put me in a fish tank and not the burning depths of the underworld."

The Twin Powers shared a laugh and then looked over to Menzuo, noticing he was deep in thought and not engaging in the conversation. "You good, Menzuo?" Allucio asked.

Menzuo placed his hand on his chin and shook his head. "I'm not sure. I can't get what Havoc was saying to me during our battle out of my head."

"What did he say?" Desmurose asked.

"Havoc kept saying that I had choices," Menzuo said. "My choices would have consequences. Major consequences."

"Every choice has consequences, bro. Did he elaborate on those choices?" Desmuorse asked.

Menzuo nodded. "Yes he did. When I asked him what choice I had, he said death. After that, Tenan opened his portal and the rest is history. I didn't have time to get anything else out of him."

"Those Pirates are crazy," Allucio said. "Always with the damn riddles. Why can't they just be straight forward with the information?"

"Because if they were, we would be overly prepared to face them," Menzuo replied. "There is always strategy when it comes to war."

"Well, I can tell you guys this much. This is just the beginning of our war," Desmurose added.

Just as Menzuo took in a deep breath, an immense surge of painful energy flushed through his body and flooded his mind. It was so powerful that his eyes began to glow. The wave of energy lifted his cape.

"Menzuo!" the voice of Solar bellowed through his mind.

"Something is wrong!" Menzuo screamed.

Allucio and Desmurose moved closer to their best friend. "What the heck was that?" Allucio asked. "Whatever you felt, I felt it too."

"I did too, and it wasn't good!" Desmurose added.

Menzuo started to breathe heavily. "Grab my hands. We have to connect with Solar!" Menzuo ran out of the room and out to the balcony with his friends close behind. "Concentrate, we have to do this quickly. Something is really off on our home planet."

"Dammit! Was there an attack?" Allucio asked.

"We're about to find out!" Menzuo said. "Close your eyes, fellas. Here we go!"

Within seconds, the energy from Menzuo, Allucio and Desmurose instantly shifted to the outer realm of the universe, following the path to Solar's energy. Their minds converged to Menzuo's hidden training realm. In the distance, the three warriors could see a man kneeling with blood flowing from his mouth. "It's Solar!" Desmurose shouted.

“What the hell happened?” Menzuo said as he and his friends appeared right next to Solar.

“Lord Fetid happened,” Solar replied. “He…he came to planet Yardania and…he…”

Menzuo placed his hand onto Solar’s shoulder. “Relax, brother. Control your breathing and tell us what happened.”

As Solar shook his head in disbelief, an injured Master Renzfly appeared within the training realm and came crawling into view. Men…Prince Menzuo…it’s all bad.”

The shock on Menzuo’s face was apparent. He remained with Solar as Allucio and Desmurose ran over to Master Renzfly’s side. “How did Lord Fetid get onto Yardania? I didn’t know that he was strong enough to leave Excervo. How was that possible?” Desmurose asked.

“That monster was way too powerful for anyone of us to stop,” Master Renzfly said as he tried to stand. His legs were too weak to hold his balance. “We tried our best to stop him, but his strength couldn’t be matched. He…he killed most of the elite guards that protected the castle, and he…he…he…my God!”

Menzuo stood, looking directly in Master Renzfly’s direction. He began to hyperventilate as the news poured in. The fear within his soul was bubbling to the surface. “What did he do, Master?”

Solar grabbed hold of Menzuo’s leg as the tears ran down his cheeks. “He’s taken Prince Denshuo.”

Menzuo’s heart dropped into his stomach. “No, no, no! Our little brother, but why?”

“But there’s more,” Solar said.

Menzuo couldn’t work up the nerve to ask, so he waited for either Solar or Master Renzfly to respond. Master Renfly finally made it to his feet and spoke. “I am sorry, Menzuo, your father…”

“Is he?” Menzuo couldn’t finish his question.

“Lord Fetid overpowered everyone and the King tried to stop him but was not successful,” Master Renfly said.

Solar finally stood too. "If it wasn't for Master Renzfly, our father would be dead."

"So he's alive?" Menzuo asked as he felt the life re-enter his body. However, it was short-lived as he looked his brother in the eyes. He could see the extreme sorrow that filled him.

Solar shook his head. "We're not sure if he will live, Menzuo. His energy is fading quickly."

"Please no!" Menzuo said as he dropped to his knees.

"Oh no!" Desmurose said. "How could this be happening?"

"This war has stretched throughout the universe!" Allucio added. "There is so much evil invading our galaxy."

Menzuo closed his eyes. He was replaying thoughts of his battle with Havoc on the moon. "Choices. This is what Havoc meant by the choices that I had to make. I chose wrong! I failed my home…I failed my father…and now… now I've failed this universe because I chose poorly!"

The thoughts of Lord Fetid taking his brother and losing his father completely flooded the young Prince's mind. As his muscles tensed, one thought ripped through him. "Mother," he whispered. "What about Queen Onnualla? Is she safe?"

"There Queen was not harmed," Master Renzfly said. "But the events of the day have left her in a catatonic state. She was last seen sitting in Prince Denshuo's room, not able to move or speak. This has really hit her hard."

Menzuo sunk deeper within the pain that filled him. "I chose wrong. How could this happen?"

"Prince Menzuo," Solar said as he clutched his ribs. "The choices you have to make as the Universal Protector are not easy, and no choice will ever be perfect. We know that you made the best choice for the safety of the universe, but you were given an impossible task."

"You didn't know of the full threat to the outer realm, but you knew what was coming to planet Earth," Master Renzfly followed. "The choice to fight the threats to planet Earth – those who would attempt to secure the Energy of all 'Good and Evil – must always be your primary focus."

"But not at the expense of losing my home planet, my brother, my birth parents or my friends," Menzuo replied. "How can I choose a fate like that?"

"As the Universal Protector, your choices will not please everyone. Today, the consequences have been dire," Master Renzfly answered. "Heavy is the head that the crown lays."

Menzuo's head dropped, overwhelmed by thoughts of failure. "I've lost our brother, Solar…and our father and mother…the King and Queen of Yardania. I have let them both down."

Solar took Menzuo by the head and then rested his forehead on his. "We will figure this out…together."

Menzuo shook his head, trying his best to figure out a solution. He slowly pushed back from Solar, holding his hand to maintain his balance. "Did Lord Fetid share anything of importance?"

Master Renzfly nodded. "He sure did."

"Of course he did," Allucio added. "Another open-ended freaking riddle. Like I said before, every Pirate Warrior loves to talk, especially the Lord."

Master Renzfly continued. "Before Lord Fetid left with Prince Denshuo, he stood over us and shared the return of his lost son. A Pirate who he left for dead in another galaxy. He said that his lost son was the insurance package he created through death, and if he were ever to be resurrected, his return to our universe would be epic. He would evolve into something with enormous amounts of power."

"Would that Pirate go by the name of Stratus?" Desmurose asked.

"Yes, that was the name that he mentioned," Master Renzfly said. "Lord Fetid said that this Pirate would be the key to destroying all life and also our fearless Universal Protector. His son would do this so that he could become the almighty ruler of this universe. The last piece to Lord Fetid's puzzle would be the life of a Yardanian Prince, and young Prince Denshuo was the final key."

"So Havoc was just a distraction," Menzuo said.

"A partial distraction, but definitely a messenger for you and for his son," Master Renzfly said. "But I have a feeling that Havoc will return at some point. With the emergence of Lord Fetid from Planet Excervo, the life of the Pirate Warriors have shifted. Their powers also exceed all Yardanian Warriors, and with our King in the state that he's in, we are left very vulnerable."

"Are there any Yardanian Warriors left to protect the planet?" Menzuo asked.

"There are many scattered throughout the outer realm," Master Renzfly answered. "I have called for their return and also for several other warriors from our sister planets to lend their services back under my guidance. We do not know when Lord Fetid will return and we have no clue when or where this Pirate Warrior known as Stratus will attack first, but we have to be prepared."

"Please let us know what we need to do, Master Renzfly," Desmurose said.

"I know what we have to do," Solar replied as he looked Menzuo right in his eyes. "We have to make good on our promise. We need to train with Master Budokane. It is the only way for us to gain the power and the knowledge to overtake what is to come."

"But how can we leave this universe unprotected?" Menzuo asked. "You heard Master Renzfly, our parents cannot give this planet the strength that it needs to survive, and now with whatever threats that have entered our universe…we can't leave."

"If you do not go, you will die at the hands of Lord Fetid and the other Pirates that he has with him," Master Renzfly said. "At this stage of your development, there is no training I can offer you to prepare you for what Solar and I just faced. I need you both to seek knowledge from the one being that can guide you to victory."

"Heading to the death world of Legerdamien is very dangerous, Master Renzfly," Menzuo said.

"But we honestly don't have a choice, my brother," Solar replied. "Master Renzfly is correct. There was nothing I could've done to stop Lord Fetid. His powers were unimaginable. We need Master Kane's guidance."

Menzuo sighed heavily. "So who will be here to protect Yardania, I mean with the King in the state that he is in?"

"The son that is next in line must take the reign," Master Renzfly said as he looked to Solar. "But because you both must go on a mission together and with the kidnapping of Prince Denshuo, I will fill in as a surrogate leader. I am the highest-ranking soldier and the current Master Warrior who can take command. But before you two leave for Legerdamien, I need you here, in your physical. Back on Yardania. You must speak to your father before you head off to Legerdamien."

Menzuo nodded. "That goes without saying. I'll be there soon. Please call on the rest of the Solar Warriors. We will see you all soon."

Master Renzfly nodded. "Please make haste of your travels."

"We will, Master Renzfly," Menzuo said. He turned to Solar. "I will see you soon, brother. I'm ready."

"I know you are," Solar said. They shook hands.

Menzuo walked over to Allucio and Desmurose. "Let's get back to The Beacon. We have a lot to tell the rest of the team."

Allucio and Desmurose grabbed hold of Menzuo and they quickly faded from Yardania.

***

Within seconds, Menzuo and the Twin Powers were back in the lab. "This is way too heavy, man!" Allucio said. "Lord Fetid has fully returned, kidnapped Prince Denshuo, damn near killed you father the King, and now a freaking Pirate Warrior is creating an even bigger threat to life in our universe. Not cool at all."

"Right, Menzuo," Desmurose added. "There are way too many threats to be facing at one time. With Paladin and his team gone, the Majesties in recovery, and the unknown status of our own team set to protect their home planets, we're extremely stretched too thin. And you and Solar are leaving for Legerdamien? I just don't like it."

"I don't either," Menzuo said. "But you heard Master Renzfly, we have no choice. Lord Fetid is all too powerful now, and we have no clue how powerful this other Pirate is. I have to risk going to the death world to become stronger and better prepare to face these threats."

Desmurose sighed. "I'm just going to say it. I think you need to stay here. It's too risky to go back to Legerdamien. You do remember that we almost got stuck there when Queen Eaizah sent us there?"

"Yeah, we barely made it out alive," Allucio added. "And we had to fight the ghosts of dead Pirates. That was insanely sickening! I'm with Dez, we have to stay here on Earth to keep it safe, and you need to stay with us. We don't know when or where Lord Fetid or these other unknown threats will attack. I believe you need to rethink your journey, brother. It's just too risky."

Menzuo looked to the ceiling, pondering his friend's words. His thoughts drifted to his lost little brother and his birth parents. How afraid Denshuo must be and what condition his parents were in. He also thought about the time when King and Queen of Yardania risked their lives to keep him safe as a child and allowed his Earth parents to raise him. It was an ultimate sacrifice that they made to protect their family lineage, one that he could not take for granted.

Menzuo looked back at his friends. "You both can stay here on Earth, but to hell with me not going to Legerdamien!" he said in a stern tone. The rage started to build within him, as his eyes glowed, showing the strength of the fight within his soul. He continued. "Lord Fetid invaded my mind after I killed his wife, protecting Earth, and the visions that he placed in my head are coming true. He's returning sooner than anyone could have planned, and these new threats are popping into our galaxy left and right. If these monsters want a war, then I'm going to return and give them everything that I can. Even if it means my life. I will not fail this universe. It is mine to protect. Havoc said that I have choices, so I choose to kick their asses!"

Allucio and Desmurose could feel the passion within their best friend. "Well damn," Allucio said. "When you put it that way, how can we stop you?"

Desmurose nodded. "You're right, Menzuo, and we're with you, but please let Master Renzfly know that we have to stay here to protect our people. Earth is our home too, and we cannot leave her vulnerable like that."

Menzuo nodded. "Sometimes, you two clowns really impress me. I am sure that Master Renzfly will be okay with your descisions to stay. Honestly, it is the right play. Let's make our way back to the group. We need to let them know what we will be doing."

They all began to make their way back to the living room where the others were. "I hope that Paladin, Blurr, Thief and Zenith found what they were looking for," Allucio said.

"Me too. I wonder if they have made it back from their mission yet," Desmurose asked.

"We'll soon find out," Menzuo replied. They took the elevator back up to the top floor, ready to let their new friends know of the imminent dangers infecting the outer realm.

CHAPTER 27

TURNING POINT

As Menzuo, Desmurose, and Allucio entered the room, strong winds sailed in through the sliding door leading to the patio. They made their way across the room and stopped short when they noticed where the source was coming from. On the patio stood Tenan with Rekluse close by his side attempting to keep him upright as he held out both hands, arms extended, slowly turning them counterclockwise. The other Majesties watched from the room, as Lydia ducked behind the sofa covering her ears.

"What gives?" Menzuo shouted above the noise, looking on intently.

Blessed came beside him. "We're not sure. He was talking with Rekluse on the patio, and all of a sudden, this small storm flashed around him."

"Is he okay?" Allucio asked.

"We're not sure. These visions he keeps having are beyond our pay grade. It's between him and the Big Man, I guess," Aganathin said. "We're here to offer support."

Desmurose quickly joined Rekluse and assisted in helping Tenan hold his ground as the winds continued to grow stronger. "Thank you!" Rekluse shouted.

Desmurose nodded and propped himself behind Tenan to give Rekluse some relief.

"I see it, I see it!" Tenan said.

"See what, baby?" Rekluse asked.

"The Overdrive," Tenan said in a hushed tone.

Instantly, a large portal opened before them, and Tenan raised his arms, lifting the portal high above The Beacon just as The USS Overdrive sailed through. The ship shot past The Beacon and banked hard to avoid several buildings before coming back around and hovering just above the roof.

Tenan fell to his knees and Rekluse knelt beside him and held him close. "You did it baby."

Menzuo, Allucio and Desmurose powered up and flew to the the roof. The aft door of The Overdrive opened and Zenith appreared. He floated down to the floor, turned back to the ship and waved his hand. Paladin, Thief, and Blurr all floated out and softly landed on the ground beside him. "Take them, they are in serious need of help."

The Solar Warriors nodded and began to each pick up a member of the Capes. They took them inside and were met by Lydia. The sight of her cousin's limp body made her frantic. "Oh my god, what happened?" she screamed.

"They need immediate medical attention. They are alive and stable, but we must hurry," Zenith said.

"What should we do?" K'nia asked.

"Take them up to the lab, I'll retrieve the medical gurneys," Lydia said.

"That's my job," B.R.A.I.N. said. "Already prepped and ready, Lydia."

"Thank you," Lydia said in a raspy tone behind tears.

Everyone joined in helping to get Paladin, Blurr, and Thief to the gurneys as Lydia began to take vitals and attach heart and O2 monitors to each of them. Blessed came beside Zenith. "What happened out there?"

"I had to place them all in induced comas," Zenith said.

"Oh my god, comas?" Lydia exclaimed, pausing.

"Finish girl, finish," Kasitia said. "You need to focus."

"Blurr successfully transversed to the Speed-Stream and took us to the Traveler's homeworld, a red planet by the name of Ryderian," Zenith said. "There, they were matched against an impossible opponent by the name of Terez."

"They?" Allucio asked. "You left them alone?"

"It was not my fight to participate in," Zenith said.

"Not your fight?" Allucio said. He began to approach Zenith when Menzuo stopped him. "You let *this* happen to them, and it wasn't your fight?"

Zenith held out a hand. "You are young and naive and don't understand the ways of this world, or any other for that matter."

"Well maybe I do," Desmurose said as he attempted to leap in Zenith's direction.

Zenith phased out of sight, and Desmurose fell to the floor, slamming to the tile and sliding into the opposite wall. "Be still as I speak. I don't want anymore distractions." Desmurose froze in place, eyes wide. "We cannot afford anymore distractions. Am I right, Menzuo?"

Menzuo's eyes fell to the floor. "Right."

"Thief and Paladin were mortally wounded. I placed them in comas to stop the progression of their injuries. Blessed, if you would do the honors of healing them," Zenith said.

Blessed walked over to Thief and began to wave his hand over both him and Paladin. "I can feel their pain. Mostly internal insults, but, their organs are failing."

"You got this boss man," Aganathin said. "Look what you did for me."

Blessed nodded and inhaled deeply. When he exhaled, a faint glow could be seen emanating from his hands. Paladin and Thief began to convulse as their bodies came to life. Lydia held Paladin down while K'nia and Kasitia stabilized Thief. After a few seconds longer, Blessed lowered his hands and stepped away. "It's done." He turned to Blurr. "I'll heal her next."

"No!" Zenith shouted. "She's not injured. There's nothing you can do for her."

"What?" Lydia shouted.

"Well why did you place her in the coma?" Blessed asked.

"She was about to kill Terez, so I stopped her," Zenith said.

"What?" Menzuo shouted.

"Wait a minute, let me get this straight. This Terez dude was pounding on them, almost killed Paladin and Thief, and then Blurr almost killed him, and you stopped her?" Allucio asked. "What gives?"

"If she would have killed Terez, all would've been lost. I darkened the Speed-Stream and did the one thing deemed impossible. I stopped time," Zenith said mildly.

"So how did that hurt Blurr?" Lydia asked.

"She had truly maximized her Overdrive stage of evolution and was invincible," Zenith said. "Terez is a descendant of the Rothandians, a race of people who are very much like humans, but they hate your kind because you are so flawed. They desire to exterminate everyone who is flawed and have been doing it for hundreds of years, using World Harvesters, who are attracted to Dark Spores. Terez is a being known as a Celestial – offspring of the stars themselves. If she would have killed him, that would have sealed a death sentence for the entire universe as we know it. In Blurrs rage, she had fully tapped into that part of her existence where time both begins and ends simultaneously. Nothing could have stopped her –"

"Except for time itself," Tenan said as he entered the lab with Rekluse. "When I had my vision, I heard Zenith – more like saw him – loading the group back onto the Overdrive, and I had no idea where they were but I was determined to bring them back home."

"I connected to Tenan through what is called teleonotioning and willed his thoughts to open the portal at just the right time." Zenith paused, and his head abruptly snapped from side to side, twitching uncontrollably. He screamed, "Argggghhhhhh!"

Aganathin raised his axe, while the other Majesties readied their weapons. "What the hell?" Allucio said.

A few seconds passed and then Zenith stopped. He looked over to Paladin, who was still resting, with fear in his eyes. "They are calling for me. I've said too much." Zenith's eyes snapped back to Blessed. "I must be going now. When Paladin awakens, tell him what I've told you, and…apologize for me in advance. I'm so sorry for what happened to her."

“To who, Blurr?” Blessed asked.

Zenith’s body began to slowly phase out of sight as he was surrounded by a blue haze. He looked down at his hands as worry bloomed across his face. “But all is not lost, another traveler is –”

Zenith vanished before he could finish, and Desmurose roused from his frozen state, hitting the tile face first. “What gives?” he asked.

Allucio ran over to him and knelt by his side. “You okay?”

Desmurose wiped his face and ran his finger under his nose. “I hope I didn’t break my nose.”

“Ahh, it’d be an improvement anyway,” Allucio joked.

“What did he mean by another traveler?” Kasitia asked.

“Sebastian!” Lydia screamed, as Paladin began to awaken from his sleep.

He sat up, and groggily looked around the room. “What happened? Where am I?”

Lydia leaned in and gave him a huge bear hug. “Cousin, you’re home…you’re home.”

Paladin looked over to Blurr, and he immediately attempted to stand from the gurney. When he did, he slid to the floor, landing on one knee. Aganathin reached down and lifted him up. “Easy, I got you.”

Aganathin helped Paladin over to Blurr’s side. He took her by the hand. Her face was still, and the monitors next to her were quiet. “Baby? It’s me, Sebas. You can wake up now.” He turned to Lydia. “She’s so cold. What’s wrong with her?”

Lydia placed a hand on his shoulder. “She’s stable, Sebas. Let her sleep.”

Blessed approached. “Come on, Paladin. We’ve got a lot to talk about.”

***

Later that night, the Capes, Majesties and the Solar Warriors crowded around the living room and exchanged notes of the past few day, catching one another up and trying their best to make sense of all the havoc reaping around them; the most puzzling of which revolved around the Blurr's current state.

"So what do we do now? Just sit around and wait?" Thief said.

"We don't know what to do right now. Zenith left before he could tell us what to do. I'm afraid that everything I tried to arouse her has failed. We're just in some crazy wait and see period," Lydia said, holding on to Thief's waist as he stood next to a love seat occupied by Tenan and Rekluse.

"Well, I'm afraid that we've still got a lot of work to do to prepare for what's coming this way. We've got to get a plan going," Slaycick said.

"Seriously? Not right now," Lydia said. "Blurr's out, and we need to regroup, have some time to…mourn."

"Mourn?" Paladin asked as he stood from the sofa. "You act like she's dead." The room fell silent. Paladin's eyes washed across the room, but no one made contact with his. "Look, I know we don't know what's going on with her, but Karla is still in there, and she needs us. Needs me."

Blessed stepped forward. "Sebastian, there's something you need to know. Before Zenith left, he –"

"Forget Zenith! I don't want to hear another damn thing he said," Paladin said. He walked back into the lab to join Blurr.

Lydia looked up at Thief. "Talk to the others, I'll take care of him."

Lydia followed Paladin, and the rest of the team huddled up. "I never got a chance to thank you for saving us, Blessed," Thief said.

"No big deal. All in a day's work," Blessed said.

"So really, boss, what's next? We've got to start thinking about this crazy Space Pirate and begin preparations for an all-out war," Slaycick said.

"I know," Blessed said. "You're not wrong, Slaycick. I just think we need to give them some time. Maybe we'll go for now and meet with the heads in D.C. The more we give them time to prepare, the less chance the population will panic."

Menzuo spoke up. "That reminds me. It may be a good time for us to tell you guys –"

"Hopefully, Blurr will pull out of the coma on her own," K'nia said, cutting him off. "Seeing as though Zenith bailed. What do you think he meant by –"

Before she could finish, she was cut off by a loud, blood-curdling scream coming from the lab. Everyone rushed in.

It was Blurr, sitting up in a cream nightgown, holding Paladin by the hands. Her skin was stark white, and her eyes were all black. "It's time, Sebastian. I cannot stay."

"What? What are you talking about, Karla? You're here, I'm here. We're fine, baby. Look at me, I'm safe. You're home," he replied, his voice fleeting.

"No, you don't understand. I've seen him. I've…seen…everything. And I cannot stay any longer. The Speed-Stream is calling me," Blurr said.

"Stop saying that, baby, you're scaring me," Paladin said. "You're not going anywhere. Remember? We're in this for life. If you go, I'm leaving with you. There's nowhere you can go that I won't follow."

Blurr's body began to glow, engulfed in a bright gold light that threatened to blind everyone in the room. She snatched Paladin and pulled him close, squeezing him. "Please…please…let me go. I have to go."

Paladin squeezed back. "No, Karla, I can't let you go. I won't."

Blurr's body began to fade and as Paladin squeezed tighter, she vanished, leaving only her gown behind in his hands. Lydia gasped as Kasitia and K'nia began to sob. Thief fell to his knees and Aganathin dropped his axe to the floor. It slammed with a loud smash that rang throughout the Beacon.

Blessed wiped his hand across his face and Reckluse turned and wrapped her arms around Tenan, breaking down in a muffled cry. Arctic stepped backward and slid down a wall, curling up into a ball and wrapping her arms around her legs.

Paladin looked at Lydia with a side-eye glance, stunned at what just happened. Lydia reached out to him, but Paladin erupted in a series of shouts of, "No, no, no, no, no, no!!!!" that could be heard across all of Hero City.

***

A week later, atop a lone hill in a flat plain just outside of Chicago, a funeral was held. All the prominent government officials of Hero City were there, as well as heads of state from Washington D.C. were present to mourn the loss of a celebrated hero.

An empty coffin housing only Blurr's costume was lowered into the ground as a twenty-one gun salute was performed in her honor. The news feeds were flooded with the news of Blurr's death, and fanboys and girls alike posted tributes by the millions in her honor across social media. Even the heavily favorited show *The Nightwatch* ran a montage of episodes for the entire week, showcasing Blurr's accomplishments.

When it was over, The Solar Warriors and Majesties left. Alice, Sebastian, and Lydia lagged behind to ceremonially fill the grave with dirt. When it was done, they headed back to The Beacon.

Days passed, and Sebastian found it hard to eat or drink; he had lost the desire to do anything without the love of his life. In spite of much encouragement from Lydia, he secluded himself to The Beacon and left the running of his businesses to other VPs and managers. A twelve o'clock shadow filled his face, covering even his neck, making him somewhat unrecognizable.

Lydia came to his room and knocked on the door. But Paladin stayed in bed and ignored her. After a few more attempts, she finally coerced B.R.A.I.N. to unlock it. "Cousin, you have to get outta here someday. Can I get you something to eat? Maybe we can watch a movie or something? Will you answer me?" Sebastian remained silent, lying on his bed, his back to her. "You know, Karla wouldn't –"

Sebastian whirled to sit up. "You don't know anything about what she would or wouldn't want, okay!"

"You know what, maybe I didn't know her like you did, but I loved her too! She took a piece of my heart when she died."

Sebastian pointed at her. "Don't say that word to me. She didn't die. She…she –"

"You're going to have to accept it one day, cousin. Maybe not now, but one day." Lydia placed her purse under her arm and sighed. "I'm going to get out. I can't stay here and just rot away. I suggest you get some air, too." Lydia turned and walked out. Sebastian waited for the sound of the door to close and fell back in his bed once more.

"Sebastian, I miss Karla," B.R.A.I.N. said.

Sebastian's eyes filled with tears. "Me too, B.R.A.I.N.," he said softly.

"I wish I had true feelings, Sebastian. I'd love to share the emotional pain I know you're going through," B.R.A.I.N. said.

"Trust me, B.R.A.I.N., you don't."

"I've been trying to rewrite some of my Prime Directives to allow me to become more intuitive and human. I think I've made some progress thus far, but nothing is working as well as I'd like it to. If what everyone is saying is right, well, I'm afraid I'll never get the chance to master it."

Sebastian sat up on the side of the bed. He touched his head. The migraine creeping upon him was pounding between his ears. "I think I'm going to go up top and get some air."

"Excellent idea," B.R.A.I.N. said.

Sebastian stood, slid on his slippers and a housecoat, and took the elevator to the rooftop. It was a cool Chicago night, as the twenty-something chill clung to his arm skin like flypaper. He pulled out a small box and opened it. A beautiful ring with a large yellow diamond glistened from the rays of the Moon. He looked up at the stars and took in a deep breath. "Why Karla?" he whispered to himself. As he gazed at the night sky, he noticed a solitary star moving across the sky. "Maybe I'll make a wish," he murmured. Just as he spoke, the star banked and took a trajectory straight for him. As it grew closer, he noticed that it wasn't a star at all but a sleek, metallic vessel resembling the shape of a dolphin with four sets of small wings along the sides and a large front canopy.

Sebastian took a few steps back and tried his best to prepare for the worst, holding a half defensive posture. The ship swung around and came to a stop just above him. The aft door opened, and a young male, no older than Sebastian step to the edge and somersaulted down in front of him, landing in a half-kneel position. He wore all black leather pants, boots and a matching black vest. His exposed arms, face and neck were beaming in a blinding glow. He stood and made eye contact with Sebastian.

"Are you Sebastian Teleford?" he asked.

Sebastian swallowed hard and answered. "Yes."

"I'm William Derry from the Torrian Alliance. You recently lost your girlfriend named Karla, a.k.a. Blurr, right?"

Sebastian's eyes narrowed. "Yeah," he replied, confused.

William's skin returned to a faint olive tone. "I've recently traveled all the way from my home galaxy of from Proxima Centuari. I think I know how to find her."

TO BE CONTINUED…

ABOUT THE AUTHORS

Braxton A. Cosby is the multi-award winning and bestselling author and screenwriter of YA Sci-fi, Christian fiction and Super-Hero novels. He is also the creator of the highly acclaimed *My Life in Story* Series. His books have garnered recognition from Readers Favorite, Children's Literary Classics, Literary Titan, LitPick, Midwest Book Review, The Reading Bud, Blogcritics, and FlamingNet. He has also been endorsed by NYT Bestselling authors Adrian Trigiani, Tananarive Due and Bill Cosby. When he's is not writing, he spends his time traveling, inspiring, and sharing his testimony of God's faithfulness. Braxton is also an accomplished actor and modle, being casts in multiple projects from comedies, dramas, and of course, superhero short films. Braxton is the CEO of Cosby Media Productions, a media content production company that endeavors to *Entertain the Mind and Inspire the Soul*. He lives in Atlanta, Georgia with his fabulous wife and 4 children.

Follow Braxton @:
Twitter:

@BraxtonACosby
Facebook:
www.facebook.com/BraxtonCosby
Instagram:
braxtonacosby
Website:
www.braxtoncosby.com

Keshawn Dodds was born and raised in Springfield, Massachusetts on February 24, 1978. He still resides there with his wife, Tamara Dodds and daughter, Sydney Sharee Dodds. Becoming known as a well-established football player in Springfield, he was awarded a football scholarship to American International College in 1997. Mr. Dodds played football all four years at A.I.C., and later graduated with a B.S. in Education in 2001 and a Master of Education in 2009.

After graduating with his Bachelor's degree, Keshawn went on to become a fourth and fifth grade elementary school teacher within the Springfield Public Schools. During his tenure, Mr. Dodds taught at the Homer and Washington Elementary Schools from 2001 - 2005. He later took a job under Springfield's Mayor, Charles V. Ryan, as a Mayoral Aide. After his time in the Mayor's office, Keshawn went back to AIC and worked there for ten years and most recently held the position as the Director of Diversity & Community Engagement. Moving forward, Keshawn is now the new Executive Director of the Springfield, MA Boys & Girls Club Family Center.

Along Mr. Dodds' career journey, he has also become a published author of a juvenile fiction series, which is known as the Menzuo - Solar Warrior's series. Keshawn has written eight books within the series, and has currently republished the first book, "Menzuo: The

Calling of the Sun Prince," in August of 2010, through Cosby Media Productions and in October of 2015, it became an Amazon.com Best Selling book. Mr. Dodds is also awaiting the release of the highly anticipated second book, Menzuo: Legend of the Blue Diamond. The rest of the books within the eight book series are due out in the years to come.

Mr. Keshawn Dodds is an avid writer and strong supporter of education. His long term goal is to become a well-known educational advocate and motivational speaker. Keshawn wants to continue to spread his words of faith towards obtaining a great education and achieving all goals that a person has set in their life. Being raised by his mother, Elizabeth Dodd, Keshawn was always instilled with what a good education can bring to a person. Mr. Dodds firmly believes that, when hard work meets dedication, success is born.

Follow Keshawn @
Facebook:
www.facebook.com/keshawn.dodds
Twitter:
@IamKeshawndodds
Website:
www.keshawndodds.com

Chayil Champion is a graduate of the University of Miami in Coral Gables, Florida where he double-majored in both English and Journalism while competing as a two-sport athlete in both football and track. After graduating from UM in 1998, Champion received his masters and doctorate degrees in education from Nova Southeastern University in Fort Lauderdale, Florida. He embarked on a career in education as an English teacher and vice principal in South Florida's Dade County and West Palm Beach County public school systems respectively before moving to Los Angeles, California in 2009.

A native from Evanston, Illinois, a suburb that borders Chicago's north side, Champion developed a love for writing at a young age, which carried well into his adult years. After penning his first book in 2009 upon his arrival to Los Angeles, Champion has gone on to write five more books, which include the Young Adult fiction novels, ***Affiliated*** and ***Going Pro***, both from The Lost Souls literary series. Champion also wrote ***Exiting The Wilderness*** and **But He Said He Was A Christian,** two nonfiction Christian self-help books. ***Majesties of Canaan: The Goliath Project*** and ***Majesties of Canaan: Secret of The Oramite*** are his super hero novels. It is the first book of many within the Majesties of Canaan Superhero Series and the second book of The Dark Spores Series where Champion has collaborated with best-selling authors Keshawn Dodds and Braxton

Cosby to form the new superhero universe and to pen the superhero novel mashup, ***Infinity*** *7*.

Outside of his love for writing, Champion, runs his own education consulting company in Los Angeles where he continues to teach and tutor students. In his free time, Champion focuses on fitness, as he is a gym rat that frequents movies and enjoys spending time with his daughter Vanessa.

Follow Chayil @
Twitter:
@chayilchampion
Facebook:
www.facebook.com/chayilchampion

OTHER BOOKS FROM

THE DARK SPORES SERIES PHASE I

BOOK 1

BOOK 2

MAJESTIES
OF CANAAN
THE GOLIATH PROJECT
A DARK SPORES NOVEL
CHAYIL CHAMPION

BOOK 3

IN A CITY OF MASKED HEROES,
DARKNESS HIDES THE TRUTH
THE
CAPE
ABOVE ALL ELSE
PROTECT THE TRUTH
A DARK SPORES NOVEL
BRAXTON A. COSBY

BOOK 4

MAJESTIES
OF CANAAN
SECRET OF THE ORAMITE
A DARK SPORES NOVEL
CHAYIL CHAMPION

BOOK 5

BOOK 6

MENZUO
Judgment Set Upon Earth
A DARK SPORES NOVEL
KESHAWN DODDS

OTHER BOOKS FROM THE CMPDSU

PHASE II

BARK
EPISODE 2: ENEMIES AND ALLIES
DANIEL PEYTON

BARK
EPISODE 3: DESCENT INTO MADNESS
DANIEL PEYTON

METATRON
THE ANGEL HAS RISEN
LAURENCE ST. JOHN

METATRON
THE MYSTICAL BLADE
LAURENCE ST. JOHN

METATRON
DAGGER OF MORTALITY
LAURENCE ST. JOHN

METATRON
THE SECRET GRID
LAURENCE ST. JOHN

www.cosbymediaproductions.com

Made in the USA
Middletown, DE
21 May 2022